8/22/22

GATOR BITE

A Troy Bodean Tropical Thriller #8

DAVID BERENS

D1607836

BERENS | BOOKS

For James Edward Summers,
my step-father,
who was in every single respect other than blood,
my dad.

He read and told me he enjoyed
every single book I've ever written.
I miss you dearly.

Get FREE Books!

As a thank you for buying this book, I'd like to invite you to join my Reader Group. You'll be up-to-date with all the latest from David Berens and you get FREE BOOKS for joining.

To join, click BerensBooks.com and your free download link will be sent immediately. It will never cost you anything, ever!

Gator Bite

A TROY BODEAN TROPICAL THRILLER #8

Prologue

ONE HOUR before the coldest August dawn Islamorada had seen in twenty-two years—the most colorful locals saying colder than a nun's brass bra—Matteo Caparelli hiked into the mangroves wearing an exquisite lavender, V-neck sweater his father had bought him for Christmas last year. He marched into the swampy tangle of flora common to the island with no way of knowing that it would be the last thing he ever wore. He had known, however, that his father had given him the extravagant gift to infuriate his mother—the newly divorced and highly jaded, Jackie Caparelli. Based on the colorful cacophony of swear words she'd used when she had watched him open the box, Matteo could tell it had worked like a charm.

Dante Caparelli would have been horrified to see his son tripping through the spongy, sucking marsh in the fifteen-hundred dollar Tom Ford Classic cashmere gift. But Matteo—Matty to his closest friends—would never make it back to hear the disappointment in his father's cigar-cough, hack-laden rebuke.

That was to say nothing of the way the slippery, tepid mud was oozing into his crocodile Salvatore Ferragamo loafers like an over-poured Wendy's frosty. Yes, Dante *would* have been furious, if Matty hadn't been slogging along toward an untimely—if not gruesome—end.

1

A Foul Gator

GARY JOHN SUSKIND walked forward ahead of Matty in high-knee style steps, dragging the construction-sign orange kayak across the top of the swamp. It was hard work for Gary, who had never been accused of being strong, or hardy for that matter. He'd broken three manicured nails on his right hand already and knew Madame Teresa up on Tavernier would be most upset that he'd treated her immaculate work with such ... disparagement. And, to beat it all, he'd put an inch long gash in his left thigh scraping up against a broken limb of one of the God-forsaken spidery trees that threatened to trip him with every step. He'd have to look into some micro-stitches for that. It wouldn't do to have an unsightly scar marring his buttery tan skin—thanks to Madame Teresa's Mystic Tan Kyss spray booth. A blemish of that kind would send his Instagram followers dropping off by the thousands. He sighed inwardly. A small price to pay to get close to the subject of his unrequited infatuation. He planned to change the unrequited part of his flirtation today.

He suspected that Matty wasn't gay, but without direct confirmation of the fact, he proceeded to woo him with lunch dates, seemingly innocuous—but actually meaningful—gifts, and outdoor excursions like this one. In a kayak, there would be ample opportunity to squeeze his thighs around Matty and maybe a chance to fake a fall from the boat and grab him around the chest. *Hmmm, wonder if my future lover would give me mouth-to-mouth if I should happen to drown?* Gary thought. He resolved to keep his options open. Suddenly, with a splash, he was knee deep in a watery void in the marsh. He squealed more effeminately than he intended and lurched sideways. The kayak kept him from going under, but he was now sopping wet.

"You okay up there?" Matty called from behind him.

Gary slapped on a smile. "Oh, yeah. All good.

Just getting kinda deep up here. Maybe we should get in now."

"Whatever you say."

Gary pulled himself up into the back of the kayak and Matty tumbled into the front. The boat rocked violently back and forth until Gary, who tried in vain to counteract Matty's motion, lost his balance and splashed out into the marsh again.

Despite his best efforts, Gary John Suskind went under. The brown, soupy swamp swallowed him and he thrashed violently, unable to tell which way was up. And then the hands wrapped around his upper arms. He realized with relief that Matty had reached in and grabbed him. His head broke the surface and he gasped. Matty was laughing and doing nothing to hide the fact. Gary's instinct was to feel hurt and dejected, but then thought better of it. He imagined this was how guy pals would react in this situation. He faked a chuckle with all the authenticity of a silicone injected Playgirl model.

"Help me up, ya big lug." He winced, hearing himself try to fake hetero-speak.

But Matty didn't seem to notice. Or maybe he didn't care.

Matty pulled hard on Gary's arms and as he

cleared the side of the kayak, he lost his balance and tumbled down on top of Matty. For one rainbow bathed, "Dream Weaver" second, he was in Matty's arms. The fire burned inside him and before he could stop himself, he smashed his lips to Matteo's voluminous Italian mouth. He tried to force his tongue in to seal the kiss, but Matty's teeth were clenched tight.

Gary—not realizing that he'd closed his eyes in the embrace—opened them to find Matty staring wide-eyed back like a man who'd taken a big gulp of what he thought was orange juice only to find it was grapefruit instead. It was not the stare of adoration or infatuation. No, this didn't remind Gary of a soft-focus movie sequence with Gary Wright crooning out his only hit song in the background. No, it felt more like the shocking twist scene in The Crying Game. Matty shoved hard, throwing Gary off of his chest. His friend's face was a red splotched, mangled mess of shock, embarrassment, and—worst of all —rage.

"What the shit was that all about?" Matty growled, his Northern accent more prominent in his anger. "Are you flippin' crazy?"

"I ... I'm sorry. I just—"

Gary John Suskind was interrupted by a thump

that shook the kayak violently. He wondered if somehow they'd gotten caught in a current and had run aground. But scanning through the dappled sun-streaks shining into the shadowy, mangrove canopy around them, he saw no sign of anything they could've hit.

"I asked you a question, fairy boy." Matty's rage growing.

Gary raised his hands. "Now, hold on just a second, Matty. I didn't mean any harm. It's just that we have such a good time together that I—"

This time, something slammed into the kayak so hard it tipped up on its side. Matty finally noticed they were under attack. The prehistoric, log-like skin of an alligator slid past them in a froth.

"Holy shit," Matty said, his feet scraping hard and pushing him back into the kayak. "What the hell is that?"

Gary would've answered, but he was in shock. Even while flailing about trying to keep his body in the boat, he knew what had hit them this time. Alligator Mississippiensis or the American Alligator. Looking for all the world like a knotty log come to life in a blur of motion, it had slammed into their boat raising the stern up at least a foot off the rippling surface. Gary didn't know much about them besides what he'd learned in middle school, but he hadn't heard of them attacking people very often on Islamorada. They were usually lazier than the tourists and liked to bake in the sun just as much, if not more. Most likely, they had gotten too close to its gator hole, or maybe even its nest and it was defending its turf. But wait, was that alligators or crocodiles? He couldn't remember.

When the kayak hit the water again, Gary fell down into the boat smacking his left arm so hard, he wondered if he'd broken it. Pain surged into his elbow sending pins and needles and numbness racing up and down his arm. Matty, however, fell backward and with his weight unexpectedly throwing him toward the opposite side, he fell overboard. The splash seemed impossibly simultaneous with the gator jerking its broad head around to see what had caused it. Before Gary could scream, the creature lunged at the object it had seen entering the water.

In a strange, but cogent moment of bravery, Gary launched himself toward the fray, preparing to kick the alligator with his borrowed patent-leather camouflage boots—clearly not made for this endeavor—until it swam away. The churning whirlpool of blood blossoming in the vortex where

Matty had gone under, instantly turned his valiant effort into a terrifying regret. The alligator's head crashed above the surface and in the split-second before Gary entered the water, to his horror, he saw a severed hand in its mouth.

2

Running Behind

GARY WAS BUMPED and thumped and turned over several times under the water. His lungs burned as he held his breath desperately trying to make sense of what was happening. A hazy beam of light snaked down through the murky water and Gary decided that moving toward it was as good a choice as he had right now. A better choice than inviting Matty out for a kayak ride, that much was now certain. He kicked hard and one of the stylish boots he'd borrowed from his best friend slipped off his foot and sank. His stockinged foot thrashed hard and he began to make slow, but sure headway toward the surface.

The prehistoric animal was still swirling around him in a blur making the underwater scene look like that maniacal boat ride in *Willy Wonka and the*

Chocolate Factory. And then the gator crashed into him from underneath. The force hit him like a rocket and thrust him up so quickly that his stomach lurched and he vomited. Luckily, he was still underwater when his breakfast of baked peach almond oatmeal exploded out of his mouth. With the alligator beneath him, he broke through the surface and was thrown ten feet like a rag doll. He slammed into a branchy tree and grabbed tightly with both hands. He gripped the reddish-gray trunk and scaled the tree as fast as he could, the gator snapping at his heels. He kicked off the second of his borrowed boots and scrambled into a crook about twelve feet off the surface of the churning swamp below. The alligator lunged at him snapping its ferocious mouth, but for the time being, it appeared he had climbed high enough to stymie the animal's attack—or maybe it was too full and heavy from eating Matty.

He laughed hard through his terror at the beast, flipping him the finger. He cackled until he was hoarse watching as the alligator flung himself up at him over and over. The way it was acting, he was now certain that the super-pissed gator was indeed actually a she and that he and Matty had stumbled onto a nest or something. He wasn't even sure if alligators laid eggs or had babies, but either way, this one was out to kill the outside threat to its offspring. It snapped its jaws at him and Gary was disgusted to see the hand—Matty's hand—flopping about between its teeth in a gruesome mess of bubblegum flesh. The sun broke through the canopy and glinted on something in the alligator's mouth. Gary realized it was a ring on his friend's now detached hand.

"You got what you want, asshole," Gary yelled. "Get the hell out of here and let me go."

He realized that he was sobbing now, tears of anger and terror mixed together with a fit of something bordering on hysteria. Finally, the alligator seemed to tire of threatening the creature in the tree and he went back to destroying the kayak. Gary watched the gator chomp on the bright orange boat, tearing pieces of it off and flinging them hard to and fro. And of all the strange things to enter someone's mind at a time when survival had become an uncertainty, Gary wondered what the hell he was thinking when he *borrowed* the kayak and invited his friend for a morning ride. If only that rich, white, sanctimonious bastard had taken the care to lock up his boat. None of this would've happened if the semi-famous writer man had just stored his glorified canoe somewhere other than propped up against the pylons under his house.

Gary yelled a curse word that he rarely used as loud as he could. He regretted that instantly as the alligator looked up from his kayak destruction and lunged at him one more time. Gary repeated the four letter word over and over, howling in the empty heat of the swamp at the menacing creature snapping its dingy yellow, razor sharp teeth at him. The gator was close enough now that he could see the ring clearly stuck on a finger—maybe a pinky—dangling out of the corner of its mouth. The family crest sparkled in the dusky shafts of sunlight that created a prison of beams around him.

He croaked out a sob, not so much out of sorrow for losing his friend, but at what might become of him if Matty's father ever found out his role in his son's demise. As the gator's attack waned and the dark gray-green beast slunk away into the swamp, he wondered what might be worse—eaten by an alligator, or wearing concrete shoes.

TWO MILES AWAY, Chad Harrison's unharmed and fully attached fingers clicked across his keyboard in a blaze of fury. He laughed out loud as he finished his piece. This article was sure to break the Keys News editor's blue pen. He scrolled back up to the title: *Hang 'Em From The Banyans: Ending Tourism In The Keys*. He knew fans of his Cap Wayfarer column would love it and the mail would support him, even if the editor did not. *Eat your heart out Malcolm Gladwell.*

He saved the file and clicked over to a new, much longer document, took a deep breath, read the last few lines, and added the words *THE END.* to the bottom. His latest Florida fiction novel was complete and would go to the proofers at Manatee Press and they would mangle it, send it back to him with a garish cover, and then after a long and laborious fight, they would restore it to its original form and publish it.

Chad knew what his fans wanted and he would give it to them, editors of the world be-damned. He closed the lid of his laptop and gazed out from his screened in porch. The waves were softly rolling and the high tide glittered in the afternoon sun. Normally, he wouldn't go out at this hour due to the sweltering heat, but it had been oddly cool for a late August morning.

"Babe, I think I'm gonna go for a quick row," he called over his shoulder.

His new—just-beyond-teenage—girlfriend of two weeks didn't say anything. She was probably still passed out from too many strawberry daiquiris and subsequent viewings of the latest Justin Bieber concert footage splashing around on YouTube or Snapchat or whatever social app was hot this week. He frequently called her "babe" not out of endearment, but because he often forgot her name, or confused her name with a previous girlfriend. It escaped him now as he was leaving the house. *Was it Lindsay, or Buffy, or maybe Chantel? Eh, who cares.*

Chad didn't care much if she stuck around long, but she was a deliciously taut, toned roll in the sack and he hadn't had much of that since Linda had packed up and left last year. He shrugged his shoulders and trotted down the steps to the scruffy sand of his beachfront backyard. Being a New York Times bestselling author did have perks, and his oversized bungalow on Islamorada was certainly one of them. It wasn't the type of beach photographed for postcards and airbrushed on cheap cotton t-shirts, but more of an interruption of the ocean for a bit of grainy, weedy, rocky sand with razor sharp bits that would slice a city-slicker's arches to ribbons. Chad wasn't a true outdoorsman, but he did enjoy the occasional dip into the wilderness around the key.

He pulled the factory distressed Blind Melon shirt he'd bought at the Dolphin Mall in the Hot Topic off and tossed it aside. He clapped his hands together and then realized something was missing.

"Where the hell is my kayak?" he asked no one as he flip-flopped from pylon to pylon searching for the missing boat.

3

The Good Work

TROY CLINT BODEAN stretched his back, which snapped and popped like a nearly finished, microwaved bag of popcorn. An odd shiver ran down his spine. Odd because it was August in the Keys and it was usually as hot and humid as a stale, sweat-soaked sauna. But there was a chill in the air today that sent his skin prickling with goose bumps.

He shook the sleep off as he pulled himself up to his elbows and peeled back the blanket he'd borrowed from the old fella—Stan Wachowski from Minnesota—currently inhabiting the brown and yellow trailer in slot 03. A retired insurance salesman whose wife had left him for a younger, more aggressive used car salesman, Stan had sold his Buick, bought a small RV and decided to head south—away from his whore of a wife and away from the frigid hell of the Land of 10,000 Lakes. The only thing he'd kept from his busted marriage was the afghan his wife had knitted presumably between hot car salesman sex sessions. Troy tossed the blanket off, unrolled the sweat-stained t-shirt he'd used as a pillow, and tugged it over his head. His shadow on the ground told him his hair was a moppy mess. *What else is new?*

Folding the blanket into a neat square, he limped his way back to the trailer to return it to Stan, but found the door locked and no sign of the man puttering around his home on wheels. Maybe the old fella had found a similarly exiled divorcee or an innocent young maid to share his bed. Troy laid the blanket on the metal folding steps that led up to the door and walked to the edge of the water just ten feet past the end of the trailer. The gentle waves here weren't a postcard of azure or aquamarine, but more of a blue, gray, and beige mixture—like a watercolor painting made with a brush the artist never cleaned. Palm trees swayed over the top of a thatch-covered pavilion with a circular cement picnic table underneath. One of the half-moon shaped benches was broken in two and reminded Troy of something he once read about a lion on a cracked altar in a fantasy land hidden in a closet.

He plopped down on the bench that was still intact and rocked his spine back and forth easing the aching muscles from his night spent sleeping under the stars—on the ground. The gentle breeze blew past him and the smell of salt and fish guts oddly made his stomach growl. But, given that he'd spent his last bit of cash on a bag of beef jerky and a bottle of water at the Quickie Mart beside the last Greyhound bus station, he wasn't sure he could do anything to tame his hunger. A seagull screeched and he glanced up toward the sound. An early morning spray of sunlight glowed on a pink piece of paper stapled to one of the tiki hut's support poles. Two of the staples had given up and the flier now flapped lazily back and forth. He couldn't make out much through his bleary vision except the bold words scrawled in permanent marker at the top:

NOW HIRING.

He stood and the bench he was sitting on wobbled, fell over, and cracked, much the same as the other one. Guess it's time to move on, he thought. He shrugged and walked over to the pole. Holding the bottom of the paper, he read the details. Something about a maintenance man for a tennis club. He shivered as he recalled the time he'd spent up in Key Biscayne. *Dang, that had been a hell of a ride.* He almost walked away but the last three sentences caught his attention.

PAY IN CASH. ROOM AND BOARD ON PREMISES INCLUDED. START IMMEDIATELY.

Bingo.

Only problem was, the job was in Islamorada, quite a few miles away. Sure, he could walk it, but there were some pretty Facist rules about hitchhiking in the Keys and he wasn't sure he had it in him to trek across the long bridges that looked so cool in pictures. His eye caught a bike wheel turning slowly from the back of Stan Wachowski's RV. The glittering green multi-speed bicycle hung on a rack behind a pink one that had a distinctly feminine look to it. He was sure before he checked that the green one would prove to be locked fast to the rack, but the pink one would be unchained and free—like the woman that used to ride it. He was right.

"Sorry, Stan," he thought, spinning the back wheel of the Pepto Bismol colored ten-speed.

Figuring the pink bike had probably belonged to Stan's ex-wife, Troy hoped the old man wouldn't miss it much, and might even wish it good riddance.

As he lifted the bike from its perch on the rear of

the trailer, he noticed an odd smell, rank and rancid. He shrugged it off, there were a lot of discarded fish entrails baking in the sun over at the marina. Troy never noticed the body unceremoniously shoved under the back axle of the trailer as he pedaled away —a body with sixty-nine strange three-holed lacerations that another Kampground visitor from Wyoming would say reminded him of spur marks as it was dragged from its hiding place.

THE COOL MORNING he had enjoyed at the Key Largo Kampground & Marina had hazed away into a late afternoon sauna. Eleven miles down US-1, he was soaked to the bone with sweat on the outside and dry as a bone on the inside. His tongue was thick and sticky and he felt like his throat was closing in on itself. As he approached The Laura Quinn Wild Bird Sanctuary, a cramp took hold of his right calf and wouldn't let go. He nearly crashed the pink ten-speed as he limped off the side of the highway toward the shade of the sanctuary. The ramshackle entrance of the place looked to be cobbled together from mismatched and repurposed lumber, much of which showed visible signs of rot. Troy's front wheel thumped along the warped and weathered planks that formed a boardwalk of sorts under the canopy of dense, rangy mangroves.

As he rolled along, his hands seized into balled fists—cramping into bony vises. Ironically, though they were both clamped tight to the handlebars, the cramps kept him from being able to apply the handbrakes and slow the pink bike. Tourists and visitors strolled along the boardwalk peering into the lush vegetation, studying birds Troy couldn't see as he barreled toward them uncontrollably. He put his left foot down in an effort to slow his ride, but as he did, it cramped as well. Later, after the crash involving a woman wearing a tie-dyed muumuu, her two inconsolably wailing toddlers, and a husband who insisted on clucking at the birds like a chicken, Troy would count himself lucky that he'd passed out, missing their loud and obnoxious exit from the park.

He woke up lying in a sparsely decorated bedroom that looked to be straight out of the seventies—mid-century oak dresser with gold inlays, white metal bed that squeaked loudly as he moved, and a threadbare yellow quilt rolled down covering only his feet. A clock was ticking somewhere, but when he tried to move his head to look for it, the timpani drums pounded in his brain. He closed his eyes and flopped back down on the pillow.

"Easy, young fellow," a voice said to him.

She sounded like an older woman, raspy and thin, but kind and motherly at the same time. He wondered if he'd died and somehow reunited with his mama in heaven. *Not likely*, he thought. He opened his eyes slowly.

"Am I dead?" he asked as the small bedroom came back into view.

Thin curtains blew in the breeze from an open window to his right. In front of the window was a silhouette of a tiny woman with short gray hair. She had ruddy skin tinged with sunburn, a dingy pink t-shirt with a pelican on the front, and a clear bag of fluid in her hand. Troy could see that a tube trailed out of the bag, drooped down toward the floor, then rose up again to end at a needle in his arm.

"S'pose not," the woman said. "Unless we're both dead."

She looked around at the room through dark sunglasses.

"Which is entirely possible at this point."

She laughed and gave the bag a gentle squeeze. Troy felt warmth enter his skin through the IV.

"What is that?" he asked, nodding toward the bag.

"Saline. Hope you ain't got any heart issues," she said, shrugging her shoulders. "Didn't see a medical bracelet or anything on ya, so I took a chance giving you this."

Troy shook his head. "Nothing that I know of."

He tried to sit up, but his head swam and his body twitched like a jellyfish, threatening to cramp again.

"Whoa, now, son. Give me a minute to get some fluid in you before you get all jumpy again." She held up a hand. "I'm figuring you probably had a big night partying and you'll need some hydration before you get your next drink. Am I right?"

"Actually, I just biked down from Key Largo and didn't have any water. Must've gotten dehydrated in the heat."

The woman rolled an imaginary toothpick around her mouth. "Uh huh. And I'm Mother Teresa."

Troy shrugged. He had no energy to argue the point and figured it didn't matter anyway.

"Nice to meet you, Ma'am." Troy held out his free arm. "Name's Troy Bodean. Never thought I'd get to meet a saint."

The woman laughed and took his hand. She was thin and bony, but her squeeze was firm and sure.

"Actually, most folks might tell you I ain't no saint, just a bird lady. Name's Laura Quinn."

"So, you're the one who owns this place?"

She nodded.

"Did you have to give that woman and her family their money back after I crashed into them?"

"Nah, they didn't pay anything," she said, waving the thought away. "Ain't no admission, though donations are always welcome."

Troy felt more warmth flowing into his arm and took a deep breath. The room wasn't swimming as much now and he was beginning to feel a little more normal. Normal but tired. His eyelids felt like sandbags and he let them close.

"Yup," the bird lady said as darkness closed in. "Just get a little rest. We'll continue this later when you wake."

And with that, Troy fell into a deep blue sleep. Blue like the water he been cruising past on his cotton candy-colored bike.

WHEN HE WOKE for the second time, the sash was lowered a bit and the sheer curtains hung limp in front of a dusky window. Pale purple skies glowed beyond revealing that he'd slept for at least three or four hours and that it was nearly night. He propped himself up on his elbows and saw that the quilt had been pulled up over his legs and the IV had been removed from his arm. A single dot of blood blossomed into the gauze taped over the needle's former entry point. His head throbbed, but softly, not threatening to drown him into unconsciousness again. He slid his legs over the edge of the bed, wincing with the expectation of the cramps returning to savage his calves, but thankfully, they never came. He tested his weight on one foot, then added the second. He managed to stand upright and was relieved that he felt—all things considered—pretty good. By force of habit, he rubbed his hands together in a motion that would wipe away dirt or grime and was met with a stab of fiery pain in both palms. He opened his hands and found they were bandaged with gauze and tape. A dark red and brown stain soaked through both, the right a little more than the left. An image of tumbling over the handlebars of the bike and reaching out to catch himself flashed into his head. He remembered his palms dragging and bumping along the boardwalk grabbing splinters in both.

"No pushups today, I reckon," he mumbled as the pain subsided.

Using his fingertips, he turned the knob to the door and squeaked it open. He was met with a hallway lined with old photographs. Most of them featured Miss Laura Quinn and various birds in states of injury or healing. More of the wall was covered with photos than was bare. Troy was duly impressed. Apparently, she was some kind of bird rescuer.

"That one's a brown pelican. We've got quite a few of them here," a voice said from behind him.

Troy turned to see Laura Quinn standing behind him. She had long black rubber gloves on that were slick with something—he couldn't tell what. Noticing his gaze, she began to peel the gloves off.

"Yeah, it's blood," she sighed. "Couldn't save that one."

An awkward silence hung between them. Finally, she was the one to speak again.

"You always prance around in your birthday suit?"

It was then that Troy came to the realization that he was naked. He covered himself with his bandaged hands. She seemed not to care that he was nude and he was thankful for that.

"I gather you noticed your hands?"

He nodded looking down at his gently clasped hands.

"You had some pretty vicious scrapes and a dozen or so big splinters." She motioned for him to follow her down the hall. "I'm almost certain I got 'em all. Just keep an eye on your hands for any red, puffy areas that linger."

He followed her into a small, fluorescent lit room. She opened a cabinet, pulled out a white towel and tossed it to him. He wrapped it around his waist as she took down a large white bottle from the top shelf. Opening a drawer, she took a plastic baggie out, counted a few pills into it, then sealed it with a zip. She handed it to Troy.

"Take three a day. Space 'em out a bit. Might wanna eat somethin' with 'em."

"Antibiotics?" Troy asked.

She nodded.

"How can I repay you?"

"No need, son. It's part of what we do here. Keep them flying." She pointed a finger up at the ceiling.

"Only question now, I suppose, is where are my clothes, and my hat, and my bike?"

She leaned her head back and chuckled with a raspy, thin laugh. "Clothes are in the bedroom. I washed 'em for you. As for the bike, you won't be goin' anywhere on that thing. You trashed it pretty good."

"Dangit," Troy said, tucking the baggie into his pocket. "What mile marker are we at?"

"You're at ninety-three. Tavernier"

Troy took in a deep breath. The air in the small room was bleachy and sterile, not at all like the bedroom he'd woken up in.

"Well, I guess I'll be hitching down to Islamorada. What is that? Mile seventy-six?"

"Uh-yah," she said, shaking her head. "I wouldn't put my thumb out around here. The police aren't too friendly with hitchhikers. You can probably catch a bus that'll take you all the way though for a couple of bucks."

Before he could tell her he didn't have the money to take the bus, she pulled a wallet out of her back pocket. He immediately recognized that it was his wallet.

"You'll find you have a bit more there than you came in with."

Troy stared at it for a long moment before taking it.

"Why are you doing this?"

"I told you, son." She smiled an ushered him

back into the hall. "It's what we do around here. Keep 'em flyin'."

Ten minutes and a tepid, slightly slimy ham and cheese sandwich later, he was in the farthest back bench he could get on a Dade-Monroe shuttle. It stank of sweat, urine, and alcohol. The nineties-era neon Miami Vice pattern of the cloth seats was threadbare and slightly damp, but there seemed to be no problem with the A/C. A cool rush of air streamed down steadily on his head. He took off his hat—the outback tea-stained cowboy hat—to feel the chill up and down his scalp and neck. For the first time in twenty-four hours, he felt reasonably good. He dozed in and out of consciousness until the driver—a woman who might have been Esther Rolle in another life—sang out.

"Islamorada, sugars." Her hand waved across the front windshield. "Village of Islands."

Outside, the sky was on fire with purple, red, orange, and yellow. As Troy stepped down off the bus, the same smell of salt and fish from Key Largo bathed him in the thick, hazy air. The bus door screeched shut and the muffler rattled as it pulled away from the stop. All was quiet and still—even the breeze had already gone to sleep. *Off-season in the Keys*, thought Troy. *Nobody here but us locals.*

He pulled out the scrap of paper he'd squirreled away into his pocket. It was slightly wet having gone through the wash at the bird sanctuary, but the writing was still clear enough. He saw that he was only a few steps from 76800—the place that was hiring. He hoped he hadn't taken too long to get here. A large round sign with peeling paint and amateurishly drawn palm trees proudly wore blue lettering announcing that he'd made it. Islamorada Tennis Club. Beyond the green chain link fence wrapping the driveway, he heard the *thwock thwock* sound of tennis balls being hit. He wiped his face with his shirt hoping he didn't look too homeless—but he knew in the Keys, that wasn't uncommon, nor was it inculpatory. Troy Bodean tucked the paper into his pocket and walked through the gate.

It was around that same time that the police were notified of the disappearance of the infamous Laura Quinn. No one would know anything was amiss until three days later when her body was found in a brown pelican nest hidden back in the mangroves. When questioned, the regular staff and interns at the Wild Bird Sanctuary would describe a strange, lanky man showing up just before her disappearance wearing a straw cowboy hat over long, stringy, black hair. When the bulletin hit the airwaves, a computer buried in a secret office, under a secret compound, in a secret location sent a highly encrypted email to a man with no official title. Very few knew anything about what he did at the bureau. Most just called him The Hunter.

4

Hammock Style

TROY CIRCLED the two-story whitewashed house looking for the source of the rallying sounds he could hear echoing around the mangrove encircled tennis courts. Green shutters framed old wooden windows and thick, pink bougainvillea climbed a wall of lattice attached to the parking lot side of the building. Some kind of bird screeched and flew out of it as he got near, causing him to duck and slap a hand on his hat to keep it in place. The courts—six clay and one hard—were not lit and most sat in near total darkness. The single hard court—a rarity south of the Florida-Georgia line—was closest to the back of the pro shop and benefited from a soft mosquito-bulb-yellow glow from the porch lights beaming out over a long row of half-broken rocking chairs.

A man in a shockingly fluorescent pink shirt dripping with rivulets of sweat was pounding tennis balls being flung at him from what Troy thought might be a 1970's era ball machine. Most flew long and smashed into the windscreen lined chain link fence beyond the far baseline. The man, whose black Nike socks were pulled high on his calf to just under his knees, looked to be making no attempt at proper tennis shots.

As Troy got closer, he saw the man's face was twisted into an angry grimace and he grunted with vehemence on every shot. And then, all was quiet, save for the grinding of the machine's gears and the man's huffing breath. Troy took a step up onto the porch next to the court and was surprised to hear a woman's screeching voice calling out from somewhere above—maybe an upstairs window.

"I think the goddamn thing's empty, Lucas. It is past ten o'clock. Give it a rest."

Her accent was thick and latin.

The man smashed his racket into the ground, splintering the head, and turned toward the house.

"I'll do what I please, woman. Just like you, apparently."

Troy heard her growl.

"It was a mistake, Lucas. Seriously. It is not like you have never flirted with a tennis bimbo."

The man jerked a matching pink headband off his forehead. His hair was soaked and flopped down in an odd way. The right side hung down past his ear, but the left was trimmed close. The top of his head was cornrowed with dark plugs in an otherwise barren plain of skin. As if feeling Troy's eyes on him, he reached a hand up and swiped the longer hair over the top to cover the plugs. Troy wasn't sure he'd seen a worse comb-over.

"Manuela, screwing the maintenance man is not flirting. It's ... well, it's screwing the help for Chrissakes!"

The man took two steps toward the porch and realized with a jolt that Troy was standing there.

"What the hell do you want?" the man demanded, pointing a finger at Troy. "Are you here to bang my wife, too?"

With the ball machine still whirring in the night, Troy cleared his throat. He reached into his pocket for the piece of paper he'd found at the Key Largo Kampground & Marina. He un-wadded it and held it up.

"I'm here about the job."

The man looked up toward the hidden voice

coming from above Troy. "Hey, hun, you're in luck. Here's a new maintenance man for you to—."

He was interrupted by the sound of the window slamming shut. Troy was sure he heard the woman's voice cursing muffled behind the closed glass.

"Did I come at a bad time?" Troy pointed his thumb over his shoulder. "I could come back tomorrow if you want."

The man put his hands on his hips. He sighed as he tried to calm his panting breath.

"No. No. It's fine. Just ... just gimme a minute."

He walked over to the ball machine and unplugged it. Troy walked out to the court and started picking up balls with the man, depositing handfuls back into the machine. The man bent over and his combover flopped down in front of his face. He swiped it back over the top without skipping a beat.

"I don't hire bums or vagrants," he said.

"I ain't neither, sir." Troy said. "Just an honest man lookin' for work."

The man took a deep breath and looked Troy up and down. "You don't look like a tennis guy. You know anything about clay courts?"

"Yes, sir. I dressed ten of them up in Key Biscayne on a daily basis for a few years."

"Key Biscayne," the man said. "Well, well, well. Hoighty-toighty. Why'd you leave there?"

Troy's mind flashed back to the murder of the Colpiller girl and the eventual kidnapping of her twin sister, Mindy. He shivered at the thought.

"Long story. Just didn't work out."

"Uh huh."

"Look. I'm a traveler. Have been for most of the time I've spent back from Afghanistan. But I'm a hard worker and I need a place to stay. Your paper here says you've got a job and room and board. If you'll give me a week, I'll prove I'm your man. If you don't agree, I'll move along."

The sound of glass breaking somewhere upstairs made the man jerk his gaze upward.

"Shit," he said, running up the steps of the porch. "Let's talk about this in the morning."

"Oh, uh, okay," Troy watched as the man ran past him. "So, um, meet you here tomorrow?"

As he disappeared up the stairs to the apartment above the shop, he called, "There's a hammock at the back of the porch. You're welcome to crash there."

Troy heard a door slam followed by angry muffled voices. He shrugged his shoulders and walked past the rocking chairs to the back of the porch. There, behind a wall of lattice, he saw an old, white hammock, swaying in the light breeze.

He tossed his backpack down beside it and went back around to the first rocking chair. Discovering that it looked to be on its literal last leg, he moved on to the next one and slumped into it. It was comfortable and the air was exactly the right temperature for rocking. He settled into a nice rhythm hoping the couple's argument wouldn't keep him awake for very long. It didn't.

TROY WOKE the next morning to find that a drizzle had watered the courts nicely overnight so running the sprinklers wouldn't be necessary. Luckily, his hammock—which he must have moved to sometime in the wee hours of the night—was tucked back under the roof of the long porch so he was dry and fully rested. It only took fourteen tries and three blisters to get the rusted yellow lawn tractor started. He hooked a wide brush onto the back with a bungee cable and pulled the ramshackle grooming zamboni out onto the first court. Before it backfired the first time, he heard yelling coming from the upstairs apartment over the pro shop.

He reached down and turned the key, silencing

the tractor. He was about to get off when he saw a leopard print suitcase come tumbling down the stairs and flop out into the gravel parking lot. The lid flew open and clothes went flying. Ladies underwear in all manner of colors and glittery sequins that would've made a stripper blush exploded out of the case as it popped open. Shortly after that, a woman in red patent leather stilettos clip-clopped down the steps with the grace of a newborn calf. Troy half expected her to tumble as well, but she managed to make it to the bottom without incident.

Then he heard the door open again and another, smaller, matching suitcase sailed over the railing and crunched down in a heap next to the woman. The assortment of bottles, cotton balls, tubes, sponges, brushes, and other unidentifiable objects that rained down around the busted luggage was more than Troy thought should have been able to occupy the small space. He took off his hat and wiped his brow. It was already hot and the sun hadn't risen above the surrounding mangroves yet.

So much for gettin' another cool morning in the Keys, he thought. As he walked toward the woman, she bent down and started tossing the strewn toiletries back into the case. He couldn't help but notice the curve of her backside in the skin-tight white denim shorts she was wearing. As she leaned further, he saw the tell-tale blue-black ink of a lower back tattoo peeking out as well. *Mamacita.*

Under her breath, Troy could hear her grunting curses in Spanish and English and halfway in between. She gripped a blue toothbrush in a white-knuckled fist dotted with hot pink nails. Her eyes squinted and she stood up, arm raised toward the upstairs door.

"This is yours, you pig," she shouted.

She spit on it, threw it in the dirt, and ground her foot on top of it, smashing it into the gravel.

"Might I be of assistance, ma'am?" Troy asked, raising his hands in surrender fashion.

"Who the fuck are you?" she demanded, whirling around to face him.

"New maintenance man."

Troy saw her eyes flick up and down his body, appraising him. Her left eyebrow twitched up slightly, and the corners of her mouth might have raised a little.

"Is that right?" she said. "Well, I feel sorry for you having to be around that asshole."

She lifted a fist and shook it at the doorway above the stairs. She looked back at Troy and once again, her eyes lingered on his chest. He cleared his throat and nodded toward the road. A black, Chevy Tahoe was pulling into the lot. It made a gravel-throwing circle to face back out of the driveway, and the passenger door flew open as it stopped. The windows were too dark for Troy to see in, but the music rattling the car's panels was distinctly Spanish.

"Yo, Manuela," a voice called out over the din. "Let's go! Let's go!"

"Good luck to you and Señor jackass up there," she said, raising her middle finger and shaking it vigorously. "I hope he treats you better than he treated me."

"Or at least as good as you treated the last maintenance man?"

Her eyebrows lowered and her mouth flew open presumably to unleash a torrent of anger at Troy, but the voice in the car yelled again and the horn honked.

She flipped Troy off, wrapped her arms around the two broken suitcases and stomped on wobbly legs toward the Tahoe. Underwear and cotton balls dropped out like a fairy tale candy trail behind her. She slammed the door and the SUV hit the gas. Gravel flew up from the wheels and Troy ducked his head, dodging the hail of rocks. When it hit the pavement, the Tahoe's tires squealed on the asphalt and they tore away North on the Overseas Highway in a storm of furious maracas and suspiciously pungent smoke.

And that's when Troy heard the gunshot from the apartment above the pro shop.

5

Goin' Back To Miami

TROY DIDN'T THINK TWICE, he just ran up the stairs, taking them three at a time. His not-so-great knee protested, but he ignored it. The torrent of obscenities and the manic screaming reminded him of Afghanistan. On more than one occasion, his fellow soldiers had displayed an artistic command of the most foul words found not only in the English language, but at least three others as well.

Troy saw the door was open, and as the wailing inside intensified, he rushed inside. He fully expected to see that Lucas Walsh had shot himself— or failed at the attempt causing agonizing, scream-inducing injury. What he saw instead was not only shocking, but slightly embarrassing as well.

The suddenly estranged tennis pro was standing

in the middle of the probably canine-shredded brown carpet, drenched in sweat, pointing a pistol at the door. Troy stopped short and threw his hands up.

"Whoa, whoa, whoa now, partner," he said, seeing the man's fingers clinch around the grip of the revolver. "Don't shoot. Let's just take it down a notch."

"And why the hell should I do that?" Lucas yelled and jabbed the barrel toward the open door. "My girl has, in the space of a couple of weeks, screwed the maintenance man, and as you probably just witnessed, run off with her asshole, drug-dealing cousin from South Beach. And you think I should take it down a notch."

Troy shrugged his shoulders. "I do."

Without blinking an eye, the man raised the pistol to the ceiling and pulled the trigger. The blast stabbed Troy's ears with pain as chunks of drywall and fluffy pink insulation showered them both. A shrill ringing echoed in his ears and he raised his hands to cover them though it was too late. Lucas fired again and more debris fell around them.

Troy yelled at the man, but his hearing was so muffled, that he could barely tell what he was saying himself. The man shook his head and wiped his dusty, tear-streaked face with one hand. It was at this point that Troy realized the dude was naked except for a t-shirt ironically printed with a bright yellow logo that read: Fuzzy Yellow Balls. No pants, no underwear, no socks, and no shoes. Just fuzzy balls of a different color.

In the new silence of the hazy room, time seemed to slow down. It wasn't exactly the hail of bullets Troy remembered in the incident that took Harry Nedman's legs and, not long after, his life, but the danger felt the same. Guns are the great equalizer. It doesn't matter where you were born, who your parents are, or what your station in life is, a round from a gun of the size that Lucas Walsh was holding, would kill ... equally. And as Troy watched the man sobbing and shaking from his head down to his—well, his Fuzzy Yellow Balls—he knew the man was on a path to destruction, destruction of himself, and possibly destruction of Troy. He lunged.

Lucas saw this as it was happening and raised the gun. The barrel swung up slowly, still caught in the slow motion of intense and deadly peril. He pointed the black, gaping hole of doom at Troy and pulled the trigger. Troy ducked his head, hoping that the Outback tea-stained cowboy hat had suddenly developed the impenetrability of a kevlar vest. The click that came from the pistol echoed in the room almost as loud as the previous gunshot. Troy felt a gasp of relief hit him just as his face hit lower than his expected target. Having ducked his head, he'd changed his planned trajectory at the man's chest. For many years after the incident, neither Troy, nor Lucas would discuss what exactly had happened when Troy tackled the distraught tennis pro.

The part they both acknowledged—after a suitable pair of shorts were placed on Lucas—during an hour of heartfelt conversation sitting at the brown, folding card table in the kitchen was that the tennis pro still loved Manuela. Even with all her faults, he told Troy, she was the best thing that had ever happened to him.

"But what do I do now?" Lucas said, like a man with his fingertips clutching the edge of a cliff.

Troy's mind drifted back to Debby. *Wow, that seems like it was a million years ago.* He tried to place when it had actually occurred, but couldn't nail it down. Suffice to say, a whole lot had happened to him between now and then.

Looking at Lucas now, he wondered if he'd actually gotten as low down and broken as this guy was when it came to loving—or maybe it was hating —the hurricane that was Debby. It might have worked out after all if it hadn't been for that pesky detail of a husband. A tear slipped out of the tennis pro's eye and slid down his cheek. This sure seemed like love to Troy, if he even really knew what love looked like.

He tapped the card table with a firm finger. "Ya gotta put on your big-boy pants and go get her. That's what you gotta do." Lucas wiped the tear away from his cheek and sniffed back the gob of mucus that was threatening to drip from his nostrils. He took a deep breath and nodded slowly.

"You're absolutely right."

He stood up and smacked his hand down on the card table. The wobbly leg crumpled sending the table smashing down onto Troy's lap. He wasn't certain, but the rusty lip of the thing might have cut his thighs. He'd check that later.

Lucas ran into the bedroom and emerged more quickly than Troy expected. He had a black, Nike duffel bag thrown over his shoulder. He tossed Troy a jangly key ring with at least a dozen keys on it. He pulled his wallet from his back pocket and handed Troy two crisp one hundred dollar bills.

"You're in charge. Keep the store stocked with fresh drinks and don't screw anything up while I'm gone." He looked down at his watch. "I'll be back before Friday."

And with that, he ran through the door and left Troy sitting with the table still propped precariously on his legs.

He lifted the jumble of keys and sniffed. "Well, that could've gone worse."

He was surprised to see Lucas jog back into the room. The man scanned the dirty apartment, found what he was looking for, and winked at Troy. He reached down to the floor, picked up the empty pistol, and shoved it into his waistband.

"Good luck," he said, rushing out into the night.

"Dangit," said Troy.

6

The Beat Of A Different Drummer

DANTE "THE DON" Caparelli folded his hands on top of the damp, dimpled paper drink menu. Across the top, the headline announced that Woody's in the Keys served the hardest drinks south of Miami. Just to the left of his arm lay his fourth generation iPhone—now a relic. His wife—God rest her soul—had nagged him about getting a new one, but Dante always brushed her off. The damn thing made calls and that was all he expected it to do. He didn't spend his precious time tapping on candies or building up medieval armies. It was all bullshit designed to keep your head tucked firmly up your ass anyways and he didn't have time for that.

But right this second, he was watching the

phone, willing it to ring and working out the words he would say into the receiver when Matty finally manned-up and called him. An ungodly smash, followed by what sounded like a dump truck flipping over erupted behind him. If he'd had his cane, he might've jumped up, but it was presently lying on the floor a few feet away. It had been there since around ten o'clock when one of the not-too-happy-with-her-tips-tonight dancers had gathered her things and stomped out the door, her dangling, sequined garments wrapping around his walking stick and toppling it to the ground. The war—the second great one—had gifted him a fused knee. He didn't need the cane for much, but oddly, standing up from a barstool was the one damn thing it did help with.

He looked over his shoulder toward the band stage. The band called Big Dick and the Extenders had played at Woody's for longer than Dante had owned it. Legend had it that they had been playing on that lot before the strip club had been built on it, but Dante knew that was a load of horseshit. Then again Jack Snipes, the ancient hippopotamus of a man who called himself Big Dick for the stage, sat in his familiar wooden chair, Fender guitar high across his chest, screeching out the lyrics to Simple Man.

He was either completely unaware that the drum set had come apart and tumbled down around him, or his hearing was so bad, that he didn't notice. Either way, the overflow of a man finished his song, then looked around to see the rest of the band in shambles, staring at the fallen drums.

"Dammit, where is Matty?" Dante murmured to himself.

He swiveled back toward the bar and picked up his phone. No messages, no calls, no voicemails, no nothing.

"Nothing from the kid yet, eh?"

"Nope," Dante said, smacking the phone back onto the yellow, peeling varnish. "I think I'm gonna need a scotch, Sully. Glenfiddich, none a that cheap bottom shelf crap."

Sully Brooklyn was—you guessed it—from the Bronx. A thick salt and pepper mustache that would make Sam Elliot jealous concealed his top lip and he often chewed the ends of it nervously. His accent was totally New York and many of Woody's regular crowd had trouble understanding the man. For him New York was Noo Yawk and everything was a good idear. Dante was never clear on why the man had left the big apple and found his way to this trailer park in the islands looking for a bartending gig, but he had poured a perfect Old Fashioned. When he asked where the sugar cubes were, Dante hired him on the spot. The last frickin' bartender kept making Manhattans and calling them Old Fashioned's.

"You try callin'?" Sully asked, putting a nearly overflowing drink in front of his boss.

Dante took a long, careful sip. "You don't think I called him? Of course, I frickin' called him."

"Alright, alright." Sully held his hands up in surrender. "Just checkin'."

"Yeah, I called him. But why should I have to do that? He's a grown man now and he's got responsibilities. If he can't even run a Friday night shift at this dump, how's he gonna take over the family business when I ain't around?"

Sully was one of the few employees that knew what the family business really entailed. No one ever said the word mafia, or mob, or even family around the workers that didn't need to know any of those details. And the back room was always locked. Always.

The sound of trash can lids being smashed together exploded from the stage almost surprising Dante right off his barstool. Sully put his hands on the top of his head and ducked.

"What the hell?" Dante smashed his fist on the

bar. "Dicky, I pay you guys to play music, not to take out the frickin' trash. What is going on right now? I don't hear music and when I don't hear music, I don't see no girls dancin' and when I don't see no girls dancin', I don't see no money comin' in, you get me?"

The Jabba-like creature pulled his cartoonish basket weave top hat off his head and scratched his stringy forehead. He shrugged his shoulders and pointed a meaty finger at the stage where the drummer, skinny, rangy, and shirtless was pulling his long black hair back up into what is now known as a man-bun. Dante considered the man-bun to be the mullet of the millennial generation. These idiots would look back someday and wonder what the frick they were thinking ... maybe.

The drummer was trying in vain to put his drum kit back together and was dropping more cymbals than he picked up.

"What is it with bands and drummers? Eh, boss?" Sully asked.

The Extenders had recently had a bad run with their beat men. Ric Hammermill had died of an overdose of energy drinks. Then Trey Dunderson had hit a water buffalo in his Fiat Uno driving through the Everglades to another gig. And just last week, Cecil VonLondersen had been in the middle of the set when some very Aryan-esque dudes in black suits had walked in, calmly removed him from the stage and walked out with him. The man blubbered for help all the way, but Dante wasn't gettin' in the middle of that. This new guy was a local and from the looks of it, might not have been a real drummer. Either way, Woody's needed music and fast.

"Sully, put the jukebox on. I'm tired of this crap." Dante pointed at Big Dick. "Figure this out before I get out of the toilet, or all of youse guys are gonna be lookin' for another gig."

Dante stumbled off the barstool, sending it clattering to the ground. He waved his hand at it and groaned as he leaned down to pick up his cane. When he stood again, he gulped the rest of the scotch and grimaced as it burned his throat.

"Sully, I'm gonna take a break. You're in charge. If all that mess ain't fixed by the time I get back, get 'em all outta here."

"You got it, boss."

Dante took his piss—a somewhat unfulfilling task these days as he was sure his prostate was acting up—and headed to the back office. He looked over his shoulder as he pulled his key ring from his pocket. Unlocking the door, he eased it open and slid into the darkness inside. He closed it behind him and locked the bolt. Then he pulled a chain lock across and fastened it as well.

Only then did he turn on the light.

7

Cinnamon Girl

WOODY'S in the Keys in Islamorada, Florida regularly receives one and two-star reviews on the most popular travel sites like Yelp and TripAdvisor. Sometimes it is a commentary on the food, or the tepid temperature of the beer, but most of the time, the review sneaks in a line about how the girls looked like biker grandmas, or offshoremen, or bearded hags. But if you scroll to a few of the more recent reviews, they all mention Cinnamon. One particularly fervent customer saying, *"Oh, Cinnamon. Need I Say More$$? Wood & Two Thumbs Up!! Cinnamon I Need You!"*

In fact, referencing the quite beautiful redhead, the sign out front at one time boasted:

13 UGLY GIRLS AND 1 PRETTY ONE.

As depraved, lewd, and lascivious as the comments were, they never really creeped her out all that much. She trusted Dante and the bouncers —*when* they showed up for work. And she never even used a fake name. How could she? Her real name was Cinnamon Starr. *I mean, really, mom?* Apparently, her father had been allergic to cinnamon, so she named her that to spite the bastard after he'd left. But now, she actually loved it. Men often asked her what her real name was and she could, without batting a fake eyelash, confidently tell them. And they never believed her.

Besides, most of the dudes that frequented Woody's were old, crusty fishermen who drank so much they could barely stand up at the end of the night anyway. When the occasional Miami punk showed up flashing gold watches, diamond rings, and crisp Benjamins all over the place, she took a break.

As Dante, his face twisted up in anger, pushed past her toward the secret room in the back of the club, she smiled and tapped him on the shoulder. He didn't notice. She started to ask what was wrong, but he slipped in and locked the door. Twice. She shrugged her shoulders and went to the bar side to have an iced tea—not a Long Island Iced Tea, just iced tea with a whole bunch of lemon in it. If it wasn't sweet and sour enough to pucker her lips, it wasn't good enough.

Her Pop Pop—God rest his soul—used to make the best Southern iced tea she had ever tasted. That, and the best bread and butter pickles, too. She could remember getting off the school bus, walking down to his house (next door to hers) and find him waving to her from the front porch with two large mason jars full of his magic brew and another jar with a fresh batch of pickles. Might sound strange to some, but she remembered those warm afternoons as the best of her life. Later, she would find out her grandfather had been putting copious amounts of cannabis in the tea making it both addictive *and* medicinal. Seemed the rest of the world was finally catching up to the wisdom of her Pop Pop and putting the weed-derived oil in every gas station and convenience store from here to Timbuktu.

She had just had her eighteenth birthday when he passed and didn't have any reason to stay in Georgia, so she'd thumbed a ride on I-75 South. She didn't stop until she saw the "help wanted" notice on the board in front of Woody's and thought she might give that a go. On her first night, she'd cleared three hundred dollars. On her second, Dante had offered her an apartment, complete with a cute purse-pooch to carry around the island. And then, on the third, he'd offered her a new car.

It had started out well enough, but she soon wondered why the nearly immediate affections were coming from this old guy. Did he want to date her? But it became clear on the fourth night when he introduced her to Matty, his son, that he was gaming this system for his progeny.

Matteo Caparelli was decent looking enough, but he seemed to be as uninterested in her as she was of him. She was eighty-eight percent sure he wasn't gay, though he wasn't exactly masculine either. Slender, average height, nice wavy black hair, dark brown eyes. He wasn't Matthew McConaughey or Brad Pitt, but he wasn't that bad either. Maybe if he'd acted interested at all … but he didn't. She told Dante as much, but he refused to take his gifts back feeling that soon Matty would come around.

"Speaking of Matty coming around," she said to Sully as he slid a tall glass of her special tea, "where is he tonight? Isn't he supposed to be running the shift?"

Sully shrugged. "Haven't seen him. But yeah. Supposed to be his night."

As the bartender walked away, Cinnamon

realized the band was in a huff. Looked like they were losing another drummer tonight. At least this one wasn't going out in a body bag.

DANTE STARED AT HIS PHONE. Thirty-seven unreturned calls to Matty's phone. It never rang more than once and always went straight to voicemail. For the first time in twenty years, a new emotion crept into Dante's mind—fear. He began to consider that something might be wrong, but what? Matty was so straight laced that he didn't figure the boy was in any trouble with the law. Maybe a car wreck or something like that. But he would've heard something from somebody by now ... right?

He pulled open his desk drawer, pushed aside the two leather-bound ledger books and found the small velvet covered box. As he opened it, the low light made the hundreds of pin-prick diamonds sparkle brilliantly. The large letter C and the engraving of the family crest decorated the sides of the ring. He slipped it on his finger. It had gotten a little loose on him since age had started to steal his vitality, so he never wore it in the club for fear of losing it or having a grungy patron take a chance at grabbing it.

The scene of Matty's graduation sprang into his memory. He had been the first of the Caparelli's to graduate from anything other than the school of hard knocks. He was proud of that boy and had been so proud to give him his own ring, making him a full-fledged member of the family. The jeweler he'd found up in Tavernier, cute, middle-aged lady, had done an incredible job on it. If Matty ever had a boy, he'd be sure to get another one from her—if she was still alive by the time his reluctant son ever got around to it.

The boy wouldn't know the full extent of what it meant to be part of the Caparelli family for many years, but it was a powerful birthright to bestow on a young man.

Dante looked up at the ceiling. "God, I know I ain't done you no favors recently, bein' part of what one might call a mafia crime syndicate, but please let my boy be okay. Yeah? I mean, I ain't killed nobody in something like ... ten years."

The office door burst open, but the chain lock caught it. Through the crack, Dante could see Cinnamon's face staring, mouth gaping at him.

He jumped up, but his fused knee sent him tumbling to the ground. When he pulled himself back into the chair, rubbing his sore leg, he looked at the door, but it was closed. Had he imagined seeing her there? He grabbed his cane, walked over, and slid the door open. Nobody there. Maybe he had … *great, now my mind is going too.*

And that's when his phone rang. Not his cell, but the phone. The family phone.

8

Dripping With Dollars

TROY BODEAN WAS JINGLING the keys to the Islamorada Tennis Club in his left pocket and caressing the single remaining hundred dollar bill in his right. *Keep the store stocked with fresh drinks, right? That's what the dude said.*

Troy was pretty sure Lucas hadn't been talking about beer, but there was a good bit of gray area there and he didn't think one or two (or maybe ten) would matter much. Before he even got to the bar at Hog Heaven to order number seven, he was ... touched. It was just enough to be a hair past subtle and not enough to go unnoticed.

Troy, against his better judgement, which had left him two beers ago, turned around. The sailor standing behind him didn't look away.

"Howdy, friend," Troy said. "Thank you for your service."

"How'd you know I was a soldier?"

It is a well-known fact that someone who has served, even for a short time, can often spot other members of the military even if they aren't in uniform.

"Well, your hair is high and tight, the stance is dang-near attention, and your sunglasses ain't Costas or Oakleys."

The man, who was flanked by two equally muscled buddies sniffed and nodded his head slowly.

"And also, the Hog Heaven is a Navy bar," Troy added.

He ignored that and moved closer to Troy dropping into a more casual stance. "What's your name, soldier?"

"Heck, I don't tell that on a first date," Troy said, immediately regretting it. "To women, that is ... I date women."

"That's okay." Navy dude grinned and moved closer until his thigh was rubbing up against Troy's. "I date women, too."

"What are you fellas drinkin'?" the bartender yelled from behind the packed bar.

Troy opened his mouth to ask for his check, but his new friend slapped a heavy hand on his shoulder and said, "double rum and diet for my new cowboy pal here. And three Red Bull and vodkas for us. I'm buying."

"Oh, no. Much obliged, friend," Troy held up his hands in surrender. "But I only drink beer. Too much of the other stuff and I get crazy."

The man leaned down until his nose was almost touching Troy's. His eyes began to wander up and down and suddenly Troy knew how women in a bar must feel at this hour of the night.

"That's kind of the point, now ... cowboy."

Troy shoved his hand into his pocket and worked his palm around what felt like the sharpest thing in there—the key to the tennis center. It wasn't a knife, but it would make the dude think about what he was going to do next. As he was about to pull the makeshift weapon out of his pants, one of the guy's friends shoved him.

"Wayne, the man said he doesn't want a drink."

"Well, I've already paid for it, John." He poked his finger into Troy's chest. "So, he's gonna drink it. Wait a minute ... are you trying to horn in on my date?"

"Date?" Troy blurted. "Now hold on just a—"

"Jesus, Wayne," the man named John said. "I'm married. You know that."

But that fact seemed to escape Wayne who now was developing what Troy thought of as matador eyes. The man was a bull, preparing for a charge.

"Then, why don't you just mind your own damn business," Wayne said.

"Oh, for crying out loud." John threw his hands up, turned, and started walking away.

Troy watched as the scene began to unfold in slow motion. Wayne flexed his hands into tight fists and leaned forward on bulging quadriceps. He took two steps before Troy decided it would be best to let John know his friend was headed his way. He yelled his name at the top of his lungs, but in the din of the party-like atmosphere, it wasn't loud enough.

John, who had probably been scanning the room like any good soldier would, seemed to notice the crowd parting around him and turned at the last second to see Wayne go airborne. In sudden sheer terror, he threw his hands out and unfortunately caught hold of the Hog Heaven logoed tube tops of two of the bar's most buxom waitresses. When Wayne hit him, he went down hard. The tops went down with him.

A roar of approval went up from the crowd of off-duty military personnel. Dollar bills, spilled drinks, and testosterone whoops began to rain down on the men grappling on the floor and around the women, both of whom had discovered a new *concealatory* use for their drink trays. As the two men he guessed might be sailors—due to the preponderance of the other Navy guys around the bar—beat each other up, Troy backed out of the circle and made for the door.

A sudden tug at his sleeve made him pull his key-knife from his pocket and almost jab it into the neck of the nearly topless girl shuffling along behind him. Her friend, the second shirtless girl, was looking over her shoulder, tears of fear welling in her eyes.

"Take us with you," the first girl shouted.

"Please, mister," the second added, "help us get out of here."

Troy swallowed and wondered how trouble had found him once again. He grabbed the first girl's hand, nodded down at the second girl's and she grabbed it.

Taking a deep breath he yelled over the newly uproarious fight unfolding just a few feet away. "Ditch the trays."

Both girls looked incredulous, the second shaking her head violently.

"Trust me," he said. "It will only be for a second. Pretend you're on that beach down at the end of Key Biscayne tanning. Hell, ain't nobody down there to watch anyway."

Girl one looked at girl two and nodded. Slowly at first, she began to lower her tray, then, as if jumping into a cold pool, she flung it away exposing her breasts to the throng of people around them. Emboldened by her friend, the second girl tossed hers up into the air.

Troy smiled a thin tight smile and said, "follow my lead."

He raised his hand, holding the first girl's into the air and began to pretend to dance as if he were the lead in a conga line. She got the hint and raised her other hand as well. Now they were all holding their hands high in the air, dancing to the beat, doing the conga toward the door.

People around them immediately began to form the rest of the line behind them and the D.J.—worth every penny of whatever the Hog was paying him—suddenly noticed and put on the Buster Poindexter version of Hot, Hot, Hot.

As the line grew, the space between Troy, the

girls, and the door grew less and less populated. When it was clear, he jerked on the first girl's arm and he and the two bare-chested barmaids flew out the door into the chilly night.

The girls were laughing as they made it free from the crowd, the second girl realized she had cash shoved into her pockets, her waistband, and her high socks—a whole lot of cash.

The night air sent a shiver up Troy's spine and he turned to look at his two evacuees. "Danged if I don't ever remember a night in the Keys that was more nippy than this."

The first girl arched an eyebrow and crossed her arms over her chest.

"Did I say ... I didn't mean ... I was talkin' about the weather."

She opened her mouth to say something, but her friend interrupted her. "Regina, I've got over two hundred bucks here. There's fives and tens and even a twenty here. And you've got just as much, I'll bet."

Regina, the first girl, looked down and realized she was dripping with dollars, too.

"Oh my gosh, you're right," she said, sorting through the bills. "Are you thinking what I'm thinking, Tina?"

"Hell, yes!" Tina said. "I'm going back in there. This is more than I've made all week."

"Let's go."

Troy watched as the newly christened strippers of Islamorada jogged back into the Hog Heaven. They sidestepped someone stumbling out and Troy realized it was his three sailor friends.

"There he is," Wayne said, through a black eye and a bloody nose. "Grab him!"

"Dangit."

TROY HAD FOUND a junk pile of a bike leaning against a tree at the edge of the Hog Heaven parking lot and had pedaled madly without looking back until he was sure that he had outrun the beat up goons chasing him. Wayne had gotten close enough to grab Troy's shirt and rip it off of him, making him the third topless person in the vicinity tonight. But he had decided not to go back and get it and was now huffing and puffing, covered with a sheen of sweat, and freezing in the night air. He had no way of knowing, but he was pretty sure it must be after midnight. He hunkered down trying to somehow keep the heat sources of his body close together and rode along until he came to the Lorelei Restaurant &

Cabana Bar—one of the few places around he knew nothing about.

"Dang Florida Keys and I'm freezin' my butt off," he muttered to himself as he pushed open the door ... and immediately regretted it.

The dulcet tones of a silky baritone voice crooned the most manly version of *I'm Feelin' Good* that he had ever heard. When he found the source of the voice, he saw a ... a performer ... wearing a skin tight, dazzlingly glittery red dress. Her hair was as black as coal and her face was made up in thick, heavy stage makeup. Pretty in her way, but Troy could tell immediately, she was no she ... she was a he. It wasn't that this sort of thing bothered him that much. Heck, he'd been on stage once back in Savannah at a drag club. No, the issue here was that he was the new guy in a veritable sea of hungry sharks staring at him as he walked in the door —shirtless.

The performer, an obvious professional, saw him and began to take the stairs down from the stage toward him. Troy was reminded of a scene he'd once witnessed on the Discovery Channel about a pack of wolves taking down their prey. They always looked for the weakest in the herd.

Troy was frozen by the sweet sound of her voice

and the singer had almost reached him when he suddenly snapped out of his reverie. He waved and backed out of the door and was on his bike again and headed south.

The sounds of a live band drew him toward yet another bar. The side of the rundown building had a drawing of an old wood-sided car and the sign above the building simply said: Woody's in the Keys.

"Now, this might be my kind of place," he muttered propping the bike up on the side of the building.

The door announced that if total nudity offends you, do not enter. He hesitated. *Another strip joint? Is that a good idea.* A cold breeze whipped through the mangroves beside the place and Troy decided that total nudity didn't offend him as much as freezing to death did.

He pushed open the door. The raw, driving chords of AC/DC's *Back In Black* echoed loudly through the bar ... oddly, with no drums.

9

Writer's Block

CHAD HARRISON, New York Times Bestselling author of eighteen zany, Florida fiction novels, four children's books, and three collections of his newspaper columns, would never be recognized on the street. Nor would anyone recognize his name. They might, however, know something about Cap Wayfarer—his multi-million-dollar pen name and alter ego. They also might know something of his ex-wife Linda Harrison since she'd been in the news lately cavorting with that hack of a writer R.A. MacDougall.

So what if the guy was the picture of a Greek god and owned a fifty-foot catamaran, on which he was often photographed shirtless, thick, wild, artsy hair fluttering around in the wind. Ugh. The guy got lucky with one stupid book about post-apocalyptic farming community. *Seriously? Who reads that crap?* thought Chad.

Finally, the phone he held next to his ear connected. "Hello. You have reached the Islamorada Sheriff's Station. If this is an emergency, please hang up and dial—"

Chad angrily punched the zero on the screen. The recording ceased. The line was open, but nothing happened. He could hear vague static in the background, so he could tell the call had connected, but no one said anything.

"Hello?" he said. "Hello, is anyone there?"

A click and a loud squelch caused Chad to jerk the phone away from his head and almost drop his expensive new iPhone—the one that was so new that he hadn't yet purchased a protective case for it. He put the phone back to his ear to hear a shuffling sound.

"Hello? You still there?" the voice on the line said. "Sorry 'bout that. Forgot to unmute my mic."

"I'm here, what the heck is going on? I'm trying to reach the Sheriff."

"Well, friend, you are in luck. This is the Islamorada Sheriff's Station. Are you having an emergency?"

Chad shook his head angrily. "No. If I had been, I would have done what the recording had told me and hung up and dialed 9-1-1."

"And that would have been a good thing," the voice had a lilting southern accent, definitely not a South Florida native. Maybe more like South *Carolina*. "Well, alright then, have a beautimous day."

Before Chad could protest, the line went dead. He stared at his phone incredulously. He hung up on me. He scrolled through his recent call list and punched the number again. Without waiting for the recording to start her spiel, he clicked the zero.

Unbelievably, the same clicking and squelching sequence unfolded and he waited until he heard the clear line before speaking.

"I have an emergency," he said.

The same Southern accent said, "then, I highly recommend you hang up and dial 9-1-1. Thank you for calling."

Click. The line disconnected.

"You have got to be freaking kidding me," Chad said, gripping his phone so tight that is spurted from his hand like a bar of soap.

He watched as it cartwheeled up out of his grip, tumbled a few times, and hit the terracotta tile in his kitchen. The supposedly indestructible glass on the front spiderwebbed immediately, sending several slivers and shards skittering across the floor.

"Son of a—" His curse became a growl as he leaned down to retrieve his phone. Using the rationale that he had owned more than a dozen phones in his life and had always paid for the insurance—but never used it, he had declined it on this newest one. A sharp edge caught his pinky finger and bit into it, drawing a minuscule rivulet of blood.

He sighed and dialed 9-1-1.

Click. Squelch. "9-1-1. What's your emergency?"

Chad felt his mouth drop open. It was the same Southern drawl that he had just spoken to.

"You're kidding, right?" he asked the operator.

"Son, do you have an emergency or not? We don't take kindly to prank callers here in Islamorada."

"Yes. Yes. Please don't hang up," Chad pleaded with the man. "I do have an emergency."

"Okay, then. Just keep calm and tell me who shot who."

"Huh? Who shot ... ? No, um. No one has been shot."

"Fine, fine. Then who had the knife originally?"

"Sir, with all due respect. There were no weapons of any kind ... that I know of."

"Ah, I see. Domestic dispute? Who hit who first? You hit your wife—or your husband?"

"No, no. Nothing like that." Chad felt he was in imminent danger of getting hung up on again. "Robbery. Yes, that's it. There was a robbery. I was robbed."

He could hear the sound of a pencil scratching notes on a pad. And squeaking, maybe the sound of a chair rocking back and forth?

"Uh huh. And what did he look like?"

"What did he look like?"

"Well, yes. Can you describe the perpetrator?"

"Oh, well, I didn't see the person."

"Didn't get a good look at him?" the operator asked.

"No. I mean. I never saw anyone. The item in question is missing."

"Ah." The voice sounded suspicious. "And did the item in question go missing when you were a little ... um ... sauced on the tequila?"

Chad could almost picture the person putting down his pencil and leaning back in his chair.

"No. The item in question is a kayak—a very

expensive kayak. I'm pretty sure I wouldn't just misplace it. It is bright orange and very big."

"Ohhh," the voice lost its suspicion. "A burglary."

"That's what I said."

"No. You said a robbery. Completely different," the operator took on a voice that he might also use when explaining to a child how a stove becomes hot. "You see, in a robbery, someone takes something of value directly from another person by the use of force or fear."

"Okay." Chad felt obliged to humor the man.

"Burglary involves a person illegally entering a building in order to commit a crime while inside."

"Well, I don't think they actually came inside."

"I'm sorry what?"

"It's a kayak. I keep it under the house."

"Locked up with a cable or chain, of course."

Chad was silent. More pencil scratching.

"I see," said the voice. "Alright. Give me your name and phone number and I'll get someone on it as soon as we can."

Chad puffed up his chest. "Chad Harrison."

He gave his number and waited for the man to ask for more information. "Okay, Mr. um ... Harrison. We will get right on that as soon as possible."

"I don't think you understand. I need to speak to the Sheriff directly. This is an emergency that should be his top priority."

"Sir, we get too many calls that *do* involve guns and knives (not true) to check out every burglary that happens on the island. Right now, we have a possible serial killer on the loose down here. Maybe you've heard of him? The Cowboy Killer?"

"Never heard of him."

In truth, he had read something in the Miami Herald about the murderer accompanied by the artist's sketch of the man that might as well have been drawn by a 3-year-old with a crayon.

"Perhaps, instead of chasing a veritable ghost around the island, I suggest you people deal with the real crime here."

"I will tell the Sheriff, and we'll get on it as soon as possible."

"He should definitely consider doing just that since this is an election year and I would hate for my column at Keysnews.com to reflect his indifference to an upstanding, longtime, and *influential* member of the community."

The line went silent. He thought he heard the man gulp, but he couldn't be sure.

"Yes, sir. We'll get on it ASAP."

"Thank you."

Chad hung up and realized that he was now bleeding from his cheek.

"Dammit," he said, tossing the splintered phone onto the kitchen table.

10

The Cowboy Killer

SHERIFF PAUL PUCKETT hung up the phone. He knew exactly who Chad Harrison was and wasn't taking any chances on the man publishing some kind of exposé in the questionably relevant Keysnews.com. The fact that a mid-list author and ambulance chasing journalist like Harrison was even threatening such a thing was serious enough, but this was an election year, and Puckett was an elected official.

He glanced at the yellow pad he'd been doodling on while Chad was giving his report of stolen goods. It read: Dinner tonight? Chinese? Or pizza?

And then a couple of circles around two words: Orange kayak.

Puckett sighed. "Mark, I'm takin' the Explorer. Gonna make a few trips around the island, see if I can spot anything that looks like this missing kayak."

"Yes, sir, Sheriff," the deputy said. "Keep your eyes open for the Cowboy Killer, too."

Puckett's eyes danced across the folder resting in his inbox—a literal inbox on the corner of his desk, not a digital one. He flipped it open to see the communique that had come across the dusty fax machine earlier this morning.

```
FLORIDA BUREAU OF INVESTIGATION
MOST WANTED
JOHN DOE
A.K.A. THE COWBOY KILLER
Unlawful Flight to Avoid
   Prosecution - First Degree
   Murder (3 Counts)
```

He scanned the details describing the man and studied the grainy, blurry, pixelated image of the guy taken from security camera footage that did little to nothing to help identify the murderer. Apparently, the guy in the hat—a straw cowboy hat—had knocked over a liquor store up the coast a bit. In the process, he'd murdered the store owner—a jovial, Santa Claus type of guy who was friendly with all the local law enforcement.

"Where you at, cowboy?" Puckett closed the folder, knowing that the Keys were an ideal place to get lost until you could hop a ride on a slow boat to Cuba.

He pulled open the bottom drawer in his filing cabinet. Pushing aside the half-empty bottle of Pepto Bismol and the full bottle of Castillo Silver Rum, he dug out the box of shells. One by one, he slid six of the special edition Buffalo Bore bullets into the cylinder.

Puckett had been around the Keys long enough to know that most folks were just passing through on their way to Key West and anonymity, or to Cuba to disappear all together. This dude had probably gotten enough money—he checked the report, a hundred grand it seemed—to make a new life in some mud hut somewhere on the beaches of Havana. He pulled on his fleece vest and realized it still had the tags on it. He'd never needed it with the average temperature in Islamorada bouncing between sticky swamp ass and just stepped out of the shower. He jerked on the tag and the paper tore loose leaving the plastic twig dangling under his arm.

Screw it, he thought. *I'll cut it off later.*

Before he'd made it half a mile from the station, the radio buzzed to life with a report out of the Homestead P.D. Apparently a Latino woman running the late shift at the Tom Thumb had reported a fidgety man purchasing a sack full of Monster energy drinks and spicy beef jerky with crisp, clean one hundred dollar bills. With some interesting translation work, the local detectives had worked out—maybe—that the man had been wearing a straw hat like the one seen in the surveillance video of the so-called Cowboy Killer. Together with the earlier report that put a similar spotting in Hialeah, Puckett knew without a doubt, there was a murderer on his way toward Islamorada and beyond.

He turned the Explorer north and cruised just below the posted speed limit of forty-five. Slowing at every parking lot, shopping center, and gas station, he scanned for anything unusual—a tough ask in the Keys. He saw an old bearded man with a spider monkey riding a unicycle, two women with tattooed bald heads and piercings of every size and shape dangling from their faces (he wondered how they got through flight security checkpoints) and a group of little people dressed in shiny wrestling outfits headed south in the back of a gigantic pickup truck on wheels taller than the occupants.

Without knowing why, he turned onto Plantation Boulevard—maybe intuition, or maybe just to change the scenery. He cruised a little slower and shined his spotlight toward the Coral Harbor Condo. He almost pulled in and wrote a ticket to the woman flipping him off from the third floor, but he didn't have time for such niceties. Half an hour later, he turned back onto Overseas Highway heading south.

Several times, he found himself drifting along at twenty miles per hour, peering into the mangroves off the side of the road. It was pitch black out there. If the Cowboy Killer wanted to hide here, all he'd have to do is take three steps off the pavement and he'd be invisible. Puckett slapped his steering wheel and pulled off the side of the road in a sandy alcove under a Key Lime tree. He knew he was close to a bunch of charter companies and tourist excursions. Maybe he'd watch the road for a bit and pull over a drunk driver or two.

He turned off his lights and pulled the lever to

lower his seat back. Or maybe catch forty winks. As soon as his hat slid down over his eyes, his radio squelched, jerking him out of a dream involving ... was it Elle MacPherson and Paulina Porizkova ... and a vat of whipped cream.

"This better be good, Mark," he said, clicking the receiver. "I was literally about to become a human banana split with two Sports Illustrated swimsuit models.

"Sorry, boss," the deputy said. "I got a call from up at Hog Heaven. Family stopped in for a quick bite to eat and found a bar full of topless women."

Sheriff Paul Puckett shook his head. "Damn tourists. It wouldn't be the first time a couple of co-eds didn't have one too many shots and do things they'll regret tomorrow ... if they remember them."

"Yeah, um," Mark said, "Seems it might be the waitresses showing their ... well, their everything. And the dad was pretty pissed when his adolescent sons got their fries delivered with a motorboat. "

Puckett sighed. "What? You mean they—? Never mind. I'm on it."

He put the Explorer in gear and squealed out onto the highway headed back north ... again.

He would be surprised to learn later that his

unsuccessful napping spot was only five feet from a large piece of bright orange rotomolded polyethylene—a tough, flexible and relatively soft plastic commonly used in the manufacture of kayaks.

11

The Non-Stripping Side

TROY CLINT BODEAN slipped into his newly-purchased, black tank-top with a 1948 Chevrolet Woody Wagon screen printed poorly across the chest in neon pink. It was scratchy and reeked of cigarette smoke, but it was better than being shirtless among the ... well ... shirtless employees of this dive bar. He watched as the band somewhat skillfully worked its way through a range of classic hit songs from the seventies to the nineties without a drummer. It was an odd sound, but after a few more beers and a couple of mistakenly poured tequila shots that the bartender had slid his way, he didn't mind the music at all.

The big fella singing was actually pretty good. As the night wore on, Troy found himself sliding down to the end of the bar where he could see across to the back room where women of varying degrees of ... talent ... took to the stage and proceeded to take all of their clothes off. It wasn't difficult to work out that Woody's was not a hotbed of hotties making a ton of money stripping. It looked more like a group of girls competing for attention on what might've been visible scar night. Most looked as if maybe they were mothers feeding their kids—or someone else's kids—or perhaps a drug habit.

He turned down dances from Mercedes, Crystal, Candy, Kitty, Jade, Destiny, and Bambi. After one particularly large shot of tequila, he had almost given in and allowed Chardonnay to gyrate on his lap to his favorite Aerosmith song, *Love In An Elevator*. Thankfully, the bartender—Sully—had shooed her away and informed Troy that he might be getting more than he bargained for with the tall, dark dancer. When Troy asked what he meant, Sully simply asked him if he'd heard of the movie, *The Crying Game*.

Troy had not, but he just nodded and decided it would be best if he didn't take the lap dance. Sully slid another tequila across the bar.

"I better not," Troy said, holding up his hand.

"That one's on me."

"Yeah, but I gotta get home and I'm afraid that one might get me lost."

"You live on the island, right?"

Troy nodded.

"I could tell you weren't no tourist," Sully said. "I'll make sure you get pointed in the right direction. Which way are you from here?"

"South. Pretty close by. You know the tennis club?"

"Ah, yep." He poured another tequila for himself. "Cheers, cowboy. I won't steer you wrong."

A dancer Troy hadn't seen yet slid onto a bar stool next to him. "How 'bout one of those for me, Sully?"

The bartender shrugged. "Can't, unless you're buying."

Troy watched as she reached down and hiked her skirt up revealing a garter stuffed with folded bills—ones, fives, tens, twenties, and even a couple of hundreds. He allowed his gaze to drift up her glittery getup, past her toned tummy, slowing only momentarily at her seemingly non-surgically-enhanced—

"Hey, buddy," she said, putting her finger under his chin. "If you're gonna gawk at me like that, you gotta at least give me a tip."

Troy grinned. "Sorry, darlin'. The tequila's to blame for that. How about if I buy this round."

He slid his hundred dollar bill across the bar and Sully looked at the girl. She nodded and he picked it up and put it in the cash register. He started to count out change, but Troy knocked his knuckle on the bar.

"Just keep that tab open," he said. "And whatever I don't drink up is for you."

Sully shrugged. "You're da boss."

The girl picked up her shot, tossed it back—no lime or salt—with no discernible grimace or shiver, and turned the empty glass over on the bar.

"Another?" she asked Troy.

Troy looked down at his full shot. He took a deep breath and drank it down as quickly as he could. It took two gulps and he couldn't help but clench his eyes shut and purse his lips. The girl laughed, but it was reserved. Something was up. There was a touch of worry in her eyes..

She had long, straight blonde hair, blue eyes, fair skin with just a touch of sunburn, and just the right amount of freckles on her nose. Troy turned his glass over and belched.

"Well, I reckon if I'm gonna buy you another round, I should at least know your name."

She held out a hand. The gesture seemed odd coming from a stripper, but she didn't really look like an old pro anyway.

"Cinnamon," she said, pumping Troy's hand once. "Cinnamon Starr. And you are?"

"Bodean. Troy Bodean. I am very pleased to meet you, Cinnamon."

She cocked her head to the side and her eyes relaxed a bit. "That's the first time a guy hasn't made fun of my name or asked me what my real name is. Most men get upset when I tell them that *is* my real name."

Troy had naturally assumed it was a stage name, but he didn't let on. "And a beautiful name it is."

He held up three fingers to Sully. The bartender emptied the last of the bottle into three shot glasses and slid them across the bar.

Troy picked his up and held it high. "Here's to swimmin' with bow-legged women."

Sully gave a thumbs up and promptly tossed his tequila into a nearby sink. Troy and Cinnamon drank quickly racing to finish first. She narrowly clanked her glass onto the bar first, raising her hands in triumph.

Troy was about to order another when the front door of the bar jerked open and crashed against the wall. He thought it was a small miracle that the black-painted glass hadn't shattered—must've been a lot of paint on that thing to hold it together.

A wiry man sauntered in, a toothpick in his teeth, his thumbs hooked into the waistband of his cutoff denim shorts. His t-shirt was sweat-stained and his skin was ruddy and tan.

"I'll be darned," Cinnamon said to Troy. "That guy's got a hat just like yours."

Something about the man looked familiar, but it hovered just below the surface of consciousness like that feeling of walking into a room and struggling to remember what you went in there to do. Troy shrugged it off and would later blame the copious amounts of alcohol he had consumed for keeping him from recognizing the dude. But in his haze, he turned around to order another drink. Cinnamon refused. Her eyes darted from Troy to the back of the bar at a closed door. Her eyes were flighty with worry.

"Say," she said, touching Troy's hand. "I gotta get out of here. Would you mind if (she lowered her voice as the bartender walked away) well ... if I crashed at your place?"

Troy blinked. "Darlin' I appreciate what your doin', but I'll be honest with you, I ain't got no cash left and besides that, I don't really like to pay for—"

She smacked him hard on the cheek. "I'm not that kind of girl."

Troy rubbed his sore chin. He shook his head to clear the cobwebs. "That's quite a right cross you got there."

"Shit," she said. "I'm sorry. I didn't mean to hit you so hard. It's just ... I don't do that kind of thing."

"Of course. Of course. That is totally my bad."

She turned and stared at a door in the shadows behind the bar. "It's just that ... I might be in a bit of trouble. See, I heard something tonight that maybe ... maybe I shouldn't have. Thing is, I don't really want to be here when Dante comes out of that room back there."

"Darlin' I'd love to help out, but I make it my policy not to get involved in domestic type things."

"Domestic?" She wrinkled her slightly freckled nose, until realization spread across her face. "Oh, it's not like that. I'm not married or even dating Dante. He was trying to get me to date Matty—wherever he is right now—but I'm not sure he's interested. Anyway, I'm starting to think that the Caparelli family is part of the maf—"

She suddenly stopped talking and stared at the

back door. Troy followed her gaze to see that there was now an older man with white, slicked back hair, standing in the door, a massive cigar between his lips. The smoke curled around his head as he stared at them.

"Please, Troy," she touched his arm. "I need to get out of here. Just let me crash on your floor tonight. I just need a day to let all of this blow over."

"Well, there's a problem with my place. It ain't exactly mine."

He proceeded to detail his accommodations and how he was just crashing in the hammock out on the back porch of the tennis club. And then he remembered that Lucas—the tennis pro—was gone. He'd hightailed it after his fiancé and would most likely be gone for at least a couple of days.

"Oh, please. Anything will do. I just can't be at my place tonight. I'll sleep on the floor," she begged, with her hands folded in front of her chin.

Nothing good can come of this, Troy thought, as he heard himself say, "alright then. I s'pose it'll be okay for one night."

He looked back at the man standing in the doorway. His eyes were squinted and his mouth curled into a frown around his cigar. He took one step toward them, but then a clanging racket like spilled pots and pans or trash can lids erupted from the stage. The other dude with the cowboy hat had plopped down behind the drums and started beating on them with reckless abandon. He'd tossed his hat to the side and taken his shirt off. For a second, Troy wondered if Tommy Lee of Motley Crüe fame had a twin brother. If so, this was the guy. When the old man looked away from them toward the cacophony on stage, Troy grabbed the girl's arm and pointed to the front door.

"Let's go."

12

A Murderer In The Room

DANTE CAPARELLI HAD plenty of experience with killers—at least, civilized ones like Shorty Malone and Al "Fat Fingers" Luccessi. He could tell when a man had taken a life. The man who he'd seen at the bar sitting next to Cinnamon was the kind who had blood on his hands. Something about the man's appearance, rugged, ruddy, wandering, and worn made Dante uneasy—a strange experience for a man who had plenty of experience dealing with serious criminal types.

And it had been a long time since Dante seen two such men waltz into Woody's. The guy behind the tumbled drum set was clearly a maniac and may or may not have killed someone as well. But, he'd gotten the drums back up and working and the music was actually sounding pretty damn good. Even Big Dick sent a "thumbs up" Dante's way as the band cranked up a bar favorite with Roadhouse Blues.

He looked back and found the two barstools where Cinnamon and the cowboy had been sitting were empty. The front door was sliding shut and Dante made to run after them, but his bad leg turned his sprint into a stumble and he was on the floor in no time. Sully flew out from behind the bar and helped him up.

"Boss, you gotta be more careful than that," the bartender said. "What with Matty not here and all, we wouldn't be able to get through the night without you."

Dante grimaced at the thought. He really needed to get more managers out here, but money was pretty tight and no one with any real work skills wanted to work in this dump. He had half a mind to pick up the Family phone and tell them to take this place and shove it.

"Did Cinnamon leave with that other cowboy fella?" he asked Sully.

The New Yorker shrugged. "Can't say for sure, but they was here before all canoodled up at the bar and now ..."

He pointed at the empty barstools.

"Did he leave a credit card or receipt or anything?"

"Nah. Paid cash."

"Tell you what his name was?"

"I think he told Cinnamon it was Bond. Troy Bond or somethin' like that."

Dante huffed. *Right. I'm sure that's his real name.*

"You want I should follow 'em, boss? The cowboy is stayin' at the Islamorada Tennis Club. He told me that much."

And the piece finally clicked into Dante's mind. Cowboy. He'd seen something earlier today about... He turned and hobbled back into his office. Slamming the door behind him, he pulled the cord on the banker's light sitting on the edge of his steel desk. He eased himself down into the squeaky chair and reached under to find his trash can. Yesterday's Keys News was folded and discarded.

He pulled it out and spread it across his desk. The latest Cap Wayfarer column had been hilarious in its naïveté—somethin' about hanging tourists from the banyan trees. Dante hated the self-righteous, Florida-native attitude about tourists. Didn't those idiots know that tourism was a massive part of how the state made its money? More than that, it always seemed to be some silver-spoon-fed millennial that floated such ridiculousness. He didn't know this Cap fella, but he was certain he was right about that much.

"Jackass," he muttered as he flipped past the front page.

Finally, he found what he was looking for on page six. It was just above the obits and just below the Peanuts comic strip.

COWBOY KILLER SLICING HIS WAY THROUGH SOUTH FLORIDA

He scanned the details and discovered that the man in question was on the run from law enforcement and had likely killed more than four people on a path of terror that led straight down to the bottom of the mainland.

Dante circled the article with a red pen and found the "If you have information" telephone number at the bottom next to a very familiar artist's rendering of the serial killer. He didn't dial the number, but he was certain he knew where the man was hiding out.

He wondered idly if the dude was planning on killing Cinnamon. Poor girl had no family nearby and really no friends that Dante knew of ... except Matty. His Matty. Matty who hadn't showed up for work coincidentally on the same day this dude wandered into Woody's.

What if this guy had killed Matty and had kidnapped Cinnamon, planning to slice her up, too. With a new rage in his heart, Dante pushed himself up from his desk. He walked to the door and shouted out to Sully over the newly rambunctious rock and roll from the band.

"Get a car down there to the tennis club," he said. "I want eyes on those two."

He slammed the door shut as Sully picked up the phone. He'd have one of their guys over there within minutes. He hoped it was one of the good ones who wouldn't blow their cover before Dante could get a real pro down here to find out what really happened to Matty. He took a deep breath and picked up the Family phone.

He punched in a number that wasn't written on any paper or stored in any phone or computer. It was a number Dante had memorized and could call without looking down at the ancient rotary dial.

The line connected, but no one spoke.

"I need *the guy*."

"*The guy*?" the voice on the line asked flatly.

"Yeah," Dante said, rolling a cigar between his fingers. "*The guy* who ... fixes things."

13

Just Rewards

GARY JOHN SUSKIND hadn't come out of his room at the Lime Tree Apartment building for more than two hours over the last couple of days. The only reason he had shown his face at all was to steal a copy of the ever-thinning Keys News paper from his neighbor.

The Cap Wayfarer column had been dead-on accurate about all the ills of tourists ravaging the sensitive state of Florida. Gary was not a native, but his mother had been and as far as he was concerned, that was good enough. He'd even sought out the writer's email to send a congratulatory note about the brilliant piece when his blood ran ice cold.

Under the article, in large red letters, he saw a reward notice.

$25,000 CASH REWARD for information leading to the recovery of Mr. Wayfarer's Orange Kayak.

A picture of the kayak appeared under the details showing the writer sitting atop it with two buxom blonde women—both nearly naked.

Since the local police department claims it can do nothing about the staggering amount of crime on the island, I am taking matters into my own hands. I am happy to handle the return of my kayak and the subsequent reward anonymously.

I will also be matching the $25,000 reward in a fund to support the candidate who runs against Sheriff Paul Puckett.

The rest of the notice was a rant against the sheriff and the local police department.

"That's not good, Shakira," Gary said to the African Grey parrot perched on his shoulder. "That's so not good."

"Not good. Not good," the parrot squawked back at him.

Gary leaned back on his designer Divano Roma futon and ran his fingers through his thick, lustrous hair.

He was in the middle of considering a call to the police to explain exactly what had happened. Surely with all the advancements in crime scene technology they could tell that Matty had been eaten by a gator along with the boat.

"That is if they ever find the kayak and whatever's left of Matty," he mumbled out loud.

"Whatever's left of Matty," Shakira, quick to mimic anything she heard, said back in a near perfect echo of Gary.

"Oh, crap, no, Shakira. Don't say anything about Matty."

"Don't say anything about Matty. Whatever's left of Matty."

Gary jumped up to grab the bird, but was interrupted by a bony knock at the door. He froze. Shakira let out a squawk, but Gary held up his finger to his lips shushing the parrot.

"I know you're in there, Suskind," the muffled voice said through the door. "Open up."

Gary watched helplessly as Shakira ruffled the feathers on her head and opened her mouth. "Don't say anything about Matty. Whatever's left of Matty."

"Shit. No, bird!" Gary lunged at the grey sending

it fluttering and flapping wildly about the tiny apartment.

The knock became more insistent. "I hear you in there, Gary. Open up. I saw the article in the paper about the kayak."

Gary nearly stumbled over his coffee table in shock. The voice outside the door belonged to Myrtle Hussholder, his landlord. She'd been the one to suggest he take his secret crush on a boat ride.

"Always romantic and they can't get away from you even if they want to," she'd told him with a sly wink.

Gary picked up a copy of the latest Broadway Journal magazine from the table and flung it at the escaping Parrot. He took a deep breath and strode across to the door. He took a second to compose himself and ran a hand through his hair.

Putting on his best smile, he opened the door. Outside on the rusted-rail enclosed walkway stood Myrtle. Gary would've been surprised to find out she wasn't at least a hundred years old.

Her dark tan, but nearly transparent skin was dotted with liver spots and her skin hung all around her with deep, elephant-like wrinkles. She had a new bandage on her face, likely another skin-cancer removal, and her eyes were watery and pale.

The grin on her face was sly, mischievous, and evil all at the same time. Somehow, it reminded Gary of the Golden Girls' Rue McClanahan. What a beautiful actress to think of at a horrible time like this.

Myrtle was in a bathrobe that was far too thin and exposed far too much for a woman of her advanced age. Luckily, she held a copy of her own Keys News over her chest. The Cap Wayfarer reward post was facing Gary and she tapped on it with a curled, knobby finger.

"Seems like you got yourself a boat, eh? Take that young boy out you been fancying?"

His pulse raced. First, he hadn't told Myrtle it was a man he'd been wooing. Second, how in the world could she have remembered that conversation? He'd spoken to her on many occasions when she couldn't remember whether or not he'd paid the rent. On several of those, he'd claimed that he had—knowing full well he hadn't—when he'd been a little short on money.

"Ah, no," he said carefully. "I'm not sure what that's all about."

"Uh huh." She folded the paper and tucked it under her arm. "Well, I just happened to be down at the Green Turtle stocking up on my wine when you and your fella cruised past with that bright orange kayak on top of your Jeep. Hard to miss since it's the only one I've ever seen like it, 'cept on the Dukes of Hazard that is."

She turned to gaze out into the parking lot. Gary's 1980 Jeep CJ-7, the "Golden Eagle" model, sat in the first space next to the handicap spot. Anyone who watched any television in the eighties would immediately recognize it as the Daisy Duke Jeep from the long-running hit show about Bo and Luke. It was no General Lee, but it was nearly as iconic. Most boys his age had fantasized about being *with* Daisy. He had fantasized about *being* Daisy. Thus, when he was old enough, he'd sought out a collector's edition of the famous Jeep. He used to like how distinct it was, but now it seemed that fact might get him into trouble.

He laughed nervously, "Oh, yes. That was us. But that kayak came from somewhere el—."

"Cut the crap, Suskind," she interrupted him. "You and I both know it was you and now it seems like you have a twenty-five thousand dollar problem on your hands."

Gary gulped down the bile threatening to escape his throat.

"I don't know what you did to that boy, but I

could sure use that kind of money. Especially since some of my tenants don't always come up with their rent."

Gary had to clamp his mouth shut to keep from vomiting on the woman. When he was sure he'd recovered, he took a few seconds to consider the fact that she hadn't already called the police. She had come to his door first. But why? *She's playing me for something*, he thought.

"Okay, Mrs. Hussholder," he said. "What now? Are you turning me in for the reward."

"Oh, heaven's no," she laughed as she let the paper fall away, exposing her body under her thin nightgown. She ran a finger down her crepey, sagging cleavage. "I'm actually thinking of another, more ... friendly solution."

Behind him, Shakira squawked, "friendly solution. Friendly solution. What happened to Matty? What happened to Matty?"

He glared over his shoulder, planning an appropriate demise for the parrot. Then he felt a fingernail tracing down his abdomen. The finger slipped into the waistband of his boxers and snapped the elastic below his waist. He jumped back a step, realizing that his own bathrobe was hanging open, exposing his stomach.

It wasn't common knowledge that he was an Instagram influencer with a fitness account aimed at men. Not many people knew he was Insta-famous with over one million followers and a daily "like" count that even top tier actors didn't achieve. Much of the reason his account was so popular was his abs —his rock hard, twelve-pack, washboard stomach. Every time he posted photographs of it, his account grew by ten percent.

Myrtle's eyes were tracing the deep grooves of his transversus abdominis muscles when he snapped his robe shut. She feigned a look of hurt and slipped her hand into a pocket. Pulling out her cell phone, she held the paper up to her eyes.

"Let's see," she said, squinting at the Cap Wayfarer reward post. "Where's that number again?"

"Hold on," Gary touched her arm. "That's not necessary."

She arched an eyebrow at him and the grin on her face became more lascivious than he would've imagined possible for a woman of her age.

"What ... um ... exactly ..." he coughed. "What exactly did you have in mind?"

She reached down and pulled his robe apart. "Did you see Fifty Shades?"

"You mean the sadomasochistic piece of garbage

that ruined the beauty of the Twilight series?" Gary asked, disdain dripping from his words. "I did."

Myrtle shoved him into his apartment, following as he stumbled backward. She closed the door behind her and let her shift fall to the ground.

"We'll start with a little light whipping and see where that gets us," she said.

"Light whipping," Shakira screeched. "Light whipping."

Gary felt his dignity fall away with his boxers. *Maybe going to jail would be better than this.*

14

Exchanging Glances

TROY WOKE TO A COOL, gentle breeze rocking his hammock back and forth under the hazy morning sun filtering through the nearby mangroves. His lower back felt like a professional wrestler had been bending, twisting, hammering, and pummeling it with a crowd-favorite signature move—perhaps called the pile-driver, or the sledgehammer, or maybe the wrecking ball. As the fuzzy goggles of way too many hard tequilas and Coronas began to fade, he realized he was not actually *in* the hammock. He was lying on the porch beneath it. *Did I fall out?* He shook his head to aid the receding fog. *Did I ever make it in?* And then when a figure lying in the hammock squirmed a bit and groaned, he realized that he was not alone.

The hallmark of any good soldier is that they can be on their feet and ready for combat within minutes, or even seconds. Troy knew that he would never have been referred to as a *good* soldier, but he was able to roll over twice, hurling himself off the porch into the scraggly bushes lining the nearby court. It wasn't much cover, but it would have to do. When he tried to get up, his knee screamed at him. A good amount of running and walking and pedaling last night had him in more pain than he'd realized.

With great effort and more than one yelp of pain, he pulled himself up to peer over the deck of the tennis shop veranda and was shocked awake at what he saw—a girl. She was seemingly naked from head to toe, except for a tiny black tank top that looked suspiciously familiar. He glanced down and realized that it was indeed his new souvenir shirt that she was using as a makeshift sheet. What appeared to be her clothing was lying in a rumpled, glittery heap beneath the hammock and he realized that he must have been using it as a pillow.

It was when he saw the sequins that he began to regain some of the blacked out memories of the previous evening. What an evening it had been. He'd started down at Hog Heaven accidentally inciting a

Navy riot and birthing two new exotic dancers, to Lorelei where he'd been a near hit on amateur night, and finally to Woody's in the Keys where a friendly stripper and a generous bartender had turned his head into a pressure cooker of pain. And finally, they had come back to the tennis club only to find that he had lost the keys and couldn't get them inside. While he looked for an open window—failing to find one —the girl had folded herself into the hammock and fallen asleep. Not wanting to leave her alone, he'd taken up watch underneath her. He couldn't remember how she'd gotten naked and how he'd lost his shirt to her, but he figured that was probably best.

He stepped up onto the porch and shook her gently.

What was her name? Cindy, or Cynthia, or ... without warning, the girl stretched both arms up and over her head, flipped over so she was facing away from him, and proceeded to start snoring softly. The black tank top dropped to the ground, revealing that she was quite totally nude—just like the front door of Woody's had promised last night. Troy leaned down, picked up the tank top, and slipped it over his head. It still smelled like a dirty ashtray, but now it had a slight vanilla scent as well.

He bent down and picked up the shiny pile of stuff under the hammock and did his best to cover her up. There was only so much he could conceal as the clothing was apparently designed to do the exact opposite. He walked around the club, thinking he'd get on his bike and head up to The Trading Post and get a few things for breakfast. When he strolled into the parking lot, he was shocked to find that his bicycle wasn't there. His first ironic reaction was to curse the random thief that had taken it (ironic because in actuality, he'd stolen—or at least borrowed it himself.) But then he remembered leaning his bike up against the corner of Woody's last night and figured it might still be there. Maybe his keys would be there as well.

Even with a bum knee, it was still just a quick stroll up the road and he figured the walk would help clear his head and ease his aching muscles a bit. Besides, the Trading Post was past that, so either way—on his bike or on foot—he'd be closer to his goal of some fresh bacon and eggs and coffee and maybe even some hot Cinnamon rolls—Cinnamon. That was the girl's name. Her real name if he remembered correctly. It was decided.

He had his mental grocery list, so he adjusted his severely scratched Costa sunglasses over his eyes, pulled his hat down low to combat the newly heating sun of a much warmer Islamorada day, and limped up to the Overseas Highway.

He turned north and started walking.

At mile marker eighty-two, he saw that his bike had indeed been borrowed by another soul in need of a ride. To his utter shock, the person had left a note and a fifty dollar bill. Troy had almost missed it, but he kicked a rock in frustration, exposing the borrower's IOU. He shrugged, tucked the bill into his pocket, tossed the note away, and continued on up to the grocery store.

He was sweating by the time he got there, and he could smell the tequila leaching from his skin. As he approached the Trading Post, a family of tourists rushed to get their kids tucked safely into their station wagon and he realized that he probably looked like a vagrant.

He was sweaty, grimy, un-showered, wearing a local strip-club t-shirt, and hadn't shaved for—well, he'd lost count of how many weeks, or maybe months it had been. But, he had cash now, so that was all that mattered. He pushed open the door and was thankful that the store's air conditioning was set on frigid.

.   .   .

CHAD HARRISON WAS out of Solspring Biodynamic Organic Extra Virgin Olive Oil—an obscenely expensive luxury he used liberally in making his daily bacon, egg, and Brie cheese on Italian bread breakfast sandwich. He had experimented with at least two dozen different brands before discovering that this particular oil made his recipe zing with flavor. He had lobbied the owner of the Trading Post for over a year before she would agree to stock it on her shelf. Hell, even the Olive Morada just up the road wouldn't carry it.

Sure, he could order it online, but he preferred to spend his money locally. He figured that was prudent, seeing as how he had become the de facto voice of the Florida natives in his Cap Wayfarer column.

He wheeled his bike into the first slot of the curbside rack, not bothering to lock it. He'd only be a second inside to grab the oil and a few more free range eggs. His mouth watered just thinking about the sandwich he was going to create. Basil, maybe he'd add a sprig of fresh basil and see what happened. He made a mental note to grab some.

Pulling open the wooden screen door, he was greeted by the familiar whoosh of ultra-cooled air and the tinkle of a real bell—not an electronic chime. *Atmosphere*, he thought. *It's all about the atmosphere.* If you had an electric door notification beeping at the customers walking in, you couldn't really sell that this place was a Trading Post. Marie had done an amazing job of taking care of the place since Ernie had passed five years ago.

He grabbed a basket—not the plastic variety found at most grocery store chains. No, this was an honest-to-God, wood, woven picnic basket with a red gingham cloth liner. He strolled down the first aisle, not bothering to wave back at the older woman running the cash register. He turned down the dairy, egg, and yogurt aisle and stopped short.

"Christ," he muttered. "Looks like they're letting the bums shop here now."

The man in front of him, rifling through the eggs like an assembly-line worker sorting widgets, was dirty. He smelled of smoke and was wearing a shirt he'd obviously stolen from a tourist. Worst of all, he was sweaty and grimy and was touching every single damned egg.

"Friend," he said, not hiding his disdain, "you gonna wash all those eggs you're defiling there?"

The man looked up, tilted his straw cowboy hat back on his head, and smiled. "I'd be happy to do just that. I didn't realize folks ate the shells or I'd have been more careful."

Chad opened his mouth to reply, but couldn't think of a sharp enough retort. He was slipping. Back in his heyday, he would've ripped the man a new one with some sly, sarcastic comeback. As it was, he just shook his head and grabbed the nearest half-dozen cage free organic eggs that looked like maybe the man had skipped over them.

"You like that brand, do ya?" the man in the hat asked, scratching his chin. "I woulda got those, but I heard they keep their chickens in a barn. Fourteen hens per square meter."

Again, Chad tried desperately to come up with a witty, scathing remark, but none was there. He tucked the eggs into his basket and turned around, not bothering to dignify the man with so much as a dismissive glance.

"That all you need?" Marie asked as she manually punched in the prices on an old five-and-dime cash register.

Chad pointed to a stack of papers at the front of the store. "And a copy of the Blue Paper."

"Okie dokie. That's seventy-five dollars."

"Seventy-five? Jesus, Marie. It was only fifty-five two weeks ago. I'm not a tourist, you know?"

The old woman shrugged. "It's your oil. They went up. Really proud of that stuff."

He shuffled a few bills across the counter and jerked the receipt out of her hand. "Highway robbery is what that is."

"You want me to stop ordering it?"

Chad huffed as he pushed open the tinkling door. He loaded the groceries into the hopper on the front of his bike and folded the paper over the top to keep the sun from beating down on them. A poorly drawn artist's sketch of the Cowboy Killer stared back at him. His eyes went wide as he looked up to see the bum who'd been fondling the eggs walking out of the store. The dude had a scruffy beard and shoulder-length black hair ... and a cowboy hat. He nodded at Chad and touched his finger on the brim of the hat. Chad jerked his bike backward out of the rack the rear wheel dipped off the curb faster than he expected and he went down. His groceries spilled out and he distinctly heard at least three—probably more like five—of the eggs cracking.

The man—the Cowboy Killer—walked toward him. "You okay there, buddy?"

Chad picked up his bike and stuffed the pile of now soggy groceries into the wire basket on the front. "All good. Thanks."

"Looks like you broke a few eggs. I'm sure they'd replace 'em."

"No worries," Chad said, hurrying to pedal away. "Not gonna eat the shells anyway, right?"

He didn't wait for the man's reply. When he reached Dion's Quik Mart, he pulled his bike to the far side of the store and watched as the man in the hat started walking. He was headed south, the same direction Chad had gone. The former investigative journalist in him began to think of the headlines: Cap Wayfarer Bags Notorious Serial Killer or maybe Thriller Writer Nabs Cowboy Killer.

He wiped a smear of egg that had somehow splattered onto the screen of his phone and dialed 9-1-1.

15

Kandy Kane's Kicks

SHERIFF PAUL PUCKETT recognized the number when it flashed up on the caller ID. He didn't waste time with his whole 9-1-1 shtick, but launched straight into what he thought the person on the line was calling about.

"I'm sorry, Chad," he said, putting a hand up. "I don't have any new information on the whereabouts of your stolen canoe."

"Kayak," Chad Harrison blurted into the phone. "It's a kayak, you moron."

Paul almost hung up, but then Chad continued in a somewhat frantic voice.

"But that's not what I'm calling about. I am calling about a murderer on the loose at the Trading Post."

Years of sitting in the station with his feet propped up on his desk made him slow to react and doubtful besides.

"A murderer you say? At the Trading Post?"

"Yes, well, he's not there now. He's actually headed south somewhere around ... around mile marker eighty-two."

"Okay, I'll bite, though I'm likely to regret it." The sheriff sat up and flipped the top off of a blue ball-point pen. He slid a yellow legal pad off the desk and into his lap. "Let's start from the top. Who did this person kill?"

"Well ... I don't know. Maybe like a man, or maybe a woman ... or both."

Paul flipped the pad back onto his desk. "Look, Chad, I know what you're doing. I promise I cruised the island myself and didn't see any obvious signs of your canoe (he called it a canoe on purpose this time to needle the man.) Furthermore, it is a federal offense to falsify an emergency call. Now, if I hear anything about your—"

"Shut up and listen, sheriff."

Paul Puckett clicked the button to disconnect the call. Within seconds, the line rang again.

"Sheriff, wait. I'm literally cruising along the road behind the Cowboy Killer."

Paul sat up. However unlikely the man's frantic story was, his law-enforcement trained intuition buzzed. "You have my attention."

"He's walking down the highway. Tall, lanky, ruddy tan, black hair and beard, and a ragged straw cowboy hat. It's the guy, I swear. Looks just like that drawing in the paper."

"And you're cruising along behind him?"

"I am."

"You're driving?"

"I'm in Dion's gator."

"What?"

"Jim Dion's gator. Like a golf cart on steroids with big knobby wheels. Borrowed it from Jim at the Quik Mart."

Paul stood up at his desk. "And he's just walking on the side of the road?"

"Yep. He just got groceries at the Trading Post."

He shot a doubtful glance over at the new officer the FDLE had insisted he hire on staff. The fresh-faced kid—what was his name, Ian?—could hear the whole conversation being taped on the emergency line. He shrugged.

Paul sat back down. "So, you're telling me the alleged Cowboy Killer, murderer of more than one person, just made a grocery run and is now ... walking down the road?"

"Uh huh."

"Not running?"

"Jesus, sheriff. Are you listening to me? Yes. He is walking down the road, carrying a bag of groceries and I am following—shit, where'd he go?"

"What? What's happening, Chad?"

"I lost him. I looked down for one second and—"

A loud, cacophonous banging suddenly blasted into the phone's receiver. It was so intense, Paul jerked the headset he was wearing off his head and flung it across his desk. The new kid, Ian, had been surprised by the commotion and had jogged over to the sheriff's desk.

"What the hell was that?" he asked.

"I have no idea," Paul replied, rubbing his ears.

He picked up the mangled headset and gently placed the right earpiece back on his ear.

"Chad? Are you still there? What happened? What was that loud noise."

There was a crackling sound and a high-pitched voice in the background yelling profanities.

"I just rear-ended a ... well, a pink Mercedes."

Paul pointed at Ian, twirled a finger in the air,

and then pointed at the front door, indicating that he wanted him to take a patrol car and check it out.

"Okay, I have someone on the way."

"But what about the Cowboy Killer? Do you want me to see if I can find him?"

"No. No. Now, just sit tight and wait for Officer Bass to get there. We'll deal with the wreck first, then we'll see if we can track down your cowboy."

In the background, Paul heard the woman's voice getting closer and more hysterical. He thought he heard a death threat mixed in with her curse-laden tirade.

"Hurry," he said to Ian as he grabbed his hat and rushed out the door.

CHAD HELD both arms up to deflect the repeated blows from the tiny, pink-sequined purse that the ... man ... was beating him with. It didn't hurt much, but the flurry of blows was relentless.

"I just freaking bought it, you jerk," he said. "I literally just bought the damn thing yesterday. Ugh, first I lose a boyfriend to a greaser and now my car, my beautiful car. Why do you hate me, God? Why?"

The tall person hitting him with his clutch, was a

man, dressed as a woman. He/she stood at least six or seven inches taller than Chad, which was mostly due to the eight inch stiletto heels he/she wore.

"Look, I'm really, really sorry, sir," Chad started.

"Ma'am," the drag queen said.

"I'm sorry?"

"Ma'am. When I'm dressed like this," she indicated the skin-tight pink sweater, black pencil skirt, and her pastel pink Jan Crouch wig, "I'm a woman."

"Ah, okay. I see," Chad stuttered. "Anyway, ma'am, as I was saying, I'm so sorry. I was on the trail of a murderer when I accidentally hit the back of your car. I mean, there doesn't appear to be any damage."

"No damage?" the woman shrieked. "Just look at this."

She pointed to the bumper and a tiny sliver of a scratch that couldn't have been thicker than a human hair, or longer than a matchstick. Chad was certain it was only the clear coat that was damaged and not the paint. A quick buff should take it out in seconds.

The woman looked down at her watch, a huge, jewel-encrusted affair. "And, wouldn't you know it, now I'm going to be late for the six o'clock show."

"I'm sorry," Chad said, meekly.

"I don't suppose you have insurance on that ... thing?"

"Well, actually, it's not mine."

The drag queen threw her head back and laughed, a maniacal sound like an evil Disney sorceress mixed with Vincent Price. "That's just rich. My baby just got defiled by a stolen redneck golf cart."

"It's not stolen. I borrowed it."

"Uh huh. Heard that one before."

"Look," Chad said, pulling his wallet out of his pocket. "I have insurance. My agent is Fran up at Allstate. I'm sure I can get this all taken care of if we can just move on."

He handed an information card to the man, dressed as a woman. She studied it for a second.

"Chad Harrison?"

He nodded and held out a hand. "You might know me as Cap Wayfarer, from Keysnews.com."

Seeing no recognition from the woman, he added, "And I've written seven New York Times bestselling novels including Trimmer Man and Good Banana."

A flash of something crossed the woman's eyes. "You? You wrote Good Banana? I absolutely *loved* that book. I've read it so much the pages are falling out. It's hilarious. Especially that part where the ape drives the boat up onto the sand and then hops out and wanders up to the beach bar. Classic Florida Keys."

Chad laughed and felt a sudden pang of terror at the tingling in his nether regions. He was neither gay, nor bisexual, or any of the other new sexuality designations, but he found he was attracted to this person.

She dug into her purse and pulled out three pieces of paper. She handed them to Chad. He flipped through them. One was her insurance card, the other two were tickets of some kind.

The insurance card revealed that the *woman's* name was Daniel Kane Kotlerson. Apparently, seeing his eyebrows dart up, she said, "I know. I go by Dani when I'm in drag."

"Pleased to meet you, Dani." Chad said, thumbing through the next two pieces of paper. "And what are these?"

"Tickets to my show. I star in the Kandy Kane's Kicks revue at the Bourbon Street Bar down in Key West—a show that I am currently running late to perform in right now."

"Sounds like a good time," Chad said with a smile, tucking the tickets and the insurance card into his pocket.

"Look, I appreciate your help, but I've got to go," Dani said to Chad. "You'll be there tonight?"

"I will."

Chad walked her back to her car and they noticed for the first time, that the rear tire on the passenger's side was flat.

"What the hell happened to my tire?" Dani yelled.

"You must've picked up a screw or a nail or something. I didn't hit you hard enough to do that. Do you have a spare?"

Dani buried her head in her hands. "That is the spare. The previous owner told me she had used it, but I never had it replaced. I'm never going to make it to work for the early show. Maybe the nine o' clock if I get a ride."

Chad looked up to see if the anyone was nearby to help with the tire or getting Dani a ride, but they were deliciously alone. *Deliciously?* He thought. *Did I just equate being alone with a crossdresser with deliciousness?* He shrugged mentally. Maybe it was ... time would tell.

"Shall we walk back to the Quik Mart to see about getting you a tow truck?" Chad asked.

Dani hooked her arm through his elbow and smiled. "Sure thing, sweetheart."

Neither of them noticed the Islamorada Sheriff's Ford Explorer pass them going south.

16

Dead Kayak

FDLE OFFICER IAN BASS had been sent to the Florida Keys on what he thought was a very important case. Though he was an adequate officer, he was far from exemplary. He was the kind of person who didn't get chosen first, nor did he get chosen last for things such as dodgeball teams, relay races, or trivia nights down at Hooters. Upon his release exam from the Chipola College Criminal Justice Training Center in Marianna, his trainer had written him a suitable recommendation saying, "Ian is a good officer. It would not hurt your team to have him on board."

With such a flat referral, he was turned down for acceptance to the Miami, Jacksonville, Orlando, Tampa, Naples, Fort Lauderdale, Sarasota,

Tallahassee, Pensacola, St. Petersburg, Clearwater, and Daytona Beach police departments. He was invited to apply in Vero Beach, but that was where the parents of his ex lived, so he'd politely declined. He finally applied for and got a position with the Florida Department of Law Enforcement as an OPS Office Automation Specialist. To this day, he is not certain what his exact duties were on that job. Mostly he fixed the computers that the other officers managed to screw up on a daily basis.

His big break came when no one—literally, not one officer—was available to investigate the trickle of rumors coming from the Keys about the mob. The current case involving the so-called Cowboy Killer was dominating the FDLE's somewhat limited resources, so every top agent was on that case.

And though it wasn't a stretch to imagine that there were dirty dealings, money laundering, and probably drug smuggling and perhaps even a touch of prostitution occurring in South Florida, there wasn't enough credible information to send a top agent to check it out. Thus, Ian was sent to Islamorada when they posted an opening for an Assistant Deputy to the sheriff. In the two weeks he had been there, he had scoured the island for the mafia and had found ... nothing. Just a bunch of fishermen, Navy personnel, tourists on their way farther south, and a vagrant or twelve. He had, however, picked up the sheriff's dry-cleaning, kept the coffee machine filled with hot, black java, delivered the proper ratio of glazed, chocolate, and powdered donuts to the office on a daily basis, and brought the newspaper in before the daily afternoon storms.

As a result of this less-than-riveting time on the island, he'd been skeptical when the sheriff sent him out to investigate the possible Cowboy Killer sighting. He'd thought it was probably a kid on a weekend bender down from South Beach or maybe on the run from a challenging exam at FIU.

He spotted the pink Mercedes with a flat tire, leaning on the side of the road. Thankfully, the people involved had decided it was okay to move the car and the ... golf cart to the side of the road. He flipped on the lights and pulled over in front of the disabled car. He walked to the driver's side and rapped his knuckles on the glass. He stood there for a good twenty seconds before realizing there was no one inside. He circled around the car and peered into the passenger's side. Empty.

He craned his neck to look over at the beefed up golf cart parked behind it. There was no one there either. He stepped around to examine the damage caused by the wreck, and besides the flat tire, he saw nothing. No dents, no dings, no nothing. He knelt down and pulled out his flashlight. Shining it all over the Mercedes bumper, he finally found a tiny, shallow gouge in the clear coat.

I had to come out here for this? He thought. He stood up and scanned the highway. Besides the random car racing along, slowing immediately upon seeing the lights, then cruising past picking up their speed again, there was no sign of the *wreck* participants. He shrugged and walked back to the Explorer. He flipped off the lights and radioed the station.

"Sheriff, there's no one here," he said. "And frankly, I don't even think there's enough damage to warrant a report. A little scratch in the paint, but it'll probably buff right out."

The crackle of static came back with Paul Puckett's reply. "Any sign of the Cowboy Killer?"

Ian huffed. "No, sir. In fact, there's not a soul around for miles."

"Alright. Well, why don't you cruise down to Marathon and back. Just see if you spot any hitchhikers wearing cowboy hats. Oh, and on your way back, I've got a pickup at Sudzy's if you don't mind."

"Roger that," Ian said with a sigh. *So much for actual police work.*

He put the Explorer in drive and eased on the highway. He hadn't gone more than two miles when he reached the Islamorada Tennis Club. He'd passed it a thousand times and almost didn't give it a second glance. But then he saw him. The Cowboy Killer.

He eased to a stop and watched through the mangroves along the front of the property as the man—wearing a straw cowboy hat, dark sunglasses, a white wife-beater tank top, khaki shorts, and flip flops—drove a tractor dragging a wide brush behind it. He made circles and figure eights all over the tennis courts. Having exactly no experience with a clay tennis court, Ian had no idea why someone would do this. Maybe the dude was on drugs or something, having a slow-speed joy ride on a stolen tractor.

He couldn't see the man's features well, so he decided to get out and have a closer look. Checking the battery life on his cell phone, he guessed if he could get within twenty feet or so of the man, he could click a few pics and send them up to the FDLE to verify the guy's identity. The fence surrounding the tennis club was rusted and hardly sturdy, but there were no obvious breaks in it that he could crawl through.

He put both hands on the top of the fence and heaved. He pulled himself up until he was able to bend his upper body over. It was at that point that his belt—the one with the pepper spray, taser, flashlight, batteries, gloves, keys, multi-tool, window punch, and his Glock 22—got caught on the V-shaped barbs at the top of the fence. He tried to wriggle free, but only ended up gouging himself in a few tender locations. Rather than endure further injury, he unclasped the belt and was able to lift himself up and over, leaving it dangling from the fence. He pulled several times on it, but something was wedged tightly and he was afraid the noise of wrenching it free might alert the Cowboy Killer.

Though unremarkable as a law enforcement officer, Ian Bass was not an idiot. He pulled his Glock from the holster and carried it along with him. After four steps, he found himself knee-deep in the murky mud and the tangle of roots common to the Islamorada mangroves. He could barely make out the tennis courts through the jungle of vegetation, but he could still hear the tractor running. The closer he got, he realized he could also hear the man's voice ... singing.

The not-altogether-unpleasant strains of *Sweet Home Alabama* rose out of the swampy marsh. He trudged along, slowly and methodically. The water was now almost to his waist and he wondered what manner of creatures were circling him just below the surface. He wondered if the blood from the cuts on his thighs would draw animals in the dark water like it did with sharks in the ocean.

Without warning, his hands pushed through a thick curtain of foliage and he fell forward. He crashed into the fence surrounding the courts and was certain his cover was blown. He quickly dunked himself down into the water so that only his eyes were exposed. Luckily, he realized the man was facing away from him and had a thick pair of vintage headphones on—blasting Lynyrd Skynyrd's Greatest Hits, no doubt.

He pulled his phone out of his pocket and held it up, waiting patiently for the man to turn back toward him. All he needed was a profile from each side and a straight on view of ... he lost his train of thought as he clicked the power button to wake his phone. Nothing happened. As a trail of water dripped down the screen, he realized with horror that his phone was not waterproof. He tapped it against his palm, willing it to work. But still, the screen remained black. All of this for nothing, he thought, feeling the oozing mud sinking into his clothes.

He studied the man for a few minutes and from this distance, he was fairly sure that he'd found the Cowboy Killer. He was sure enough that he would radio Paul Puckett once he got back to the SUV and have him put a call in to the FDLE. Jurisdiction notwithstanding, this was a case for the big boys up on the mainland.

Turning around he heard a sound—a familiar sound to any that have lived near the Everglades for any length of time—that made his heart stop. Some call it a purr or a cough, most describe it as a chumpf. It is distinctive and clear and can mean only one thing—there's a female gator nearby ... and she's in heat.

Watching the murk that rose up to his waist, he stilled himself, scanning for motion. Maybe he had imagined it. Nothing was moving and the water was dead calm ... for about three seconds. And then, the massive muscled bulk of an enormous alligator thrust out of the water at him. He dove to the side and somehow squeezed between two larger trunks out of reach of the gator. The beast's jaws slammed into the left trunk and she bit into it with a fury, screaming as she did.

Ian Bass filled his underwear with his own mud. And then he ran. The trudging, agonizingly slow lunges he made through the water couldn't possibly be fast enough, but somehow, the monster hadn't eaten him yet. He glanced over his shoulder to see the gator still attacking the tree trunk. Daggers of sharp flora stabbed at his arms and legs, one particularly sharp thorn from some ancient tree caught the side of his face and he was sure he'd need stitches in that one.

Just ahead, he saw something. *The Explorer? Thank God!* He surged forward and then breaking into a small clearing, realized it wasn't the SUV. It was ... a beach. He stepped out onto a slim, one-foot wide section of scraggly beach. The horror pounded in his brain. He'd gone the wrong way. He hadn't made it to the road because he'd gotten turned around and trudged all the way across the island to a small, isolated beach.

There was jungle to the left and right, he couldn't pass either way. He thought he might wait to signal a passing boat, however, the fishing capital of the world was suddenly deserted. No one, nothing but gently splashing waves for miles and miles. He realized the alligator's furious noise had stopped.

He turned around and studied the dense jungle behind him. Nothing was moving. Maybe the gator had given up and gone away. It was at that point, he realized he was still holding his gun.

"Shit!" he yelled into the air.

He took a deep breath, emboldened by the newfound courage of a .40 caliber weapon in his hand, and stepped back into the mangroves. Ten yards in, something bumped against his leg. He yowled, knowing he was going to die and emptied the Glock into the object.

When all he heard was the clicking of his trigger, he stopped and looked down. With hysterical laughter, he realized it wasn't the gator.

"You killed a kayak, Ian," he said to himself. "Nice work buddy."

A bright orange, mangled, and now mortally wounded kayak bobbed up and down next to him. He laughed again and kicked the kayak.

"Ow, shit, my toe," he hopped up and down, sloshing the water around him.

Suddenly, the gator, growled and surged up out of the swamp behind the boat. The dagger-like teeth of the massive maw of the mama gator slammed down onto the kayak, chewing, tearing, shredding the orange fiberglass.

Ian emptied his bowels again along with his bladder this time, but he didn't stick around long enough to see if the gator could smell it.

Coronas And Key Limes

BETWEEN THE JANGLY CLOSING BARS OF his favorite Skynyrd tune, Troy Clint Bodean heard something thrashing around beyond the fence behind court number nine. He lifted his sunglasses, tilted his hat back on his head, and pulled the borrowed headphones from his ears. He waited and watched. Other than the usual rustling of the wind and the occasional torrent of birds taking flight out of the trees, he heard nothing out of the ordinary. He thought for a second he might've seen something slinking around in the shadows, but whatever it was had gone back into hiding.

He shrugged his shoulders and put the earbuds back in. He grinned at the song that had replaced the southern rock stalwarts legends. Jimmy Buffett had sneaked his way into the playlist and had begun extolling the virtues of a fully loaded cheeseburger. Troy's stomach growled and he wondered how Cinnamon was coming along with the sack of ingredients he'd brought back from the Trading Post. As if she'd known he was thinking that, she poked her head out of the apartment window facing the courts.

"Hey, cowboy," she called with a wave, "breakfast is served."

Troy gave a thumbs up over the rumble of the tractor as he pulled it back into the garage. He turned the key off and froze. As a longtime resident of swampy places, he was all too familiar with the sound a mama gator made. He was certain he'd heard it when the sputtering of the tractor died down. Sweat dripped down his forehead in the greenhouse-like heat of the shed. The wind creaked through and the door drifted open.

"You comin'?" He heard the girl's voice echo across the courts.

Dangit, woman, he thought. *Now ain't a good time.*

His view was obstructed to the right and left of the open door. He felt sure the gator had slunk out in the open to investigate the noise he was making brushing the courts, but he couldn't see it.

Calculating the distance across court number eight to the fence, he realized that with his not-so-good knee and the land speed of a Florida alligator being something around thirty miles an hour, he decided he couldn't outrun it.

He scanned the inside of the shed for some kind of weapon. He wasn't sure he could kill the thing, but he might be able to fend it off or slow it down long enough for him to get to the fence. The tools of the tennis trade didn't offer much in the way of a good weapon inside the building. Leaf blower, line brush, bags of clay, extra line rolls, nails ... and a hammer.

He picked up the hammer and for reasons only known to men, he swung it up and down a few times, testing its heft. *Probably only good enough for a whack to the skull,* he thought. Getting a firm grip on the handle, he took a deep breath. He knew when he lunged out, his knee would revolt against the quick burst, but it couldn't be helped and he willed it to press on.

He jumped out of the garage and hit the ground hard. In protest, his knee buckled and went limp under him. He slammed into the clay and rolled forward in an awkward somersault. The hammer went flying as he clutched his now screaming knee in pain. He rolled over onto his back, scanning for the attacking gator. He raised his hands against what he was sure would be the dagger-lined maw slamming down on him.

Nothing happened. He looked left, right, back. His head swiveled around looking for the alligator.

"What are you doing down there?" Cinnamon said, her voice echoing over the settling calm over the courts.

Troy couldn't help but smirk in relief. Though he was sure he'd heard a gator chuffing around out here, there was clearly no sign of her now. Or maybe he'd imagined the whole thing.

He picked himself up and dusted off the caked on layer of clay. His knee ached, but it wasn't as bad as he thought it would be. He turned around and waved to the girl poking her head out of the second story window.

"Just caught my flip-flop on the edge of the door," he said. "I'm gonna wash off this dust and I'll be right up."

"Don't be too long," she said. "Your eggs will be cold."

He looked around one more time to reassure himself there was not an attacking beast coming up behind him. Nothing but the gentle sway of the mangroves and a distant bird singing in the breeze. As he limped through the open gate, he heard a plop to his right. He jerked his head around and saw that a nearby lime tree was dropping the sweet, ripe fruit on the ground. He scooped up a couple to squeeze into an afternoon Corona.

CINNAMON RINSED the plates as Troy leaned back and rubbed his full belly.

"That was dang good, young lady," he said, stretching his arms above his head. "You'll make a fine wife one day."

"Hey," she said, crinkling her nose, "that's sexist and I don't appreciate it. I'd rather be a chef than a homemaker."

Troy raised his hands up in surrender. "Didn't mean any offense. You'd make a great chef, too."

She grinned and winked at him. "Maybe I could be both."

Troy coughed and sputtered and searched for the words to change the subject.

"Don't worry, cowboy." She laughed and threw the dish towel at him. "I'm not looking for anything like that any time soon. What I really want to do is perform."

"You mean, like, at Woody's?"

"Ugh, no," she said. "That place is a dump. I'd like to be a real dancer, not a stripper. But right now, I need the money. When I get enough, I'm out of there."

"Can't say as I blame you."

A beam of sunlight streamed through the window over the kitchen sink. Dust motes floated around in the not-too-awkward silence that had settled between them.

"I see you brought in a couple of limes," she said, rolling the green fruit around in her hand.

"Thought they might go good in a Corona on the beach."

"Now, that is the first smart thing you've said all morning."

"You got a suit?" Troy asked, and then realized that, of course, she hadn't brought anything with her.

"Nah," she said, stripping her t-shirt over her head, "but this oughta do the trick."

Her spangly, sparkly, sequined bikini from her work the night before at Woody's glinted in the sunlight.

Troy felt his mouth drop open, though he tried hard to keep it from doing so. It is anecdotally known most strippers look amazing under dark black lights, but then in the light of day, they resemble something between the creature from the black lagoon and the swamp thing. Cinnamon not only looked good, he noticed, she looked even better in the early afternoon glow.

"Why don't you take a picture," she said, breaking his daze, "it'll last longer."

"I am ... I'm so ... you have to forg—"

She grabbed his arm, pulling him up out of the chair. She pecked him on the cheek and tapped the top of his hat.

"I'm just teasing," she said. "It's sweet. You get the beer on ice, I'll look around and see if I can find a couple of towels. Is there a decent stretch of beach near here?"

"If we cross the highway, the other side is nice enough. Usually pretty quiet."

"Perfect. I need to work on my tan lines." She grinned and put a finger under his chin to close his mouth again.

Like almost any other early afternoon on US 1, traffic was scattered and sparse. The sun was bright and hot and before Troy could react, Cinnamon reached up, grabbed his hat and plopped it onto her own head. He almost raised his arm to take it back, but dang if she didn't look super cute in it. He grinned and put one foot out onto the road. As soon as it touched the warm pavement, the sound of a vehicle roaring recklessly past made him stumble back, almost dropping the styrofoam cooler.

"Hey, watch it, dude," he yelled, feeling like an old man in Bermuda shorts with black socks pulled up to his knees. "Slow down, man. It's the Keys!"

An Islamorada Sheriff's SUV barreled past them, barely staying in his lane.

"Jesus! That was close. He should at least turn his lights on, right?" Cinnamon asked.

She threw an arm up and flipped the bird toward the disappearing Ford Explorer.

"I reckon," Troy muttered, squinting at the car now far off in the distance. "Ah, well. Let's just get down on the beach. I'm ready for a beer."

18

It's Blackmail, Sugar

GARY JOHN SUSKIND choked the bile back into his throat. It burned like he had swallowed a shot of gasoline and sand. Myrtle Hussholder lay under him covered in a sheen of sweat that smelled of mothballs and gin. She moaned as if she was alternating between ecstasy and agony, but when Gary slowed down his rhythmic thrusts, she slapped the side of his face.

"You're not done until I'm done," she screeched at him as she sniffed back the endless drip of mucus from her bulbous nose.

Apparently, she was sensitive to his cologne or maybe his bird.

"You're not done. You're not done," the parrot,

Shakira, echoed at him from her perch beside the bed.

He fought back the urge to vomit all over the woman and closed his eyes. As long as he kept a strong mental picture of a young Tom Cruise in his signature white shirt and socks from *Risky Business*, he was able to perform for the old hag. But she kept squeezing her thighs around him and he could feel the sagging skin slapping his hips.

He began to wish the alligator had eaten him along with Matty. Just as he was losing his will to go on, a loud pounding shook the paper-thin front door. He heard a key jam into the handle, the door jerk open, and the chain lock catch it in mid-swing.

"Gary, what the hell?" a voice called into the living room.

"Oh, Christ," Gary hissed to Myrtle. "It's my boyfriend, Dani. You've got to get the hell out of here."

"Not until I'm done," she gasped for air. "I'm not even warmed up yet."

Fighting another gag, Gary pointed toward the door. "If Dani finds you here, neither of us will get to finish."

"Well, what do you recommend?" She frowned.

"You don't have a back door, and that window is two stories off the ground."

Gary looked around.

"Closet. Get in the closet."

He stood up, grabbed the woman's flimsy nightie and flung it at her. She was sitting on the edge of the bed licking her lips at the sight of him urging her to hurry. He realized he was still naked and grabbed a pillow to cover himself.

"Gary! Open up. I need to borrow your Jeep!"

That didn't make sense. Dani had a car. Why the hell would— the sound of the door being forcefully opened, followed by the sound of the chain breaking and the broken parts skidding across the floor interrupted his train of thought. *Oh, crap.*

He grabbed his aged landlord by the shoulders and slammed her back on the bed. He jerked the sheet up over her head and leaped in beside her. He was just pulling the quilt up over her bulk to camouflage the fact that she was there when Dani burst into the room.

"Hey hun," Dani said, rifling through Gary's things piled on the bedside table. "Where are your keys? Why'd you lock the chain? You never lock the chain."

"Wait. What? Why do you need my car?"

"I got into a little fender bender," Dani said. "Actually, I'm not sure if there was any damage to the car, but my tire went flat and I don't have a spare. I need to use your Jeep tonight to get down to Key West. I'm already late to the show."

Gary shook his head and flung his arm in the direction of the closet. "I have no idea where my keys are ... um, maybe in my pants over there in the hamper."

"Well, can you get up and help me find them?"

Little did Dani know how much trouble he'd had getting up over the past—he looked at his alarm clock—ugh, two hours. He watched as Dani found his pants, dug into the pocket, and pulled his hand out holding the keys.

"You okay with me taking it?

"Yes, yes, of course." Gary nodded vigorously.

"Not even warmed up," Shakira said, repeating some of Myrtle's best lines. "Oh, baby, gimme a kiss."

Dani, thinking it was Gary who had said it, walked to the side of the bed, leaned over, and pecked him on the side of the cheek. And that was when the old woman's allergy to Gary's CK One cologne reached a tipping point. She sneezed loudly three times back to back. If he'd had more than a second to react, Gary would've been shocked and repulsed by the amount of snot he felt spray all over his thigh. He didn't have that time because Dani's mouth flew open and he grabbed the duvet and flung it aside, exposing the naked sack of a woman, curled in the fetal position next to Gary under the sheets.

Dani threw his hand over his mouth, gasping at the sight. He barked like a seal a few times, obviously shocked by the sudden appearance of not only a woman in his boyfriend's bed, but a woman who reminded him of Ed Asner.

"What ... the ... hell ... is going on here?" Dani jabbed his finger accusingly at Myrtle with every word.

Gary threw his hands up. "It's not what you think! I swear."

"I don't care." Dani was shaking his head furiously back and forth as if trying to throw off what he'd seen. "We are through. I should've trusted my instincts. I knew you weren't gay. You haven't been with me like this (he pointed his finger at Myrtle again) in so long!"

Gary knew that the reason he'd been distant with Dani was because he'd been falling for Matty, but none of that mattered now that he'd become alligator food, so he kept it to himself.

"Of course I'm gay. You know me. You know I love you. Seriously, even if I wasn't ... I mean ... this is not *that* at all. It's just ... it's ..."

Myrtle Hussholder, who looked like she was ready for a cigarette and a drink, raised her arms over her head and arched her back. Her underarms were unshaven and gray, stringy hair poked out in every direction.

"It's blackmail, sugar," she said, grinning like a Cheshire Cat. "The second oldest profession on Earth."

She grunted and huffed as she slid out of the bed. Grabbing her nightgown and wrapping it around her body, she tapped Gary on the shoulder as she walked out.

"I'll be back later for more, sonny," she called over her shoulder. "And if you have any second thoughts about our little agreement here, I'll call the cops and tell them everything."

She waddled out the door, pulling it shut behind her.

"What the hell is she talking about?" Dani demanded. "Why is Jabba the Hutt blackmailing you?"

Gary pulled on a pair of linen pajama pants. He led Dani to the kitchen table, sat him down, poured two tall glasses of strawberry sangria left over from their party last Friday night, and told his boyfriend about the stolen kayak.

"So, just take the stupid boat back and tell Mable to kiss off."

"It's Myrtle, and, well … I can't do that," Gary said, gulping the sangria and pouring himself another one.

"Why not?"

Gary sighed and tried to think of the best way to break the news to Dani that he'd been out on a kayak ride with another man—a *stolen* kayak and a man who was now dead and eaten by a rogue alligator.

19

Work With Me

TROY FOUND himself resting back on his elbows, propped against a small white cooler protecting four unopened Coronas. The sweet and tart taste of Key lime brushed his lips with every sip and the rivulets of condensation dripped lazily down the side of the half-full bottle ... or was it half-empty? Felt like the former ... right this moment.

The ease of the afternoon took him back to a simpler time. What had it been? Ten years ago? Fifteen? Heck, he didn't know and didn't feel like adding it up. Seemed to him like this crazy life of his had all started to go sideways back when he took up residence on Pawleys Island. He glanced over at Cinnamon. She reminded him of Karah in so many ways—except her hair was a little lighter, her smile was a little more worldly, and her legs might've been a little longer.

"You going to keep gawking at my body, or are you going to hand me another beer?"

Troy grinned as he realized she'd been looking at him while he reminisced about days long gone. He gulped the last sip of his own beer down, took her empty bottle and replaced it with a fresh one, complete with a slice of the local limes he'd found.

"You seem preoccupied," she said, scooting closer to him. "What's on your mind, cowboy?"

He pulled the straw hat off his head and looked at it. "I ain't no cowboy. Far from it. I found this old thing on a ..." He thought better of telling the whole truth of the matter. "... on an old fishing boat drifting past my house."

She took it from him and slipped it back on his head. "It looks good on you. I can't imagine you without it."

"I've had lots of people tell me that," he said, adjusting the hat into its usual position—just slightly tilted down over his eyes. "Been thinking 'bout givin' it up. Partin' ways with it."

She cocked her head to the side. "What would make you want to do that?"

He inhaled slowly and let the deep breath ease

out of his nose. "Been thinkin' lately that right around the time it came to me ... well, that's when all the trouble started followin' me around."

"Trouble? Like, what kind of trouble?"

He opened his mouth to tell her, but closed it when he realized he was about to tell the tale of a bunch of dead bodies piling up around him everywhere he went.

She squinted her eyes. "You're not that cowboy killer are you? I've been seeing all that on the news, but you ... you don't strike me as that type."

He laughed. "Nope. I'm no killer. Did a short stint in Afghanistan, but my knee took a bit of shrapnel in the worst way."

"So, what were you? A Navy Seal? Green Beret? Or one of those super-secret spy kind of guys?"

"Actually, I was a pilot. A glorified taxi for the brass really."

She considered this for a second, then said, "Then you can take care of me."

He nearly did a spit take. "Do what now?"

She hooked her arm through his elbow. When he looked into her eyes, he saw that she was joking on the surface, but something underneath said she was concerned ... afraid.

"Take care of me. You were a soldier. That means

you have to defend citizens, right? Well, I'm a citizen and I need defending."

"I haven't been a soldier for a long, long time," he said, finishing his beer. "I'm guessing that might've been before you were born."

Her smile faded. "I have to work tonight and I'm afraid of what they'll do to me."

"What they'll do to you? Who? Customers? Just a bunch of drunks," Troy said.

"No. Not them. I can handle them." She dropped her bottle into the cooler. "Something weird is going on around Woody's. My ... well, sort of my boyfriend is missing. He hasn't called me in like three days and that never happens. I've tried to call him, but his phone goes straight to voicemail. It's not like him at all. I think something really bad has happened to him."

"That sounds like somethin' you gotta call the cops about."

"No!" Suddenly her tone was sharp. "I can't do that. I think he's been murdered or something."

"Then it is most definitely time to call the police."

Troy stood up, slid the lid back onto the cooler, and picked it up. She grabbed his arm. "I need your help. What do I do?"

"Listen, I've been here before, darlin'. More than once." He took a few steps toward the highway behind them. "We gotta get back to the apartment and we'll call in the cavalry. If we don't, it's just gonna get worse and worse. Trust me."

Tears welled in her eyes. "No. Please don't."

"Why not?"

She took a deep breath. "He's Dante's son."

"Who's Dante?"

"The owner of Woody's. A member of the Caparelli family."

Troy shrugged. "Okay. I'm not sure what that has to do with anything, but—"

"The Caparellis are ... they're mafia ... at least, I think they are. If I go to the cops with this, they'll start looking into the family. And if Dante finds out I'm the one who called them ... I'll probably be the one to disappear."

Troy's mind flashed back to all those moments through the years when this exact same scenario unfolded before him. It all flashed before his eyes like a bad movie or a whole bunch of Dateline episodes back to back. Somebody had died, someone needed his help, he got messed up in the whole dang thing. He looked up at the brim of his hat. *Why are you doin' this to me?* he thought. He was shocked to hear what must've been the hat say, *you're the only one who can help*.

"Just come to work with me tonight. Hang out at Woody's, I'll buy. I mean, maybe Matty is really just on a bender with some friends in South Beach ... or maybe he's met another girl and is cheating on me. I'd be fine with that. Or maybe he'll even be there or they will have heard from him. I just need a friend. I don't want to go alone."

For a long moment, Troy thought about hitching his way right on out of town. He'd come to what might be called the *debate* moment in any good story. He had a choice and he knew if he made the wrong decision, someone could die ... or maybe not. Maybe it was like she said. This kid, Matty, was probably sitting at the bar drinking a Sex on the Beach, or a Cosmopolitan, or something equally ridiculous. He let out the air he'd been holding in his lungs.

"Alright," he said, shrugging his shoulders. "I'll come down in a bit. Just need to shower off the sweat and sand."

She grinned and wrapped her arms around his neck, hugging him tight. "Me too. Wanna share?"

Before he could answer, she took off walking at a fast clip across the road toward the tennis club.

"Oh ... dang," he muttered to himself.

. . .

HE WOKE up to find the sky a deep shade of long-post-sunset purple. No sunlight was left, but the moon cast enough light for him to see. A warm breeze rocked him back and forth. He wasn't too surprised to find that he'd fallen asleep in the hammock on the veranda waiting for Cinnamon to get ready for work. He walked up the stairs to the apartment and found the door closed, but not locked. Inside, he found the kitchen light on, but otherwise the place was dark and quiet. A Corona—he would soon find out was the *last* Corona—sat condensating on a handwritten note. He popped it open and picked up the note. Though the water had blurred the writing a bit, he could still read it.

Please meet me at Woody's. I left you sleeping because I figured you must really need the rest. I really hope you'll come in tonight. I need you.

"Well, well." He sighed and took a big gulp of the tepid beer. The clock on the stove told him it was well past midnight.

It wasn't late enough for Woody's to be closed. There was still time for him to head up there. The debate played in his head. As of now, he was pretty much the same guy he'd planned on being when he got to the island. If he hopped in the bed and rolled over, he'd be that guy in the morning, too. But if he picked through his things for a reasonably clean shirt and walked up to Woody's, he might not be.

He opened the fridge and found two packets of ketchup, an empty jar of green liquid that had once held bread and butter pickles, and—probably most importantly—no beer. He closed the door and sighed.

"When have I ever walked away from trouble?" he asked the empty room.

He could almost hear the walls say, "Hasn't happened yet."

His best short-sleeved button-down linen shirt was a little wrinkled, but then again, a good linen shirt always was. He smelled under the sleeves, then smelled his own underarms, and decided it would have to do.

When he walked out of the small, one room apartment, he felt a little chill in the air ... or maybe it was in his spine. The debate had been won, but he wasn't sure if the right side had prevailed.

20

Kayak Hunting Season

GARY TIED the string on his pajama pants and gulped down the remaining sangria in his glass. There was so much to tell Dani that he wasn't sure where to start.

"Okay, so, let me start at the beginning," he said, reaching out to hold his boyfriend's hand. "There was this guy."

Dani jerked his fingers out of Gary's and folded his arms tight across his chest. "A guy? Okay. Go on."

"Just a friend, Dani. You know I would never ... it was just someone I met doing that show down at ... okay, never mind." Gary felt his heart racing. A little flirting with another man was the least of his problems right now.

"And just what does this have to do with your

hag of a landlord and you shagging her in the bed where we made love for the first time?"

Gary felt the acid in his stomach starting to boil with the tart alcohol and anxiety mixing into a volatile cocktail.

"I might have stolen a kayak."

Dani's face, though still stone-like, remained frozen, but the creases of confusion folded around his eyebrows.

"Well, more like borrowed it ... without the owner knowing about it."

Dani stood up and turned toward the door.

"Wait," Gary jumped up and grabbed his shoulders. He turned him around gently. "I took the man, my friend, Matty, out for a kayak ride."

"On the *borrowed* kayak?" Dani asked.

"Yes. And now the owner wants it back. He's put up a twenty-five thousand dollar reward for it."

"So what?" Dan threw his hands up in frustration. "That is no reason to be boffing your disgusting skin-sack of a landlady. Just return the stupid boat and we'll be done with all of this."

"Yeah. There's a problem with that scenario," Gary said.

"The kayak is ... dead."

"Dead?"

"Eaten ... or at least mangled pretty badly ... by an alligator."

Dani considered this for a moment. "Then you'll just have to man up, go to the owner, confess everything, and buy him a new kayak. That will sure be a lot better than being on the wrong end of the whole reward business. At least maybe that way, you'll stay out of jail."

Gary took a deep breath. "There's a problem with that, too."

"Jesus, Gary," Dani huffed. "What are you not telling me? Just spill it."

"The man I mentioned before ... the alligator ate him, too."

Dani spit out a few curse words that Gary didn't think his boyfriend had ever said in his life. He was sure sailors thought twice before using some of the words he heard that day. Dani slumped down on the futon in the living room.

"Then, we need to go to the police."

"No can do," Gary said. "Matty's dad is mafia or something like that. If they found out I had anything to do with Matty's death ... I'm not really sure what they would do, but I don't really want to find out."

Dani's eyes glazed over, apparently deep in thought. "Where is the boat now?"

Gary shrugged. "In the mangroves. We were down around eighty-two."

"Do you think there's any chance anyone will find the remains of it?"

"I mean, if they were really searching for it … maybe."

Dani went back to his thinking pose. "We'll hide it. We'll trace your steps, find what's left of it, and get rid of it."

"Okay, first things first, there's a giant alligator out there who ate the man I was kayaking with. Second, if we even find it, what the hell would we do with it?"

Dani's lips turned up into a sly smile. "I have a friend who owns a dive boat. We'll sink it to the bottom of the ocean. No one will ever see it again and you can tell your landlady to kiss off."

"That's absolutely the most ridiculous…"

Gary's voice trailed off as the plan began to sink in. It wasn't the worst idea ever. He was pretty sure he knew where they had been when the alligator attacked. And this time, he wouldn't go without certain *precautions*.

"Okay. I'm in. When should we go?"

Dani looked at his rhinestone-encrusted watch

and grimaced. "Well, I've missed my show for sure. Might as well head there now."

"Fine. I need to get some clothes on."

Dani followed him into the bedroom. He changed into a pair of dark jeans and a long sleeve pullover to protect his arms against the thorns and stings common in the mangroves. It wasn't often a place that killed you with one big bite. Usually, it was the thousand or more tiny wounds that did you in. Gary reached up on the shelf, back in the corner and found what he was looking for, wrapped in a black cloth. Behind it was a box of shells. He'd bought it back in a time when men of his sexual preference were not well received in public—a barbaric time called the early eighties. There had been a short period where he thought if he was outed, it might come to violence. He unwrapped it and dropped the cloth on the floor. It was a revolver, that much he knew. Other than that, he had no idea what brand, or what size the bullets were, or—most importantly, how to fire it.

He was able to check and see that there were no bullets in it. He reached up again and patted around until he found the box of shells proclaiming that they were .38 Special, 130 Grain, Full Metal Jacket bullets ... whatever that meant. He turned around to find that Dani had changed clothes as well.

He was wearing an outfit that looked as if G.I. Joe had dipped himself in glue and then jumped into a vat of sequins and glitter.

"That ... is ... ridiculous," Gary said.

"Almost as ridiculous as you thinking we're taking that gun with us."

"Dani, you didn't see the size of that alligator. I'm not going out there without it. I'd rather do time for stealing a kayak."

"If you take that, I'm not going," Dani said, crossing his arms and sitting down on the foot of the bed.

"Fine then. I'll go without you."

Dani jutted his chin toward the ceiling. "Fine."

Gary sat down next to him and put his arm around him. "But it would be a shame for you not to wear that fabulous outfit now that you have it on. It kind of turns me on."

Dani seemed to be fighting the urge to smile. Finally, he shook his head and rolled his eyes.

"That's the first smart thing you've said all day. Okay. We'll go, but don't put any bullets in it yet. I don't want your gun going off prematurely."

Gary raised an eyebrow and opened his mouth

to reply with the obvious joke, but Dani lifted a finger and put it on his lips.

"Later, silly boy. Let's go get this kayak, then we'll talk more about guns."

Gary pecked him on the cheek. They tiptoed out of the apartment and softly down the metal stairs. The last thing they needed was Myrtle poking her head out and seeing them leave. Gary fired up the Jeep and pulled it out onto the highway.

"Now there's a garish outfit if I've ever seen one. Too bad, really. Not a bad looking guy. Do you think he's ... ?" Gary said, pointing at a man walking north on the side of the road.

"Pfft. Wearing a wrinkled linen shirt, khaki cargo shorts, flip-flops, and a straw cowboy hat? Not a chance. That guy is as straight as a Mormon missionary."

Gary laughed and waved to the man. He touched the brim of his hat in reply.

21

A Basketball Jones

IAN BASS PEELED OPEN the Islamorada Sheriff's Department's last bandaid and applied it gingerly to the cut between his left thumb and forefinger.

"So," Sheriff Paul Puckett said, sitting back in his chair, his hands folded behind his head, "tell me again what happened to your uniform."

Ian tried his best to shrug off the question. "When I stopped to check out the accident, a truck ... a tractor trailer ... raced past and splashed me with mud."

Puckett rolled an imaginary toothpick around between his teeth. Seeing doubt creep onto his face, Ian added, "or sewage or something. I think there was a backed up drain there."

"Uh huh." Puckett stared at him for a few seconds, then sniffed and sat up. "Check in the back. I think we might have a spare."

He began clicking the keys on his computer doing his best to look like he was busy. Ian knew from the past few days that the sheriff was likely playing solitaire. His suspicion was confirmed when he cursed and muttered something about the deck missing all of its aces.

Ian tucked the white t-shirt into the gray sweatpants he'd bought at the Dollar Tree to replace his soiled police issue shirt and pants. He walked back to the stockroom and found a uniform folded on the top shelf behind the paper towels and Folgers coffee. He pulled it down and checked the tag on the shirt. *XXL. Great.* He draped it over his shoulders and felt like one of the happy patients who had completed a successful season of the TV show, *My 600-lb Life*. The shirt bagged out all over like loose skin. He did his best to tuck the extra material into the pants—waist size 44. Cinching the belt as tight as it would go, he knew he probably looked like a clown.

As he rolled up the sweatpants, he considered what he'd just been through and worked out what his next action might be. He'd seen the Cowboy

Killer—or at least a man fitting his description—down at the Islamorada Tennis Club. But the guy sure wasn't acting like he was on the run. Maybe it was just a dude wearing a cowboy hat, but that seemed like a huge coincidence. He figured he'd drive back out that way and do some proper surveillance—from the road, rather than the swamp. God knows he didn't want to run into that behemoth of a gator again.

He also saw the kayak that most likely belonged to the writer that had taken out that ad in the paper offering a twenty-five thousand dollar reward. Though Ian wasn't hurting for money, he wasn't exactly getting rich working for the FDLE. He had given some serious thought to telling the sheriff about the kayak, but hadn't made up his mind about that yet. Twenty-five g's was a lot of money. If the dude at the tennis club turned out to be the real Cowboy Killer, he'd clue Puckett in on the location of the mangled boat.

The sheriff looked up when he emerged from the back and immediately started laughing. *Ugh, what is this*, Ian thought, *the third grade*. When he finally collected himself, Puckett said, "Oh, that's funny. I'm sorry, just couldn't help it. I'll get Mark on the horn to order a new uniform for you today. Should be here by the end of the week."

"Great. Thanks," Ian said, putting his keys, wallet, and cellphone into the overly-deep pockets of his new uniform.

"I guess you're not quite as big as Big Jim was," Puckett said, wiping a tear from his eye. "Same height though, it looks like."

Thankfully, the pants, though voluminous in the waist, were the right length. At six-foot-two, Ian wasn't exceptionally tall, but he was taller than the sheriff and the other officer on staff.

"Say, that reminds me," the sheriff said, sitting up and flipping through the pages of a nearly empty calendar, "the town three-on-three charity event is coming up soon."

"Three-on-three?" Ian asked.

"Basketball," Puckett said. "There's a tournament with all the local fire departments, rescue squads, wildlife management officers, and sometimes even the Coast Guard. Draws a big crowd. Proceeds all go to charity."

"No thanks. I'm terrible at sports."

"Well, hell. That doesn't matter, son. Do I look like I can play basketball? It's all for the kids."

Ian put his hat—the lone undamaged item from

his original uniform—on his head and walked to the door.

"I'll think about it."

"I'll pencil you in," the sheriff made a big motion of scratching something into his calendar. "You going out?"

"Yeah," Ian said, thinking he didn't really want the sheriff to know he was headed back down to check in on his cowboy, "just gonna cruise up and down. It's almost time for the drunks to be out."

Paul Puckett smiled the wide, toothy smile of a politician who wasn't actually happy. "Go get 'em, tiger."

Ian closed the door without replying.

"WHAT DO you think about that kid, Mark?" Puckett asked the deputy who hadn't made a peep during the whole exchange.

He raised his eyebrows at the question, but didn't answer. The phone rang and he picked it up.

"Okay. No, he's not ... but ... no, sir. We haven't—" Mark put his hand over the receiver. "It's the writer guy. Chaz."

Puckett rolled his eyes. "Crap. You mean Chad Harrison?"

Mark nodded. "I'll put him through."

"No, no, don't—" The sheriff was interrupted by his phone buzzing. Double crap.

He picked it up. "Sheriff Paul Puckett speaking."

"Well?" the voice on the line asked.

"I'm sorry, what's the question."

"Stop playing games, sheriff," Chad said. "You and I both know what I'm calling about. Has your lousy excuse for a police department done anything to find my kayak?"

Puckett took a deep breath, "Actually, no. We have no resources at this time to devote to finding your—"

"Resources?" Chad blurted through a laugh. "Do you know who you're dealing with, sheriff? I've looked up the numbers from your last campaign. There was a pretty big discrepancy between the two reports I saw. I wonder if I dug a little deeper how much that would affect your upcoming campaign?"

Triple crap. "I have no idea what you're talking about."

"Let me read from the report I found. Turns out your ex-wife had a box of documents that she was more than happy to deliver to me."

Jesus, Mary, and Joseph. What did she do to me? Chad was reading aloud the sordid details of the missing campaign funds, but Paul Puckett wasn't listening. He knew it all already. There was a very nice 2018 XLE Lite 20MBC Bunkhouse Travel Trailer parked in his driveway because of that fund discrepancy.

"So, sheriff," Chad said, finishing his triumphant tirade, "do you think we could find the resources now?"

Paul Puckett slammed the receiver on his desk three times startling Mark out of his chair. "Oops, sorry. Dropped the phone. What I meant to say was, we'll get a full search on tonight and have your kayak back to you by tomorrow ... or the next day at the most."

"Why, thank you, sheriff," Chad answered with a sneer in his voice. "Your constituents appreciate that. I'll be calling tomorrow."

"Yes, sir. I'll be waiting."

He slammed the receiver down. "Mark, who in the hell could possibly know where that stupid boat is?"

The disinterested deputy looked up. "No clue. Maybe you should just buy him a new one."

The sheriff opened his mouth to say what a stupid idea that was ... until he realized ... it wasn't a half-bad idea after all.

He clicked away from his failing solitaire game and opened a browser window. He was shocked to see how much a new kayak would cost. He wasn't sure what came after *triple crap*, but that's exactly what he was thinking.

22

A Sassy Nation

TROY WAS HAVING trouble keeping up with the bartender who was sliding Corona after Corona across the bar to him. He was happy that he wasn't paying for them, nor was he running up a tab. In fact, the owner of Woody's, Dante Caparelli, was generously taking care of them. What Troy didn't know until much later, was that Dante was using the alcohol to relax his inhibitions about giving him information.

The band was in rare form, having somewhat settled in with their new drummer. The guy was wearing his hat again tonight and Troy again thought there was something very familiar about him. But, that feeling continued to ebb out like low tide with every golden beer he drank.

"They actually don't sound too bad tonight, eh?" Dante asked.

"Yup. Not bad at all," Troy replied, working hard to keep from slurring.

He hadn't been this drunk in a long time and his danger radar began to tingle. Dante seemed to notice apprehension growing in Troy and signaled the bartender to deliver two filled-to-the-brim tequila shots.

"I probably sherdn't," Troy said, forgetting his efforts to speak clearly.

Dante clutched his shoulder tightly. "I insist."

"Alrighty then," Troy picked up the glass. "What should we toast?"

"My son," Dante raised his glass. "Wherever he may be."

Troy wrinkled his brow. "You don't know where your son is?"

Dante threw back the shot and slammed his glass down on the bar. Had Troy been more sober, he would've noticed the anger in the motion. Instead, he followed suit and chugged his own shot.

"I don't," Dante growled. "But when I find out where he is—"

"Donny, Donny, Donny," Troy said, slapping the old man on the back, "you know kids. Why, when I

was a young man, I used to take off for days at a time
—to go fishing mostly. My old man didn't care much
—not like you do—but it used to give my mom fits."

Dante ordered two more drinks and another
beer for Troy. He slid the shot over and Troy picked
it up.

"My boy isn't like that," Dante said. "He's more
responsible than a cowboy like you."

"Can't argue with that," Troy agreed.

"Say ... you wouldn't know anything about where
my boy is, would you? Being a rambler like yourself,
maybe you've bumped into him?"

Troy gulped his shot and laughed. "Don. Can I
call you Don?"

"It's Dante," the old man slammed his fist on
the bar.

"Okay. Okay. No need to get testy, Donny. I don't
reckon I know your son, but if I see your guy, I'll tell
him you said, 'hello'. Now, if you'll excuse me, I gotta
hit the head."

Troy got up and stumbled past the bar to the
restroom. When he put his hand on the door,
someone grabbed it. Even through the haze of
drunkenness, he was aware enough to grab the
person's wrist and jerk them into the bathroom with
him. He slammed the door behind them and turned

the lock. When he flicked on the light, he was startled to see it was Cinnamon.

"What are you doing?" she demanded, jabbing a finger into his chest.

"Takin' a piss," he said, pointing at the urinal—which was filled with ice, an old trick used in many a bar to mask the smell of alcohol laden urine.

"I can see that," she said. "I meant why are you talking to Dante?"

"Donny? Me and him have been having the nicest chat," Troy whispered and pointed toward the closed door. "And he's been buying everything."

He grinned triumphantly and wobbled. Cinnamon caught him, barely in time to keep him from tumbling down to the slick, yellow tile. The tile had originally been white, but years of accidental and intentional misses had stained it to its current shade.

"I can see that," she said, crossing her arms. "So, what? Are you guys big buddies now?"

"I reckon we might be. Shame what happened to his son."

Cinnamon's tone snapped dangerously close to anger, but there was too much fear for it to go all the way. "He's talking to you about Matty?"

"Yup. Say, you mind if I pee while we talk. I'm about to bust over here."

She huffed and opened the door. "I'll be at a table by the band. Come straight away, don't talk to Dante anymore."

Troy flashed her a thumbs-up, but by the time the door had closed, he had forgotten their entire conversation. When he finished, he walked out to find Dante standing there holding two beers.

"There you are, friend," he said, smiling like a snake to a rat. "Ready for another round?"

Troy swayed when he reached for the beer and fell into Dante. The beers slipped out of his hands, crashing down on the floor in a heap of broken glass, spewing foam all over the man's expensive suit.

"You jacka—" The old man's words were drowned out by the band ripping into an AC/DC song.

The drummer was in rare form, slamming the drums like he was trying to make them bleed. Troy whooped and started walking toward the stage. He caught sight of Cinnamon sitting at a table and tried to sit down with her. The only problem was, his balance was seriously compromised and as he lowered himself into the sticky, vinyl covered chair, his knee gave out. He spilled forward, knocking the table over and tumbled onto the ground with it.

"Oh, my God," she said, kneeling to help him up. "Are you okay?"

"Right as rain, darlin'," he said, grinning. "But if it's alright with you, I should probably get goin'."

"Sounds like a good idea," she agreed. "Let me get my stuff. I'm going with you."

"Absolutely not," Dante's voice was loud over the roaring guitars. "It's the busiest night we've had in two weeks. You're not going anywhere."

Troy might've heard the threatening tone of Dante's voice, and he might've realized that she was trying desperately to signal him that she was scared and didn't want him to leave, but the band apparently had cranked their amplifiers up to eleven as the guitar solo began. The entire crowd was cheering and hollering at them and the drummer was standing on his stool, kicking the cymbals with his feet. Troy also didn't notice the vice-like grip Dante had on Cinnamon's arm. He was done and as such, began to crawl toward the exit. No one noticed him leaving ... no one except the Islamorada Sheriff's Department's newest officer, Ian Bass.

As Troy stumbled south, the Ford Explorer

followed at approximately three miles an hour, with its headlights off.

THE COWBOY KNOWS *something about my Matty*. Dante Caparelli had never been more sure of anything in his life. He picked up the family phone and waited for the line to connect. When it did, he told the person on the other end of the line that Matty was missing and that he knew who had done it.

"You said you were sending *the guy*?" he asked.

"He shoulda been there by now."

Dante's blood went ice cold. Troy's words echoed in his head. "...if I see your guy, I'll tell him you said, 'hello'."

This dude was definitely the Cowboy Killer. Not only had he probably killed Matty, but now ... had he somehow found and killed the family assassin? Nah, surely not. He tried to assure himself that there was no way that bumbling idiot had pulled that off. And if *the guy* was in town ... Dante's face broke into a smile.

"Happy trails, cowboy," he said, hanging up the phone.

23

Home Sweet Home

CINNAMON WATCHED HELPLESSLY from the stage, unable to signal Troy as he stumbled out the door like a newborn giraffe. She'd been naked up here many times, but for some reason, she felt more exposed now than ever. She finished her dance under a shower of folded one dollar bills and raked the money up into careless wads under both arms. Some of it drifted away, but she didn't care, she was ready to get the hell out of here.

Dante had been staring at her since before Troy came in and his expression was as dark as Stephen King's early horror. In fact, he looked a bit like an older Jack Torrance after the Overlook Hotel started to poison his brain.

The money was good tonight, better than it had

been in a long time, but she decided that she didn't feel safe. It was time to make a quick and quiet exit. She didn't have a ride, but it wasn't too far to her apartment and she didn't want to wait for a cab or try out the newest ride sharing company —Thum.

She surreptitiously gathered her things and tucked them into her bag and waited. When Dante staggered off his bar stool to use the bathroom, she grabbed her purse, threw a couple of dollars to Sully behind the bar and dashed out the front door into the warm, humid night. When the raindrops started to fall, she regretted her decision and started to jog —a feat hampered by the nine inch neon pink stilettos she was wearing. The rain came down in sudden sheets soaking her to the bone.

Her left heel broke sending her splashing down into a mucky puddle and she felt tears welling in her eyes. She was thankful that the road was dark. No one would see her in her semi-naked, muddy state ... or so she thought.

TROY WAS ALMOST certain that the bell for third period science class was responsible for waking him. He jolted upright, sure that Sister Connelly would be rapping his knuckles with her splintered yardstick for his insolence.

"I'm sorry, Sister," he groaned, waiting for the whack on the back of his hands.

He pried his eyes open and was suddenly struck with vertigo so strong that he reassessed his situation. This wasn't the third grade. No, it was Afghanistan and his chopper was going down. The sound wasn't a school bell, but rather an alarm klaxon telling him he was out of fuel or an engine had blown up ... or they'd been hit by enemy fire. When his eyes finally adjusted and he found his balance, he sat up. A distant, yellow light shone through the hazy night and his surroundings crept into focus.

The cloud of alcohol parted enough for him to realize he was swaying in the hammock on the veranda of the tennis club. The evening came back to him in bits and pieces, but he wasn't exactly sure how he'd gotten home.

He knew he'd been at Woody's talking to the owner ... What was his name? Dante. Good guy. Bought a bunch of drinks.

His thoughts were interrupted by the loud ringing sound again and he saw his phone lying on the ground under him. The screen showed a number he recognized. He bent over to answer it and having forgotten the sneaky ways of hammocks, tumbled forward in a flash and somersaulted over until he lay flat on his back, staring up at the yellow flood light on the corner of the building.

His phone persisted in buzzing, so he swept his arm out until his fingers were able to grab it. He put it to his ear and clicked the button to connect.

CINNAMON WIPED the rain from her face and dialed Troy's number again. She wasn't sure who else to call and she wasn't really sure why she'd decided to call him. But when he answered, the relief swept through her like a tidal wave. The wave quickly turned into a trickle when she realized how intoxicated he sounded. His words slurred and he didn't make much sense. She almost hung up, but she noticed there was a pair of headlights trailing her through the downpour.

"Somebody is following me, Troy," she said, clutching the phone tight to her face. "What do I do?"

"Cops," he grunted. "Gotta call the cops."

"I don't want to hang up," she said. "And besides, they wouldn't find me until it was too late."

"Cops," he repeated. "Just call 9-1-1. Can you go inside somewhere? Grocery store or Walmart or somethin'?"

She shook her head. He really was drunk. "Do you know what time it is? Nothing is open right now."

"Two? Maybe three."

"What?"

"Is that what time it is?" he asked. "Don't have a watch. Haven't worn one since I got back to the States."

"Just stay on the phone with me, Troy," she said, looking over her shoulder.

The car was still there, but it had slowed a bit more—which wasn't all that strange, the rain was heavier than ever. She had taken off both shoes and was trudging through several inches of water. Scanning around, she couldn't see anything but mangroves and jungle and dark ocean. After a while, she lost sight of the car and up ahead, she saw the driveway to her tiny, pale yellow apartment building appear. She jogged past the rotten Lime Tree Apartments sign and hurried up the metal stairs to the second floor. The breezeway was covered and she was elated to be out of the rain. Even though the car had seemingly disappeared, she rushed to find her door. Some of her neighbors' lights were on, but no one was usually awake at this time of night.

"Thank God for that," she muttered to herself, rummaging around in her purse for her key.

"Well, hello, doll," a voice screeched, causing her to drop her bag, spilling the soaking wet contents all around her bare feet. "Late night, eh?"

"Hi, Mrs. Hussholder," Cinnamon smiled and knelt to scoop up her things.

"*Miss* Hussholder," the old woman growled. "Mr. Hussholder was a degenerate who ran off with a 16-year-old girl two years ago."

"Sorry, Mrs. er, Miss Hussholder."

"None of that matters," said Myrtle Hussholder, leaning against the rail outside her door. "What I need to know, is if you're ever going to pay your rent? Every last one of you is late this month. What the hell is wrong with young people today. Always entitled. Always wanting something for nothing. Makes me sick."

Cinnamon dug around in her purse and pulled out a wet, wadded pile of money. She shoved it at the woman—it couldn't have been more than a hundred dollars.

"I'll have the rest soon, Miss Hussholder," she said, finally finding her key and jamming it into the lock. She jiggled it and turned and the door swung open. "I'll have the rest for you by the end of the week. I'll pick up another shift or something."

She lunged through the door and slammed it behind her. The old woman banged on the window over Cinnamon's second-hand couch. "You better, honey, or you're outta here with the rest of the vagrants."

She dug her phone out of the dripping contents of her purse and found that the call was still connected.

"Troy?" she asked. "Troy, are you still there?"

On the other end of the line, she could hear him snoring. She smiled and shook her head, disconnecting the call.

Cinnamon stripped out of the clothes, muddy, soaked, and falling apart—throwing sequins all over the linoleum. She turned on the tap in the bath and let it run for a few minutes until it was hot and not too brown. Thankfully, she found a half a bottle of Pinot Noir that Dante had given her for Christmas. She didn't bother to get a glass. She eased down into the steaming water, took a long slow drink of the expensive wine and slowly began to relax.

Her phone buzzed in the other room, but she never heard it, she was asleep against the cold tile.

24

A Cowboy, An Assassin, and a Cop

RAIN POUNDED FDLE Special Agent Ian Bass as he tugged on the ridiculously oversized pants sagging down around his feet. He had cinched up his belt as tight as it would go, but even on the last hole, it wasn't quite enough to keep the pants from falling if he moved the wrong way. He could also see specks of blood popping up on the sleeves of the uniform from the myriad of cuts and scrapes he had gotten earlier trying to get a closer look at the Cowboy Killer—who had apparently taken up residence at the Islamorada Tennis Club. He had originally thought that was a strange plan, but as he jogged around the building trying not to lose his pants or get too soaked in the sudden downpour, he came to the conclusion that it wasn't a bad plan at all.

It was quiet during the off-season, hidden from the road by all but a small driveway, and completely unremarkable in every way—unless someone was looking for him, they might never know he was there. Luckily, Ian Bass had discovered his hideout and was planning to take the dude down. If he could pull this off, it was potentially a career making capture. He'd be promoted for sure and given a better position than that rat hole of a police station under Puckett.

He parked the Islamorada Sheriff's Ford Explorer up on the road under a tree with Spanish Moss hanging down in a curtain. There was no way the cowboy would be able to see it from the building.

The tennis pro shop and the apartment above were quiet and dark. He didn't see any lights on anywhere except a bare yellow bulb hanging from the back corner of the roof. A swarm of mosquitos clouded the light even in the rain and Ian laughed at the stupid notion that the yellow was invisible to bugs. Maybe there was some science to it, but out here in the middle of nowhere, even the amber glow would draw the little buggers in—and when one finds it, they all come out.

He stepped up on the veranda on the back of the building, thankful to be out of the rain that was beginning to slow to a hard drizzle. He shone his flashlight (one hand on his belt, to keep his pants up) in the windows of the shop. He saw tennis rackets, tennis clothing, tennis towels, tennis balls, tennis trinkets, tennis magnets, and a few Islamorada logoed items as well ... but no Cowboy Killer ... or anyone else for that matter.

The place was deserted. He wondered if maybe he'd spooked the guy when he'd been sloshing around in the swamp nearby almost becoming gator chow. Maybe the murderer had flown the coop. If the rain hadn't been plinking around so loudly on the tin roof of the back porch, he might've heard the snoring coming from the hammock.

It was, however, just quiet enough for him to hear a car pull in ... slowly. *Hot dog*, he thought. *He's here. I'll be able to get the jump on him and bring him in.* He doused his flashlight and edged around the building so that he could see the car. The driver had turned off his headlights and was coasting into a spot near the building. It was too dark to see the driver, but the car was a dead giveaway—a beige, rental sedan. Nondescript. Chosen to blend in.

He put his hand on the mic attached to his left shoulder. Backup in the form of Sheriff Paul Puckett was just a quick call away. But knowing the old man, he would take all the credit and use it to win the upcoming election. He eased his hand down and tucked his flashlight back into his belt. He unclipped his gun and when he did, the belt let go and his pants flopped down around his ankles.

"Jiminy Cricket," he hissed, kneeling to pull them back up.

The car pulled past him and stopped, but it didn't turn off. Ian noticed the plates were from New York. He hadn't remembered hearing anything about the Cowboy Killer being a Yankee, but then again, maybe it was just a rental car far from home.

He knelt down and pulled his gun from the holster, careful not to loosen his belt again. Squinting his eyes, he could tell there was someone in the driver's seat, but the rest of the car appeared to be empty. The engine shut off and the quiet was deafening. Actually, the buzzing and humming and croaking and creaking of the island was deafening. Ian could feel his heart thumping so hard, he was sure if the wildlife hadn't been so active, the killer would've heard it.

The door opened with a soft squeak and rocked back and forth a couple of times. Ian heard a sound he knew well and it sent his adrenaline into overdrive. A distinctive click. *So, the guy has a gun. Well, so do I,* thought Ian. Besides the human-shaped targets at the academy, he'd never shot a person before. He really didn't want to do that anyway. He wanted to bring the Cowboy Killer in alive—it would be a great photo for the front page of newspapers all around Florida. All around the country for that matter.

He watched as the guy eased around his car, oblivious to the misty rain. His head, still shrouded in shadow, turned back and forth. It was odd behavior, not like someone who was crashing here. It looked more like he was checking to see if anyone was home. Or wait, maybe he knew Ian was coming for him. Somehow he'd gotten tipped off. Maybe he'd seen the Explorer. *Crap.*

True to his moniker, he was wearing a hat. But this one wasn't a cowboy hat. It was some kind of Fedora, like a gangster from the twenties would wear. He must've switched hats earlier. The man took two steps toward where Ian was crouching and froze. The killer's eyes were still silhouetted in the shadows, but it seemed like he was looking right at Ian's hiding place.

"I can see you, ya bum," the man said, his accent more Long Island than Islamorada Island.

Ian swallowed, but remained still. His gun was pointed at the man, but his hand trembled and he felt a bead of sweat drip down his palm.

"And I can see you, too." Ian said, trying hard not to let his voice crack, but failing.

"Old man says you been spending too much time with his son's girl."

Ian opened his mouth and then his brain registered the words. "I'm ... I'm sorry ... what was that?"

The guy laughed, a raspy, throaty sound, like a three-pack-a-day smoker. "Don't act like ya don't know. I know your type. What? You found a gun and all the sudden you're a serial killer? Fuhgeddaboudit. I'm gonna use your own gun—or whoever's ya stole—to put a bullet in your skull. And then you're gonna get a little visit with some gators. Capiche?"

Ian was chilled to the bone at the thought of confronting another alligator, but the man's words made absolutely no sense at all. This was all wrong.

The man he'd seen on the tractor didn't match up with what he was hearing from this guy. Something wasn't right here.

"This gun is police issue," Ian said, "And you're not going to be visiting anything but a jail cell. It's time for the killing to stop, cowboy."

Ian couldn't help but say his last line with a trace of Arnold Schwarzenegger. He was smiling when the man suddenly started walking toward him, raising his arm and firing two times. A quick, and professional *pop-pop*. The bullets struck the side of the tennis shop, sending white and green splinters flying all around Ian's head. His ears rang from the loud bang. He stood and took two steps backward, raising his own gun.

With impeccable timing, the ballooning pants he'd borrowed from the Sheriff's back room, dropped to his knees. He stumbled back and fell to the ground. When his elbow hit the ground, his gun fired. Certain the killer was closing in to finish him off, he crab-walked backward into the shadows, wet gravel and muddy rocks scraping his bare legs. He bumped into a tall lattice wall, covered with pink Bougainvillea. The space between the lattice and the side of the building was just big enough for him to squeeze into. He was completely hidden, but he realized he couldn't lift his arm up to point his gun ... and his pants were at his ankles.

He fought to control his breathing and waited for the Cowboy Killer—or whoever the hell this guy was —to come by and kill him. The rain stopped and he held his breath to listen. Nothing. No sound at all— except the rattling, wailing, swaying nature all around him.

He eased himself out of his hiding place, jerked his pants up to his waist, pulling his belt tight, and pointing his gun out into the darkness. He put his back up against the side of the tennis shop and tiptoed around to the corner. He took a quick look out at the parking lot, sure the bullets would ring out again, but nothing happened. He took another look and saw the car, still sitting in the same spot, the driver door still open.

A few feet away, he saw the man lying face down on the ground. He pulled back around the corner and waited a few seconds. Then, taking a deep breath, willing himself not to pee his pants, he pointed his gun and stepped out into the parking lot. The man was still, not moving at all. Ian crept closer and kicked the man. Nothing. No groans, no moans, no nothing.

He knelt down and pushed the man over so that

he was lying face up. To Ian's surprise, the man had a single, nearly bloodless bullet hole right between his eyes. But he didn't shoot the man. Who had? And then he remembered falling and his weapon discharging. Of all the random things to happen, his shot had hit the guy ... in the head no less.

He felt for a pulse. Nada. This guy was stone cold dead. He was suddenly elated. He'd shot the Cowboy Killer! Looking at the man's face, though, he was quickly filled with dread. Of all the descriptions and sketches and renderings of the famous serial killer, this man fit none of them. He was weasley and gaunt and had no facial hair at all except a thin mustache on his upper lip. Ian reached down into the man's pockets. In his front left pocket, he had a pair of fingernail clippers and two sticks of wintergreen chewing gum ... and that was it. Nothing else. No I.D. No money. No nothing.

"Who the hell are you?" he asked the dead guy.

He stood up and paced a few times beside the body, considering what to do next. *Call the Sheriff? Nope. Call the FDLE? That would be better. Maybe Nick is working tonight and can get me some kind of record on this guy from facial recognition. I might even be able to send pics of his fingerprints and get a hit.*

"Okay, fella," he said, holstering his gun. "Looks like we need to take a ride back to my place."

He hooked his hands under the man's armpits and dragged him across the lot and up the driveway to the Explorer. He shoved the man into the back and threw a blanket over him. He had his keys in the ignition when he remembered the man's gun. *Might be able to get something on that, too*, he thought. He jogged back down the drive and quickly found the man's gun—a Ruger 22 LR, the last kind of gun he would expect a serial killer to have. Putting all the pieces together from the encounter, Ian decided this guy was some kind of assassin.

"Everything okay, officer?" a voice drawled out of the dark.

Ian raised both guns, pointing them in the direction of the voice. "Freeze! Come out with your hands up?"

"If I freeze, I can't exactly move to come out," the voice said, no tinge of humor in it.

"Just get your butt out here where I can see you." Ian said, waggling the guns.

His heart leapt when the dude, the real Cowboy Killer, came out of the shadows. It was the guy he'd seen riding the tractor earlier, and yes, he was wearing the straw cowboy hat.

"Sorry, officer," the man said, slurring his words slightly. "I just saw you carrying your friend to your car and thought you might need some help."

"Everything is going to be just fine, friend," Ian said. "Come with me."

As he followed the man up the hill, with the guns pointed at his back, he thought he heard him say something under his breath.

"Dangit."

25

Not A Finger

GARY JOHN SUSKIND and Daniel Kane Kotlerson —or rather *Dani*, because he, or she, was currently wearing a woman's pink camouflage blouse and pink leopard print tights—trudged through the thick mucky mangroves, just off the Overseas Highway. The moon shone through the trees casting beams of eerie blue light over the swampy water.

"I literally cannot believe you would drag me out here in this," Dani said, pushing past a thick vine. Her boots were covered in muck that looked like a dirty Wendy's Frosty.

"I can't believe you would actually wear something like that unless you were on stage," Gary said, his tone more joking than judgmental.

"Let's just find this thing and get out of here," Dani said. "I do not want to be out here."

"Hey, you're the one that insisted on coming. You could've stayed at the apartment, but no, you had to get all dolled up and tag along."

"Aww, you think I look nice?"

Gary smiled, seeing that Dani was pleased with herself. "Yes. Yes, I do."

"Good," she said. Then raising an eyebrow she added, "Remember that, because if I ever hear of you boating around with another man again, you won't think there's anything nice about me at all."

Gary leaned over and pecked Dani's cheek. "Yes, dear."

They both had LED flashlights and swung them around erratically, hoping to see the missing orange kayak. For more than an hour, they waded back and forth, thinking they were covering a lot of ground, but if it had been daylight, they would've realized that they were covering the same square acre of land over and over again.

"I think we're walking in circles," Dani said, stopping to catch her breath.

"No we're not," Gary answered unevenly. In actuality, he wasn't sure where they were going.

"Do you know where we are?" Dani asked. "Because it seems like we might be lost."

"Well, um..."

"Oh, dear sweet Jesus, we are lost, aren't we?"

"I never said that."

Dani's hands began to flail wildly. "We are going to die out here in the middle of this Godforsaken muck-hole and they won't even find enough of us to bury us properly. Of all the stupid things—"

"Dani. Quiet." Gary snapped suddenly.

"I will not be quiet, thank you very much. Bring another man out on a boat ride and you expect me to be quiet. Uh, no. And now I'm out here, lost, cold, and getting bitten by God knows what disease-ridden insects because you wanted some strange. You did this to me and I will—"

"Dani! I mean it." Gary hissed. "I thought I heard something."

Dani stopped talking and held her flashlight up under her chin giving her a creepy, horror movie look. "What was it?"

"I have no idea, now stop talking for one second and listen."

"Oh, that is it, mister," Dani said through gritted teeth. "I'm done. Your tone is offensive and vulgar and I will not stand for it."

She turned and started sloshing away from Gary.

"Dani, stop. Come back here."

"Too late, Gary."

Gary pointed his flashlight in her direction. "Dani, how do you know that's the way out of here?"

She stopped, swung her flashlight side to side. Everything looked exactly the same. They were most definitely lost. She turned around and began walking back.

"Fine," she said. "But when we get out of here—"

Without warning, she fell and went completely underwater. Besides the ripples where she went down, there was no sign of her. Gary ran over, poking his hand down into the water.

"Dani?" he called, turning in circles. "Dani, where are you?"

With a splash, Dani broke the surface and gasped. Gary grabbed her arm and pulled her to her feet. She coughed and hacked and spat brown water out. Her blonde wig was gone and her black eye liner was streaming down her face.

"What happened? Are you okay?" Gary asked.

"I tripped," she said, looking back behind her. "One of my boots got stuck in the mud and I fell."

"Oh, no. I'm so sorry. Are you okay?"

"Except for the fact that it's gone and I'll have to get new Wellies, yes, I'm fine."

"That and your wig, too."

Surprised, Dani reached up and found that the wig was indeed missing. Tears began to well in her eyes. Gary pulled her close and hugged her.

"Baby, I'm so sorry. Let's just get out of here." he said. "We'll deal with this tomorrow."

Dani nodded and they turned to go. Gary pointed his flashlight in the direction Dani had been walking. "I think you were right. I think that's the way back to the road. Just be careful. Let's try to stay above the water on the way out."

Before they took a step, the water bubbled again and a long shape broke the surface. Dani squealed and started to run, but Gary grabbed her arm tight and pulled her back.

"Hey, it's okay. Look."

He ran the beam of his light along the shape. It was bright orange.

"It's your kayak," Dani said.

"Well, not *my* kayak, but yes, it's the kayak."

"Oh, thank God," Dani said. "Now we can leave here and never come back."

"If we can get it out of here," Gary said. "Here, see if we can turn it over."

They reached their hands down under the water and heaved until the kayak tipped over and righted itself. It was hardly sea-worthy with big gashes and cracks up and down the front.

"That's where the alligator got it," Gary said, pointing his light at the damage.

A brilliant sparkle lit up as he moved his flashlight over the bite marks.

Dani, walked toward the front and bent over. She picked something up and dropped it quickly.

"What? What is it?" Gary asked.

Dani had slapped her hand over her mouth and she said something, but Gary couldn't understand.

He moved closer. "Hun, take your hand off your mouth."

"A finger," Dani said. "I think it was ... your friend's finger."

"Oh, gross," Gary said. "But what was that sparkling?"

"I don't know. Maybe a ring or something."

Dani took a deep breath and felt around the inside of the boat. She pulled her hand out and Gary shined his light on the object. Definitely a finger— Matty's finger. It had a large, golden ring on it with several jewels, maybe diamonds, mounted on the top. Before Gary could say anything, Dani reached down under her arm, opened her purse, and dropped the finger inside.

"What the hell are you doing, Dani?"

"I've lost a very expensive wig and a very expensive pair of rain boots. I'm sure I can pawn this thing and replace them."

"That is downright disgusting," Gary said.

"No. Disgusting is what you did by bringing another man out here, watching him get attacked by a vicious amphibian beast, and then leaving him to get eaten and die. That's disgusting."

Gary was about to argue that he didn't have a choice. If he had stayed behind to help Matty, he would've died as well, but before he could, the water churned up under the boat and a long row of razor sharp teeth erupted from below the surface.

Before he could move, an alligator—maybe the same alligator—had snapped its jaws around Dani's waist. He rolled and pulled her under in a thrashing, splashing, crashing explosion of reddening water.

Gary was stunned, frozen in horror and shock. It was déjà vu all over again. He'd watched the same exact scene unfold with Matty and now with Dani. Only it wasn't the exact same scene, this time, he had a gun. He reached behind his back, pulled the gun from his waistband and pulled the trigger until it clicked.

He must have clipped the gator because it screamed and dove, taking Dani with it.

"Dani!" he yelled, running after it as best he could. "Dani!!"

He lunged forward and bumped into something. He aimed his gun and squeezed the trigger again, but it was empty. Between gasps of air, he pointed his flashlight at the object, thinking that it might be the alligator, or maybe Dani's body, but it was neither.

It was a glittery, sequined pink purse—Dani's purse. He glanced around. All the commotion and splashing had caused the kayak to sink again, and there was no sign of Dani ... or any ... part of Dani. She was gone. Everything was gone. He tossed his gun away and it plopped into the water and sank.

When all had quieted again, he heard the not-too-distant sound of an engine ... a car ... and it was close. He walked in the direction of the noise and discovered that they had been about twenty feet away from the Overseas Highway and his Jeep. He got in and tossed Dani's purse into the passenger's seat. Shivering, shaking, scared out of his mind, he screeched onto the road and tore off into the night.

26

I Ain't No Fortunate Son

"TROY CLINT BODEAN, SIR."

"And that's your full legal name? No aliases or anything like that?" the police officer asked, scribbling notes on a yellow pad.

"Reckon that's the only name I've ever gone by," Troy said. "My brother used to call me T-Roy, but that has been a long, long time ago."

"T-Roy?"

"Yup. You know, like Troy, but with the T and the Roy separated."

The man—apparently some kind of special agent—tapped a few keys on his laptop while Troy waited. He was a small, kind of rat-like fellow, with dark eyes, dark hair, and oddly large, oversized clothes on his wiry frame. It looked a bit like he might be wearing someone else's uniform, which worried Troy a little. That and the fact that he'd brought him back to his apartment rather than a police station or federal building or the like.

It was a small apartment building that smelled like mildew, cat urine, and low tide—which wasn't all that unusual for Islamorada. The man who called himself Ian Bass, claimed he was an FDLE Agent on special assignment in the Keys. He said he was an undercover officer tracking unusual mob activity in the area and was close to a breakthrough in the case. But that was when he'd gotten a hunch that some kind of serial killer was on the loose.

He clicked a few keys on his laptop and read from an open document.

"The so-called Cowboy Killer is responsible for the deaths of at least three people including Earl Heskett, owner of Benny's World of Liquor, Phil Claxton, the Vice Mayor of Pembroke Pines, and Haley Joel Osment."

Ian looked over his shoulder, "Not *the* Haley Joel Osment, but a girl who's mother apparently had such a crush on the actor that she named her daughter after the actor. Strange world we're living in Mr. uh..."

"Bodean. But you can call me Troy."

He sniffed and turned back to his screen. "Says here that multiple eye-witnesses say the killer has a tattoo on his upper back near his right shoulder that says, 'Tasty Cherries.' You got anything like that?"

"Nope. Don't got any that I know of."

"Do you mind showing me?"

Troy unbuttoned his rumpled linen shirt and showed the man his unmarked back. He felt a little odd when the man snapped a few pictures of it with his phone. He took several more, profile, front view, back of the head, and so on before attaching the photos to an email to send off to the FDLE. Troy also saw photos of the man he'd seen Officer Bass stuffing into the back of the Sheriff's vehicle on the same email. That man didn't have any tattoos either and didn't look anything like the artist's rendering of the Cowboy Killer Ian showed him.

Ian spun his chair around and stood up. "Okay then, I guess you can go," he said, holding his hand out indicating the door. "Stay out of trouble. Oh, and I don't think I'd go back to the tennis club if I were you. I feel like this guy might have been looking for you."

"Lookin' for me?" Troy asked. "Why in the world would anyone want to find me?"

"Don't know the answer to that question," Ian shrugged. "But he was packing like an assassin."

"An assassin? What in the ... why would anyone want to kill me?"

He thought of a few times that he'd crossed paths with evil people in his life, but most of them were gone—either dead or in prison.

"Uh huh," Ian said. "So, I'd lay low if I were you. Find someplace other than the Islamorada Tennis Club to hole up for a while."

"But I don't have anyplace else to go."

"Well, there are plenty of hotels around. It might be a good idea to get a room for a few days, don't make contact with anyone, keep a low profile, order takeout, that kind of thing until I figure this thing out."

He started to tell Ian he didn't have any money to get a hotel room, but before he could, his phone rang. He'd almost forgotten he had it on him. He reached into his pocket and pulled it out to show Cinnamon's number on the screen. He looked at it, looked up at Ian, then back at the screen.

"You gonna answer that?" Ian asked.

Troy nodded and clicked the button. "Hello?"

On the other end of the line, Troy could hear noise, but no one seemed to be on the phone. He put his hand over the mic and mouthed the words, 'butt dial' to Ian. Ian squinted, apparently confused about what that meant.

Troy felt the need to explain. "It's where the person's phone is in their back pocket and perhaps when they sit down to dinner, or maybe on the couch to watch a movie, their bottom activates the phone and makes an unintended call."

"I know what it is, you idiot," Ian snapped.

"Well, I didn't mean no offense, officer."

Troy put the phone back to his ear. He strained to listen and could finally make out a few muffled voices, one of which he thought might be Cinnamon. Snippets of words broke through and sent a chill up his spine. He heard something about an alligator eating someone just before the call disconnected.

He punched the button to redial her, but the call couldn't connect. He tried several more times before looking up at Ian.

"It won't go through."

"It's the cell tower strength. It really sucks here in the apartment. Probably the lead paint messing with the signal," Ian said. "It's always better out by the road. I've got to go, so why don't you try to call back up there … and maybe get a cab to take you to a hotel."

Troy nodded and walked out the door. He walked up to the road near the entrance to the apartments. Under the faded sign announcing Lime Tree Apartments, his signal got up to two bars. He dialed Cinnamon again and waited.

TEN MINUTES EARLIER

CINNAMON STARR WOKE up in a tub of freezing cold water with someone banging insistently on the door to her one bedroom dung heap of an apartment. At first, she had been convinced she was dreaming about being a performer in the hit Broadway show, Stomp, but as the fogginess of sleep left her she realized that show was passé and hadn't been a thing since Friday, December 12th, 2012.

She pulled the stopper on the tub and let the water drain as she toweled off. Wrapping her hair in it, she draped her robe around her, grabbed her phone (without seeing the fourteen missed call notifications,) and tiptoed to the front door. She put her eye up to the peephole to see who was doing all the loud knocking.

Her neighbor and sometimes shoe shopping buddy, Gary Suskind from the apartment down the way, was standing outside, soaking wet, muddy, and pale. He shook like a man who had chugged one too many Red Bull's and his eyes were sunken and dark.

"Gary, is that you?" she called through the closed door.

"Yes, it's me," he hissed. "I know you can see me through the peephole. Let me in please. It's an emergency."

She unlocked and unchained the door and before she could get out of the way, Gary shoved his way in and slammed it behind him. Naturally, it didn't latch correctly. It hadn't worked right since she'd moved in two years ago and Myrtle seemed less than interested in having it fixed. As it was, Cinnamon had to heave upward on the knob as she pulled it shut and engaged the deadbolt. Otherwise, it swung open—as it had now.

Gary paced back and forth like a family member waiting anxiously for the bad news from the attending emergency room doctor. He steepled his hands in front of his lips and Cinnamon made a mental note to ask him what shade of pink he'd used on his fingernails. She thought it would coordinate perfectly with her latest Dusty Rose, rhinestone-sequined thong acquisition from JuJu's Bodyscapes.

He moaned and groaned and mumbled to himself and for a few moments she wondered if he was on drugs. He didn't usually partake of anything stronger than weed, but who was she to judge. He was carrying on about an alligator and a kayak and the most random things, maybe even a dead body.

She stood up and positioned herself on an intercept course to his southerly path across her Grandmother's Persian rug. She was surprised when he didn't slow and bumped into her and they toppled to the floor like lovers—him on top, her on bottom. She never noticed that her phone had tumbled out of her pocket and skidded across the vinyl wood flooring until it came to a rest under the couch. She also never noticed that it had connected to a call from one *Cute Cowboy Troy*—the name she had assigned to him in her contacts. Gary wasn't a massive guy, but falling on her in such an unexpected way caused her to cry out.

"If you two are going to be shagging and screaming at each other, at least shut your door. I've had two noise complaints and both of you know that three is an instant call to the cops."

Cinnamon craned her neck to see who was speaking and unfortunately got a rather unpleasant view upside down of the lower contents of Myrtle Hussholder's thin nighty. She felt bile rise up in her throat and heaved to throw Gary off. Jumping to her feet, Cinnamon ran her fingers through her hair. As she regained her composure, she realized Myrtle's eyes were tracking up and down over her body. Looking down, she saw that her robe had come untied during the fall and she was full frontal nude in front of the woman—who oddly, didn't seem to be repulsed, but rather ... pleased. *Eww*, thought Cinnamon. But before she could raise any sort of protest to the old woman's gawking, Gary had grabbed her hand, jerking her out of the door. And that is how the one good-looking stripper on Islamorada came to be riding down Overseas Highway in a 1980 Daisy Duke model Jeep CJ-7 with the only man she knew—who had no interest in getting in her pants—in her bathrobe and house shoes ... and nothing else.

Five minutes later, Gary swung the Jeep into Robbie's of Islamorada. Robbie's was nearly world famous for their waterfront restaurant, daily tarpon feeding, party boat and charter fishing, snorkeling, parasailing, sunset cruises, boat rentals, jet-ski adventures, and serendipitously, kayak tours. But at this time of night—just before closing time—it was a dark, creaking, nightmarish place. The only customers left were local fishermen hunched over stale beers and the dozing drunk tourists who had passed through the "fun and rowdy stage" into the "two seconds before blackout" stage. One of them came stumbling out of the restaurant in what had to be a hard bourbon daze. He swore into his cellphone and promptly smashed it into the lighted sign above the pier.

It looked exactly like a scene from a tropical thriller novel or murder mystery show on the ID Channel. Gary parked his Jeep in the first open spot —it was marked for handicapped customers, but at this point, he counted himself as mentally disabled. He buried his face in his hands, and began to sob.

"Gary, hun," Cinnamon said, running her hand across his back, "what's wrong? Why are we here? I mean, I'm not all that sad to be out of sight of that crone, but—"

"It's Dani!" he cried, interrupting her. "He's gone."

"Oh, Gary," she said, "I'm so sorry. We both know that relationship wasn't going to last. What was it? Another woman? Er, another ... man?"

"No!" He looked up, mascara was running down his cheeks. "Dani didn't leave me. The alligator got her. Same one that got—"

He stopped talking suddenly.

"Alligator? What? What are you talking about, Gary?"

A massive pelican splashed into the water in front of them startling Cinnamon so that she almost wet herself. For Robbie's to be such a fun-loving, daytime water sport activity spot, this place sure was creepy at night.

"The alligator ate the kayak," Gary wheezed, his eyes shining like those of Jack Torrance after a few weeks at the Overlook Hotel.

She squeaked when he grabbed her shoulders and shook her. "And poor, sweet, beautiful Dani. The damn thing ate Dani, too."

And that was when Cinnamon ruined Gary's luxury noble fluffy wool seat covers.

27

Splashing And Thrashing

TROY PUNCHED Cinnamon's number again and again, but it went to voicemail every time after a couple of rings. He wasn't an expert on such things, but he figured since it was actually ringing, that her phone was on and receiving the calls—and she wasn't rejecting them. The music at Woody's was pretty dang loud now since they'd added the wacky drummer ... maybe she just couldn't hear it ring.

There was a time in his life, a time that was long gone down the dusty road of the past, that he would have simply walked on home and let things play out. But the years between the war in Afghanistan and his arrival in the trailer park, island town of Islamorada had taught him a healthy respect for the fact that there were a whole bunch of messed up people out there. People who would do bad, after-midnight things to a pretty girl like Cinnamon. People who would take pleasure in her pain and not give two-pennies of a care about her at all.

As he tucked his phone back in his pocket and stared blankly at the empty, windy, wet stretch of Overseas Highway stretching out in front of him, a thought occurred to him regarding Cinnamon's active, yet unanswered cell. He'd seen more than enough cop shows to know they had ways—ways as foreign and unknowable to Troy as the Heisenberg Uncertainty Principle or the Schrödinger equation —of tracking the location of an active cellular phone as long as it was equipped with GPS. And since, he'd just come from the apartment of an FDLE officer, he figured that the man might have access to such tracking equipment. If he didn't have it in his apartment, he could probably make a quick call to someone in another, more important location, who did.

He jogged back toward the Lime Tree Apartments and took the metal steps two at a time up to Ian Bass's apartment. Only, he underestimated just how slick the well-worn edges of the stairs would be and on the last one, his foot slid off, scraping his shin against the edge. At the same time, his bad knee buckled in pain as his foot slammed into the next step down. He yelped in pain and simultaneously lost his balance. He fell backward, clanging his way down, banging into every step along the way. In the silence of the night, it sounded like a group of grossly inaccurate high school cymbal players had decided to practice the rousing conclusion of John Phillip Sousa's *Stars and Stripes Forever* right there on the stairs.

When he reached the bottom, he lay flat on his back for a few seconds, catching his breath and waiting for the telltale stab of pain in one or more broken bones. As he slowed his breathing, he realized the rain had stopped and there were a few stars beginning to poke through the late-night clouds. The smell of fish and trash and cat urine told him he was lying in a popular feline restroom. He dreaded to think what he might be laying in, so he slowly eased himself up to a sitting position. As he did, a door on the second floor flew open and he heard a screeching sound that reminded him of the loose drive belt on the pickup truck he'd owned back on Pawleys Island. It got louder until he saw the source of the awful racket.

A woman—wait, was it a woman? Or a troll? The hag wore a paper-thin undergarment—Troy choked back the bile in his throat—and held a cast-iron skillet in one hand. She shook it over her head as she yelled at him. It took a few minutes before he could make out what she was saying and even when he thought he had it, he only caught a few words. Something about the police and jail and vagrant. He knew better than to wait around until he figured out exactly what she was saying.

He got up and started running ... er, limping down the highway. He wasn't sure exactly where he was going. The cop had said not to go back to the tennis club, Cinnamon wasn't anywhere to be found, and he didn't have any money to get a hotel room or a drink. As he walked, the various points of pain that were likely areas of his body that would be bruised tomorrow began to throb. He slowed and eventually came to a stop. He desperately needed to think. He sat down and ran through the events of the past few days.

The cop had said that the fellow at the tennis club must have been after him, but that didn't make sense. Troy didn't have any money, didn't cause anybody any trouble, and didn't have any enemies— or friends, for that matter—that might want to do him harm. Cinnamon might have gone back to work. He could walk to Woody's and see what was up with her. But the more he thought about that, the more he was sure she wouldn't go back in there ... at least not tonight.

He decided to take his chances and go back to the Islamorada Tennis Club. At least there, he would have a hot shower and a bed to crash into so his aches and pains could have a chance to recede. And he'd be careful approaching the place. He knew enough about stealth to check it out before any potential threats detected his presence.

Half an hour later, he was tiptoeing through the edge of the mangroves on the north side of the tennis property. It was deeper and muckier than usual after all the rain and for a second he wondered if he'd made a huge mistake trudging into the swamp with his bad knee. But slowly and surely, he made his way toward the one visible yellow lightbulb on the backside of the pro shop. He poked a hand through the foliage surrounding court number one and pulled it back slightly so he could see the porch. Nothing. No movement. No sign of anyone there. He was about to push through and go into the apartment when something bumped against his leg.

He jumped, sending a knife of pain into his knee and he sat down hard. He found himself chest deep in the murky water staring at something long and bumpy floating just above the surface. He lurched backward hard, suddenly terrified that the gator he'd heard poking around outside the fence was about to make a meal of him. He kicked with his good leg and it thumped into the side of the thing.

It made an odd, hollow sound and Troy realized the object wasn't moving. He tested it with another gentle kick. Still nothing. He squinted his eyes and saw through the dirt and grime on it a patch of bright orange peeking out. He moved closer and used his hand to sweep across the top and revealed even more of the object's true color. It was smooth along most of its length, but his hand caught on something sharp down near the front. He pulled away, thinking he'd been bit, even knowing this wasn't an alligator. He glanced at his finger to see he'd cut himself on whatever this was.

"Well, that'll be infected by morning," he muttered.

And then it struck him as he stood and looked at the floating, orange thing in front of him. *It's a kayak*, he thought. *Or a paddle board or something.* He reached under the closest edge and heaved up. With an unceremonious splash it flipped over and he could see that it was, indeed a kayak. To his untrained eye, it looked like it might be an expensive one. But then he saw what he'd cut himself on. The front of the thing was a jagged mess. It had been torn and cut and shredded like the *Orca* in Steven Spielberg's classic, *Jaws.*

"I think we're gonna need a bigger boat," he quoted the famous line. "Or at least one with fewer holes."

As if hearing his doubt of its seaworthiness, the kayak gurgled and began to sink. He chuckled and it echoed in the trees with an odd sound. He made a mental note that he'd come out here tomorrow and get it out of here and take it up to the dump.

The strange echo of his laugh came back again, which he thought was weird since he hadn't laughed again. The next sound was closer and Troy realized, with new terror, that it wasn't a chuckle he was hearing. It was a chumpf.

"Dangit," he wheezed, and tried to slowly move away from the kayak, back toward the road.

It was a long, long way, and his knee pounding. If the gator had discovered him, he knew he wasn't going to make it out alive. He moved as slowly as he could, careful not to make anything bigger than a ripple in the water.

As his back bumped up against a larger tree

trunk, the water beside the kayak exploded and a narrow, jagged mouth slammed into the orange plastic. Troy decided that silence wasn't his major concern. He pulled himself up to stand, wobbly on top of the tree roots. At least up here, he could move a little faster.

He turned and played a game of "the water is lava" across the bare feet of the mangrove trees, hopping and jumping as best he could. He looked over his shoulder at the thrashing sound and in a moment he would never forget for as long as he lived, he locked eyes with the *alligator*.

Lifeless eyes, black eyes, like a doll's eyes. When it comes at you, it doesn't seem to be livin', Troy thought.

The alligator paused for a split second, perhaps assessing the new creature in front of him. And then he lunged. Troy ran. Somehow, his feet found solid purchase all the way across the swamp to the highway. He burst out onto the road and ran north, ignoring the pain in his legs, without looking back.

He was sure he heard the alligator grunting and snapping at his heels all the way to Woody's.

28

The Big Reveal

CHAD HARRISON AKA Cap Wayfarer always enjoyed eating at local establishments and turning down the requests for pictures and autographs he received. He once grabbed a photographer's ridiculously overpriced Hasselblad camera and tossed it into the lobster tank at the Islamorada Fish Company. As a matter of actual fact though, such requests and intrusions were becoming less and less frequent since it had been over eleven years since any of his books had rated into the top one hundred bestsellers on any mainstream list. And being recognized wasn't what it was in the eighties. His file photo at Knoxnews.com was a picture his second girlfriend—or was it third—had taken of him sitting in his prized Sun Dolphin

Aruba 10 Foot Sit-In Kayak. The color— Opulent Orange had cost an extra two-hundred and fifty bucks—almost as much as the sticker price on the thing.

Tonight, he'd brought his current girlfriend out to eat. Thankfully, she was too young, and perhaps too stupid, to know anything about fine dining, so he'd brought her to one of the tourist traps along the highway. It was reasonable and usually the service was okay, but Chad was particularly upset that no one, not even the vacationers sitting at the table down by the pier, recognized him. He sighed as he perused the menu of fried and tossed and breaded bottom-feeding fish offerings.

"Oooh," his girlfriend said, flipping her platinum blonde bangs to the side, "I'm gonna get the grouper basket."

She said it in a way that made him think she considered it to be a specialty, a prized dish, an award winning entrée. He pursed his lips and hid the fact that he was repulsed by the plebianistic offerings on the twenty-two page menu.

And that's when the ding alerted him to a new email on his phone. He was thankful for the interruption to their riveting conversation. He stood and put his phone to his ear.

"Sorry, doll," he mouthed, holding his hand over the speaker portion of the iPhone, "Gotta take this."

She nodded dutifully, batting her eyelashes over wide eyes in response to how important her boyfriend was and flashing *don't-you-wish-you-were-me* glances at all the people who just happened to look her way—at this particular moment, there weren't any, but she saved the special look for another day.

"Should I order for you?" she called as he walked away.

"I'll have whatever you're having," he said and pushed through the front door.

The email was from the paper. It read like a generic notice, but it was only sent (via non-bcc'd-email addresses) to him, Dori Handler, and Rex Kiser—the three editorial writers on staff.

He mumbled aloud as he read the email.

Something, something, something. The McGlashen group that acquired Blight House Inc., publishers of Knoxnews.com, WaveRunners, and Tropical Thriller Press is filing for bankruptcy. Staff writers are still employed for now, but to keep delivering quality journalism and reporting, some downsizing must occur.

Your current pay period will end at midnight

tonight and any and all unpublished articles that you have delivered to the editor will remain property of Keysnews.com.

"Holy crap," he said aloud to the nearly deserted parking lot. "They fired me with an email."

He immediately dialed the editor and though it was after hours, he knew Ed was still in the office pumping out mind-numbing pieces about the service workers upcoming basketball game or the pie-eating contest at Mary's Bakery and Pasties down on Marathon. Naturally, his call went to voicemail. After punching zero until he reached the appropriate mailbox, he screamed the most vile curse words he could think of to the recording and then in a fit of rage, turned and flung his phone as hard as he could. It hit the large red sign bearing the restaurant's name—ROBBIE'S. It shattered into at least four big plastic pieces and thousands of other microscopic glass bits—all of which splashed down into the Tarpon feeding station down on the dock. The fish woke and began a soon-to-be-disappointed frenzy attacking the shell of Chad's phone as it drifted down into the black, murky water.

With his heart pounding and his breath coming in ragged staccato, he realized that had been a very bad idea. He was about to take his walk of shame back into the touristy waterfront eatery when he overheard voices. Without making it obvious, he inclined his head toward a white Jeep sitting in the handicap spot next to the front door.

An oddly dressed man was crying into his hands as a woman sat in the passenger's seat consoling him. The roof was off, so as Chad got closer, he could hear more and more of their conversation.

"...and that's why I can't go to the police about the kayak. Stupid, orange piece of ... it's a vessel of death. That's what it is."

Chad's pulse raced. Sweat beaded on his forehead as adrenaline pulsed into his veins. He felt like he did when he was on the trail of a hot scoop or uncovering a political scandal involving sex and drugs and dirty money. He stole one quick look at the thieving passengers for identification purposes and felt sure he would be able to identify the woman ... actually, she looked strangely familiar, but didn't all the bimbos from Miami. The man never lifted his head from his hands as he sobbed, but Chad figured it wouldn't matter if he could get the damnable Sheriff of Islamorada down here fast enough.

He ducked into the restaurant, leaned over the host stand, and grabbed the reservation and to-go order telephone he knew was stashed there. He startled the girl at the stand, who had been leaning back, smacking her gum, and tapping her phone furiously—perhaps connecting rows of candy, or promising some kind of late-night sweets for her boyfriend. She yelped and slapped the back of his hand, making him drop the receiver.

"This is official police business, honey," he snapped. "So, why don't you take your sexting somewhere else while I take care of this."

Her face darkened and if her jaw hadn't dropped open, he might've suspected that she'd swallowed her gum. As it was, he could see it floating around her back teeth, bobbing up and down with the pulsing of her angry tongue. She stormed off, stomping her flip-flops as hard as she could on the sandy, pine floor. Chad grabbed the phone again and dialed 9-1-1. When he heard the line connect, he didn't wait for the sheriff or whoever was manning the phones tonight to answer.

"They're here. I'm at Robbie's down by seventy-seven. I've got eyes on them and I'll keep them contained until you get here."

He heard a groan on the other end of the line. Sheriff Paul Puckett said, "Christ, Chad. Is that you? What in the Sam Hill are you talking about?"

There was a pause and Chad could almost hear

the man looking up at the schoolhouse clock perched on the wall above the door.

"Sheriff," he snapped. "I know you have an important game of solitaire to get through, or perhaps a second reading of the latest edition of Guns and Ammo, but this is actual, important police business. I just overheard a couple parked in front of Robbie's discussing an orange kayak—my orange kayak."

The line disconnected. He stared into the receiver and banged it against the well-worn host stand. A piece of wood splintered and went flying off the top edge. Chad slammed the phone down and swiveled to return to his table. He almost bumped into a man's chest—a chest as wide as his leather sectional sofa imported from Italy. The man, dressed in a skin-tight black t-shirt, had biceps that pulsed with ropey veins circling them in steroidal anger. Tucked behind him, hands jammed defiantly on her hips, was the hostess still smacking her gum.

"That's the guy, right there." She pointed a furious finger at him and her earrings jingled as her head bobbed back and forth.

As the man's beach-ball-sized hand covered Chad's face and dragged him toward the front door, he was thankful that at least he would be outside where he could keep an eye on the kayak thieves. He skidded to a stop only three feet from the front of the white Jeep they were sitting in. Picking bits of gravel out of his skin, he could almost hear them talking again over the ringing in his ears.

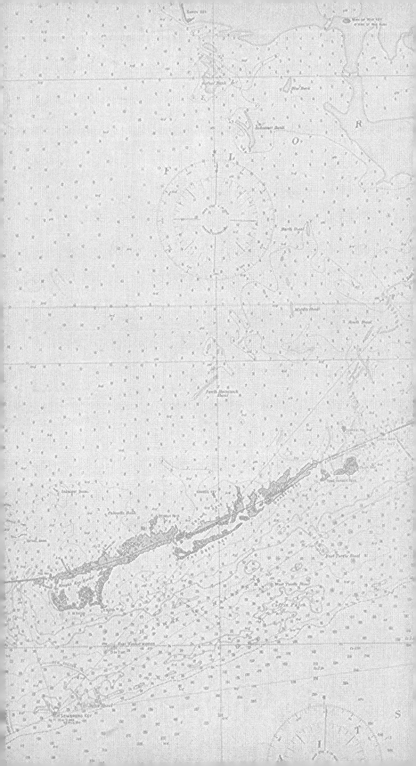

29

Nobody Home

GARY LIFTED his head off his steering wheel long enough to see the bouncer—a cute young football player from FIU named Mike—throwing another drunk out of the restaurant. The poor drunk tourist wearing a faded powder blue polo, torn khaki shorts, and one leather sandal bounced across the sidewalk and scraped into the gravel lot in front of them. Gary wondered if he'd wake up there in the morning and wonder how in the hell he'd gotten there.

He wiped his nose and turned to Cinnamon. She was a good girl, sweet and kind—too sweet and kind for the drama he was dragging her into.

"You know what?" he said. "I'm actually okay, now that I think about it."

"You're okay?" Cinnamon asked with a huff. "Your boyfriend is dead and you're ... okay?"

Her eyes filled with tears. Gary wasn't sure what that was all about, but he shrugged and took a deep breath.

"I mean," he said, "there isn't much I can do. The kayak is gone, Dani's gone, Ma—"

He stopped short. He had told Cinnamon about Dani, but hadn't said anything about Matty. She didn't need to know anything about that. He decided not to mention it.

"I guess you're right," she said, her tears escaping her eyes and trailing down her cheeks making small, hot tracks of mascara. "My boyfriend—well, my guy friend anyway—is gone, too."

"Really?" Gary asked, happy to change the subject. "What happened?"

"Well, he's missing," she said wiping her eyes. "He might've just run off. He's done that before. But usually he tells me when he's going to be gone. I think ... I think something ... bad has happened."

Gary shivered. "Worse than being eaten by an alligator?"

She nodded her head. "Maybe. I work for some pretty shady characters down at—"

She was interrupted by the sound of Gary's cell

phone blaring out *It's Raining Men. Sorry*, he mouthed and pulled it out of his pocket. He groaned at the screen, tapped the button to decline the call.

"That's the revue calling about Dani. The owner of the Bourbon Street place on Duval is asking where his star singer is and I don't know what to tell him. I mean, he's been calling non-stop."

"Surely, they've got someone else who can do it." Cinnamon said, matter-of-factly.

"Honey, I don't think you know how good Dani really was," Gary started, but then began to sob uncontrollably before he could add to his sentiment.

"Hey, hey," she said, running a hand over his back to calm him down, "It's going to be okay. We'll figure this thing out. I'm not sure what happens next, but—"

"I'm going to jail," Gary jerked his head up. "That's what's next."

"That is absolutely not true. You haven't done anything wrong and ..."

Her words trailed off as she saw a look of horror spread across Gary's face. He wasn't looking at her, he was staring out the front windshield. She turned and was startled to see the drunk guy standing up, looking at them over the hood of the Jeep.

"Gary," she whispered, trying not to move her lips, "let's get out of here, please."

He jammed the gear shift backward, and stomped the accelerator to the floor. Gravel and rock flew out from the tires as the wheels fought for purchase. A spray of debris shot out and rained all over the drunk. Bruises and welts and scrapes began to appear immediately as the man raised his hands to block the barrage of rocky hail flying at him. As they tore out on the highway, the night wind rushing through their hair, they could hear him screaming in the parking lot far behind them.

"WHAT DO YOU MEAN, you ain't heard from your man?" Dante Caparelli growled into the *family* phone. The long, evil silence on the other end of the line told him he'd overstepped.

For a second, he considered hanging up, or maybe even apologizing for his gaffe. But no. This was his son and the family was supposed to be sending a professional to take care of it.

"Are you tellin' me that a two-bit, serial killer with a stupid hat and a drinking problem managed to outsmart *the guy*?"

"We don't know anything of the sort," the voice

said. "Sure we haven't heard anything, but that don't mean nothin'. When he's done with the job, he'll check in. Until then, you gotta sit tight and don't do nothin' stupid. If it'll make you feel better, we'll do some checking and see what gives."

Do some checking? See what gives? Dante was furious now. To hell with the consequences. He was about to demand more, but the line clicked and went dead. He slammed the phone down on the receiver. He picked it up and slammed it down again. And then he did it again. Red chips of plastic splintered off the phone and skittered across his desk.

His door swung open after a cursory knock. The music from the club blared through the opening and Dante wondered what the hell the band was doing. His bar manager—he'd promoted Sully in the absence of his son—had a dark expression on his face.

"Boss, it ain't goin' so well out here," he said, jerking a thumb over his shoulder. "The customers are pissed that Cinnamon ain't here. The band is ... I don't even know what the band is doin'. Oh, and we're out of Corona."

"Fix it," Dante growled.

"Beg pardon?"

The old man stood, put his palms flat on the top of his desk. "I made you the manager so I wouldn't have to deal with bullshit like this. Go do your job. Fix it."

Sully's face twisted into a mix of confusion and fear. He looked like a man about to jump out of an airplane for the first time unsure of what he was feeling. Could be excitement, could be fear, could be hysteria. He nodded and backed out of the office door.

When it closed, Dante turned his hands over. He had several sharp pieces of the shattered receiver sticking in the soft flesh of his palms. One had a trickle of blood oozing down from it toward his wrist. He brushed them away.

It had been a long time since he'd gotten blood on his hands in more ways than one. The owner of Woody's before him had been *reluctant* to sell. That had been a few years ago and Dante was fairly sure that no one would ever find his remains behind the club, under the dumpster.

He leaned back in his chair, pulled a cigar from his suit pocket, and rolled it around in his lips. He slid open the file drawer and removed a small, snub nose revolver from the back. He spun the cylinder slowly checking for bullets. Three. More than enough to drop a cowboy in his tracks.

Dante tucked the gun into his suit pocket, made the sign of the cross touching his forehead, then his chest, then his shoulders, and only then did he stand to leave his office. He was a new man, a man on a mission, a man determined to find that cowboy and put a bullet or three in his head.

He straightened his coat that hung slightly lower on the side holding the pistol. After a quick two fingers of his prized Knappogue Castle Sherry that he picked up for just such an occasion, he opened his office door and stepped into the cacophony shaking the peeling wallpaper from behind the stage on the nearly empty stripper side of Woody's. Sully was standing in front of the stage shouting at the shirtless drummer beating on the poor drum kit like it had stolen something from him.

Dante shook his head, put his hands over his ears, and lurched toward the front door trying to escape the dual crashing cymbals that were currently *Rockin' in the Free World*. As he reached to push his way out, the door whooshed open. He lost his balance and tumbled into the parking lot, falling hard into the gravel. The jolt to his already tender palms sent him down to his chest, knocking the wind out of him.

He rolled over onto his back and took slow deep breaths until the pain subsided. The streetlight mingled with the yellowing bulbs lighting the ancient Woody's sign above the front door blinding him. He squinted as a figure leaned over him, silhouetted in the glare.

"Howdy, partner," the voice behind the shadow said. "You okay there?"

Dante raised a painful arm to block the light. To his shock, he was looking at the man with the straw hat, the dude who had killed Matty and probably the family's fixer, the Cowboy Killer.

"Say," the man said, holding a hand down to help Dante to his feet, "have you seen Cinnamon?"

Dante grinned with no mirth. "Yeah," he said. "I got just what you're looking for in the back."

30

The Nose Knows

TROY COULD HEAR the muffled sounds coming through the dank darkness of the back room Dante had led him into. Whatever was happening on the other side of the wall was neither musical nor enjoyable in any way. It sounded more like Keith Moon had traded in his Ludwig Black Oyster Super Classics on a couple of upturned aluminum trash cans and was beating on them with a pair of pipe wrenches. The classic melody of *My Generation* was lost in the barrage of percussion, trying desperately to stick its head above the noise like a drowning swimmer being bowled over by wave after wave of water.

His wrists were zip-tied behind his back with another looped between them through the slats of an old wooden kitchen chair. He wrenched his hands back and forth but only succeeded in cutting his skin on the sharp edges of the narrow, but strong ties.

"Okay, cowboy," Dante said, bringing Troy back to the interrogation the old man had begun more than thirty minutes ago. "Let me get this straight. You say you didn't have anything to do with the disappearance of my son."

Troy could see photographs over the old man's shoulder. There were vintage, over-exposed pictures showing signs of yellowing at the edges with young men in suits standing around classic cars on crowded city streets. One picture showed a younger Dante holding a baby in his arms, a lit cigar between his teeth. Behind him, lying in a hospital bed, was the woman who had apparently given birth to the child. Next to that, a more modern pose in front of a typically mottled blue abstract studio backdrop showed a young man in a graduation gown. The student's oily, pimply face betrayed that it was probably a high school graduation rather than a college one. On a single shelf below the pictures, two plastic bowling trophies stood watch like the Pillars of Hercules. Between them were a few paperback books, weathered, worn, and well read: *For Whom The Bell Tolls, A Time To Kill, The Deep Blue Goodbye, Double Whammy*, and—of course—a copy of a King James Bible.

"As God is my witness," started Troy, "I don't know nothin' about your boy—a fine fellow, I'm sure."

Dante chewed on the insides of his cheek, seeming to consider this carefully. "Uh huh."

A sudden silence on the other side of the wall followed by random shouting gave the old man pause. He looked at the wall as if trying to see through it. He turned back to Troy. "And you haven't had any run-ins with any other ... men?"

Troy squinted his eyes. "I'm not sure I take your meanin'. If you're asking if I'm partial to fellers, then the answer is no. I prefer the fairer sex."

Dante's mouth opened slightly, but no sound came out. "No, not that, you imbecile. I mean dealings with ... bad men. Has anyone strange come around hustling you lately?"

Troy suddenly remembered the strange happenings with the cop and the attacker at the tennis club. He certainly figured the man the cop had put in the back of his SUV must've been a bad man. He was about to tell Dante the story when the old man's cell phone began chirping inside his pocket.

"Yeah?" he growled into the phone. "Are you kidding me, Sully? What the frick am I payin' you for? Fix it."

Troy couldn't hear the voice on the other end of the line, but judging from Dante's exasperation, he guessed the person was not delivering good news.

"Fine," Dante said, pushing himself up out of his squeaky chair. "Stall 'em. I'll be around in a second."

He shoved his phone into his pocket. "Can't get good help these days. You got a job, Mr. uh ..."

"Bodean. But you can call me Troy. And yes sir. I am gainfully employed as of the moment."

"Yeah."

The old man sniffed, straightened his wide, diagonally striped tie, and buttoned his jacket. He whisked open the door to the room and Troy could feel the cool night air wafting in. Judging from the little he could see, he reckoned they were in some kind of room around the back of the building—a storeroom or an office of some kind.

The door slammed and he was alone in the dark, only a single amber bulb burning above him. He remembered back a few months ago—was it more than a month—on the long, monotonous bus ride down to the Keys, he'd gotten into almost the exact same situation with that kid who'd killed the liquor store owner. Something in his brain hung up on the memory of the murderer and their kidnapper. He could almost see his face, but it eluded him. It was the same feeling you got when you walked into a room and forgot why you'd gone there. It would come to him, but right now, he was blank, trying desperately to dig it out of the fog in his mind. He figured a psychologist might tell him he'd buried that along with the more shocking memories from Afghanistan.

He tried to jerk his hands free again, but this time only managed to cut himself. He could feel the warm trickle of blood dripping down on his fingers. He recalled that Cinnamon had told him she was certain these men were mafia or mob or something like that. He wondered if he was going to be thrown into the ocean wearing concrete shoes or maybe taken out into the Everglades and tossed into the swamp with a hunk of raw meat tied to his neck. Either way, he was sure he didn't want to wait around to find out.

But he had no idea how to get out of his current predicament, nor did he know where he would go when he did. He wondered if Cinnamon was safe or if she'd already met the fate she had feared. Between the low sounds of mayhem coming from the other side of the wall, he heard a low, buzzing sound on the old man's desk. It was insistent and mocked him as he scooted his chair—one jarring bump at a time —over toward the metallic bumblebee hissing at him. With great effort that left sweat dripping down his nose like an Olympic ski jumper racing toward takeoff, he moved closer at a pace he thought of as slower than a snail riding on a turtle's back. The noise stopped, but then started again, insisting that he was getting warmer.

He leaned down, and gave a silent apology to his dentist—who he hadn't seen in many years, gripped the top drawer handle with his teeth and pulled. Thankfully, it wasn't locked and slid open easily. Inside, he could see his cell phone lying among a few random papers, a dozen paper clips, a half-empty box of staples, and a small, snub nose revolver. A chill went through Troy's spine as he considered all the bad things the gun had probably been used for, but before he could process them all, his phone buzzed again. Unfortunately, it was face down, so he couldn't see who was calling. Without thinking, he slammed his head down, trying to grab it with his teeth—another silent prayer that he wasn't going to lose any of his pearly whites. His hat bumped into the desk and fell from his head, toppling over onto the desk. He was able to get the edge of his phone into his mouth and flip it over. It wasn't ringing anymore, but he did have a missed call from an unlisted number.

He jabbed at it with his nose, trying to open the screen, but the rivulets of sweat just smeared across the fingerprint scanner. Troy wondered if his nose would be sufficient to unlock the phone. He sat up and rubbed his face across his sleeve and prayed to the Gods of telecommunications that his nose did indeed have the necessary information to get him in.

He pressed his slightly dryer snout onto the fingerprint scanner. Predictably, it failed and asked him for his passcode. He tried desperately to tap it out with his proboscis. He raised up to see it had also failed. He tried once again only to see that the phone was locked for a minute and that he could try again after that.

After the longest sixty seconds he had ever experienced passed, he tried again. He could hear Winston Churchill reminding him that success consisted of going from failure to failure without loss of enthusiasm. He wasn't sure where he'd read that, but it came to him just as his phone told him it was now locked for five minutes.

The screen lit up with a timer counting down and Troy watched it, alternating between the door and the phone as the seconds ticked at the pace of a snail riding on a turtle's back through a field of frozen molasses on roller skates with rusty ball-bearings and wheels coated in grease.

31

A Dead Man's Purse

CHAD HARRISON'S date for the extravagant night out at Robbie's had apparently decided to leave after he'd been thrown from the bar in a fashion normally reserved for vagrants and overly intoxicated tourists. As such, she'd gotten into his car—an extraordinarily pretentious, and exorbitantly pricey Rosso (red) Competizione Tri-Coated Alfa Romeo 4C Spider—and driven it out of the parking lot, missing the exit and crunching it over the curb at high speed. Unfortunately, the yellow concrete curb was two inches higher than the exotic car's undercarriage. The damage was extensive, but she never noticed over the eardrum bursting Van Halen blaring from the radio.

Chad picked the gravel shards thrown up by the

knobby wheels on the white Jeep from his forearms and face. A thousand trickles of blood dripped down his cheeks painting him like a geisha girl or perhaps a member of the Walking Dead. He wasn't sure if that show was still relevant, but decided he might try to watch a few episodes and write an article on them.

He sat for a few minutes on the pier, his feet dangling over the water where the tarpon feeding took place in the daytime. There were no fish there where they had swarmed around his phone earlier —he guessed maybe they were diurnal and only fed during the day. He wondered if that was their nature, or if they had been trained to the behavior like Pavlov's dogs.

He glanced over his shoulder at the highway, wondering where the heck the police were ... they should've been here by now. He glanced at his watch. It had been over an hour since he'd called. He gritted his teeth and spat into the water. A single, tiny fish came up, nibbled at the drop, and disappeared into the darkness below.

No one was coming. The police didn't care. His girlfriend didn't care. His boss at the paper didn't care. Nobody cared and no one was going to do anything about his kayak. No one but him. He pulled himself up and looked around. He'd need a cab or—no, no way to call one. His phone was in bits at the bottom of the ocean, and they sure as hell weren't going to let him use the phone inside.

He needed transportation and fast. The Jeep was long gone, but he'd seen which direction they'd gone and thought maybe he could catch up with them if they were still on the island. His eyes landed on an old green bicycle propped up against the ice machine beside the restaurant. Probably one of the staff's primary modes of transportation. He didn't give two flips less about that and held no remorse as he pushed the bike up to the highway and got on. It had been a long time since he'd ridden a bike and it took him more than a mile to get comfortable with the rusty rhythm of the thing. But it wasn't long before he was cruising at a decent speed, his head swiveling back and forth looking for the thieves in the white Daisy Duke Jeep.

GARY JOHN SUSKIND and Cinnamon Starr screeched into the deserted parking lot at Dion's Quik Mart just minutes after leaving Robbie's.

"What are we doing here?" Cinnamon asked, her

eyes dancing around the convenience store searching for meaning.

She thought maybe Gary was meeting someone here, or perhaps purchasing something like duct tape or rope. When she'd gotten into the Jeep with him earlier tonight, she hadn't considered him dangerous, but the longer she was with him, the more she saw the signs—subtle and muted, but most definitely there—that he was coming unhinged. His face was the screwed up mask of a man who was watching his pants catch on fire, but insisted that everything was fine and that he preferred to be warm. The real answer was far less significant than she imagined.

"Gotta use the little boy's room," he said, "And grab a Fresca. You want one?"

She shook her head as he unbuckled his seat belt and jogged past the two sentinel fuel pumps watching guard under the aging, sodium bulb wash of light.

One of the bulbs was flickering, threatening to die giving the whole place a horror-movie ambiance. Cinnamon was beginning to wonder if she was living in one. She punched the door lock down on her side and reached across to do the same to Gary's wondering why that made her feel safer. The upper portion of the Jeep's windows were basic vinyl coated fabric with floppy clear windows. Jason or Freddie would slice through them without hesitation and be on her in a second.

She pulled down the visor, looking for a mirror and found, to her surprise there wasn't one. She grabbed the rear view mirror and torqued it around to face her.

For the first time she could remember in a very long time, she looked rough. Her eyes were ringed with red and bloodshot from the stress. Fine lines were beginning to show at the creases of her eyes and cheeks. Her makeup had given up and her nose was shiny.

"Oh, hell no," she said to her reflection. "Girl, you're not going to be laying on a coroner's table looking like death."

She dug around in her purse and found a bottle of Visine. She squirted a heavy dose into each eye and blinked the extra away. Streaks of tetrahydrozoline hydrochloride traced lines down her cheeks making her look like she'd been crying. She tossed the drops back into the purse and raked her hands back and forth looking for her powder. A little on the nose to freshen up ... but between the folded dollar bills, the unopened package of tissues, the flesh-colored bandages for the backs of her heels, the keys to her apartment and car, and the other random junk she told herself she was going to clean out on a daily basis, there was no powder. She remembered that she had applied it back at Woody's before going on stage. *Crap. Had she left it there? Probably.*

She snapped the purse closed with a frown. She leaned closer to the mirror and rubbed her face. *Nope, this wouldn't do at all.* She slumped back into the seat and folded her arms over her chest. She tried to cross her legs in defiance as well, but her heel got stuck on another purse on the floorboard. Must be Gary's. She grabbed it and pulled it into her lap. The heavy pink patent leather bag was stuffed to the brim with even more random junk than she had in hers. She was secretly pleased to discover that she wasn't the only hoarder on the planet.

Two nearly empty tubes of lipstick, three gummed up sticks of mascara, an open and desert-dry package of makeup removers, several different colors of eyeshadow ... she rummaged a bit more sending much of the flotsam and jetsam spilling out into the seat around her.

"Really, Gary?" she said out loud. "No powder?"

She was about to give up when she saw a glint of

something metallic. Like a bird drawn to a glittering piece of tinsel, her hand thrust into the nether regions of the purse and grabbed at it. The shiny object turned out to be a gold buckle, on a wallet. Oh, geez. He forgot his wallet. He won't be able to buy his Fresca, she thought. Upon further examination, she found the buckle was broken. The wallet flopped open revealing a dozen or more credit cards and a—her heart stopped beating. The driver's license beneath the clear plastic window showed a glowing, wide-grinning picture (better than most DMV photos) of ... Dani.

"Shit!" she said, chucking the purse into the floorboard.

To her horror, she'd been rifling through the purse of a ... of a dead person. It was Dani's purse. She rubbed at her hands to try and wipe off the ... well, the death. Tears formed at the edges of her eyes.

The remaining objects in it flew in random directions all around her shoes. Keys, cotton balls, tissues, various single earrings, and ... a ring ... a familiar looking ring. She wiped at her eyes and reached down to pick it up. When she did, she was startled to see the ring was on a severed finger.

"Oh, crap!" She exclaimed, dropping it back into the bag.

Eventually, her curiosity got the best of her and she used one of the tissues to pick up the finger to examine it.

The ring was heavy, a manly thing, not what she would've expected Dani to wear and the finger didn't have nail polish—she knew enough about Dani to know that she wouldn't be caught dead out without nail polish.

She rolled it around like Indiana Jones examining a long lost artifact of Mayan treasure. It was a bulky thing like a high school or college ring, or one of those monstrosities worn by professional athletes upon winning a championship.

She rotated it and stopped in sudden recognition. Fear burned into her throat like a hot wire wrapped around her neck. The crest on the side, she had seen it many times before. She knew this ring well. It was Matty's ring and ... oh, God ... Matty's ... finger? She looked up to see Gary walking out of the store. She slammed her hand down on the lock, checking to be sure it was engaged on both doors.

It was Gary. There hadn't been an alligator attack. She had no idea why, but she knew for sure that Gary had killed Dani ... and before that ... Matty.

She wanted to scream, but he was there, staring into the driver's side window.

"It's just me, girl. Open up."

She screamed.

32

Can You Hear Me Now?

TROY FELT the edges of the plastic ties around his wrist digging in. Warm rivulets of something—might be blood, might be sweat, he couldn't tell—dripping down his wrists to his fingertips and dropping in splashes on the floor like an old kitchen faucet. His phone was still locked and counting down the seconds—one-hundred forty-seven of them to be exact—until he could attempt to use it again. The noises coming through the wall connected to the stripping side of Woody's reminded Troy of a 2-year-old discovering the cabinet with the pots and pans and reveling in the noises they could make when banged together. Even as muffled as it was, it still made his molars shake. He wondered how anyone sitting in the bar itself would be able to hear after the ear-splitting performance.

He was lost in trying to decipher the angry shouting voices buried in the clatter when his phone rang. He jumped in surprise and wondered if he could answer it if it was locked. Cinnamon's name appeared at the top and he wasn't sure if he was relieved, shocked, or something in between. A very small part of him felt like a teenage boy seeing that his crush was calling.

He dragged his nose across his shoulder, which was almost as sweaty as his face—the old man liked his office to be toasty warm ... or maybe the A/C was out. It didn't help much, but at least he wasn't dripping onto the screen when he leaned over and swiped.

As he jabbed at the phone with his nose, he wondered why in the world the phone manufacturer would make the green "Accept" button so infuriatingly small? Didn't they know there would be kidnap victims trying to push it with other, less accurate body parts? On the third try, he hit it just right and the call connected.

At exactly that moment, the door to Woody's jerked open and the not-quite-right and ridiculously loud opening bars of Led Zeppelin's "Whole Lotta

Love" burst through like a wrecking ball pushing Dante Caparelli into the room. The old man flew in as if a tsunami was carrying him on stumbling feet. Troy could barely hear Cinnamon's frantic voice coming through the phone. With more practiced accuracy, he leaned down and punched the *Speaker* icon. Her shouting made Troy jerk at his wrists again, trying to free himself to no avail.

Dante, as if pushing back a physical wall of sound, shoved on the office door until it slammed behind him. Cinnamon's voice was suddenly clear over the dampened cacophony outside.

"... you there? Where are you?" She was yelling into the phone, on the edge of hysterics. "I need you!"

"Hey, I'm here." Troy said, ignoring the fact that Dante was listening. "Slow down. What's goin' on?"

She didn't slow down. In fact, she sped up to a speed and pitch usually reserved for 33RPM records being played at 78RPM's on a vinyl player. Troy looked up at Dante, who squinted his eyes, shrugged his shoulders, and held his hands out, palm up as if to say he had no earthly idea what she was saying either.

But eventually, she ran out of breath and that slowed her long enough for Troy to hear another voice on the line. It was distant and quieter and punctuated with loud thumps. It was a man's voice—a man that did not sound happy or calm.

"Darlin'," Troy shouted. "I can't understand what you're sayin'. You gotta speak clearly so I can hear you."

That seemed to do it. Her words suddenly broke through like a radio station locking in on an old dial stereo.

"I'm trapped. I'm stuck in the car and he's outside!"

Troy's skin went icy as if he'd made an impulsive decision to join in the Polar Bear Plunge. Despite the hot and humid conditions in the room, he felt a shiver run up and down his spine. He knew this feeling all too well. The PTSD which hadn't bothered him for a while began to snarl and growl at him from the back of his mind—an evil, burning demon that threatened to petrify him. He shoved back at it. He had to. If he didn't get a grip on the situation, Cinnamon could be in grave danger.

"Who's outside? What's wrong? Are the keys in the car?" he asked, trying to keep his voice under control.

Dante just stared at the phone, his mouth hanging open, eyes still narrow slits.

"I'm in his car at Dion's." Her voice was followed by some thumping and sounds of rummaging. "I don't see the keys. You've got to hurry. I think he's going to hurt me."

Troy opened his mouth to ask who was going to hurt her, but before he could get it out, her voice rose to a new level so high that he wondered if any dogs nearby would start barking.

"The window just tore! He wants in ... he's going to get in. God, Troy, please help me." She said through sobs. "He killed Matty! He killed Matty and now he's going to kill me. Troy, please—"

"Don't let him in!" Troy yelled.

Duh, he thought. *What a stupid thing to say.*

And with that, Troy heard the man's voice, closer, louder. Cinnamon shrieked and Troy was sure the man had her. And then, in time with the final cymbal crash of the biggest hit from "Led Zeppelin II," the line went dead.

Dumbstruck, Troy looked up at Dante who was equally surprised. The old man stared at the phone, his mouth working in a silent speech trying to comprehend what they had just heard.

"He killed Matty," Dante finally said, then repeated it slowly, emphasizing each word. "He. Killed. Matty."

Troy nodded his head.

Slowly, methodically, Dante pulled a pair of scissors out of his desk drawer. He clipped the ties around Troy's wrists.

"Looks like you're off the hook, cowboy," he said as Troy gently rubbed away the sweat and oozing blood.

The band outside the room started a new song, something Troy did not immediately recognize, but it was full of drums and raging guitar. He wasn't sure what the old man would do now, but he at least felt like he might avoid the pair of cement shoes and boat ride he was sure was coming. Dante slid the scissors back into the drawer and closed it with a screech. A red phone on the desk rang. He picked up the receiver, glared at it, then slammed it down so hard, it splintered sending shards flying across the desk.

Over the new number the band had launched into that Troy now recognized as something from the early Bon Scott AC/DC catalog, Dante looked up at Troy and shouted, "But who the hell is Dion?"

33

Yekaterina's Got A Gun

IT HAD STARTED AS A DULL, monotonous, quite normal evening at Dion's Quik Mart. Yekaterina Kuznetsov—who often went by the shorter, slightly more American version, Katerina—cursed the digital cards for not lining up correctly in the fifteenth solitaire game of her overnight shift. With the tourist season not quite in full swing, customers were few and far between. Most of the people she rang up each night were locals looking for lottery tickets, cigarettes, and beer. But there was the occasional vacationer headed down to Key West looking for lottery tickets, cigarettes, and beer.

Tonight, she hadn't seen anyone at all until the flamboyantly dressed young man had hopped in looking for the key to the restroom. She handed it to him along with the short chain attaching it to the brass dolphin sculpture. No one worried about the statue being stolen as it was missing its tail and its dorsal fin effectively making it a thick, hotdog shaped paperweight. But Katerina took the young man's car keys as collateral anyway.

"Do not steal it," she said, wagging a finger at him. "And when you come back to get your keys, you buy something, no? Is for paying customers."

He smiled and gave her a thumbs up gesture and danced out of the store. She clicked back to her game—the sixteenth one now—noting with glee that her cards were all lining up perfectly. Most of her business was tourist driven and she had settled into the normal island rhythm of coasting until the season started. She glanced up at the calendar and noted that there were seventy-four days until Fantasy Fest—the next big peak of visitors. Between now and then, she would make do with a few off-season travelers and the elite local clientele who liked the beer she kept at forty-four degrees. Her husband, Morty, God rest his soul, had insisted on building the four-thousand square foot beer cave with sections designated for domestic, imported, craft, and the occasional local brew. She had argued that he was building above the level of alcoholic common to the islands, but his business savvy had proven him right. In the long run, they made over seventy-five percent of their sales from beer and gas.

She raised a hand toward the ceiling. "I told you, I told you," she said to her husband's ghost above her. "You were right."

When she looked down, she noticed her cards were bouncing around the screen in their satisfying victory dance. She was just about to click the reshuffle button when movement outside the store caught her eye. She was horrified to see the man she'd given the bathroom key, banging the broken brass dolphin into the side window of the Jeep parked at gas pump number two.

Oddly, there was no broken glass. Katerina had no experience with Jeeps and the fact that some of them had nearly impenetrable vinyl windows— impenetrable to dolphin paperweights anyway. The man was frantic hurling it against the Jeep over and over again, screaming at the poor girl in the passenger seat. Katerina could see that the young woman was recoiling away from the attacker in fear. She picked up the phone and dialed emergency.

Later, when she was giving her statement down at the Islamorada Sheriff's Station, she would complain that she called them ten times and always got a busy signal. They would say that wasn't possible and she would insist it was, showing them her outgoing call list in which she had dialed 1-1-2 eleven (not ten) times. The friendly sheriff, whom she knew from his bimonthly visits to pick up his beloved Samuel Adams' Utopias Ale—which she up-charged two-hundred percent to six-hundred dollars a bottle—pointed out that the number for emergencies in the United States was 9-1-1. Katerina had clapped her hand over her mouth as if she'd made a blunder akin to accidentally spoiling the end of a twisty thriller novel and apologized over and over to the officers on the scene. They put her in a cruiser and took her to the station where they could properly check the license on her firearm. What firearm you ask?

When Katerina had failed to get an answer from her misdialed attempts to notify the police, she threw her phone down and decided that the woman —who had now climbed into the driver's side seat to avoid the man who was running around the Jeep in a circle of blows from the dolphin—was in grave danger.

She glanced back at the ceiling as if to tell Morty he was right again, but when the woman outside shrieked loud enough that she heard her through the plate-glass front of the store, she went into action. She flipped the combination on the lockbox quickly and opened the gun safe. The massive pistol lying wrapped lovingly in the dimpled foam lining, gleamed at her. She hadn't touched it since before Morty passed, and was pretty sure he had cleaned it daily—whether it needed it or not. Thankfully, he had shown her how to put bullets in it, but that was about it. She had resisted learning anything more about the vessel of death.

"Pull this thing back, point the small end at the burglar, and pull the trigger," he said, shrugging his shoulders. "That's about it."

She remembered waving him off in dismissal as she slid the bullets into the cylinder. She had no idea what kind of gun this was, but it was silver with dark wood on the handle. It was as long as her arm from her elbow to her finger and she had to use two hands to pick it up. She took a deep breath, imagined drawing the sign of the cross over her body as she couldn't let go of the gun to do it or it would've dropped to the ground. Steeling herself, she burst through the door, pointing the revolver more or less at the man who was still racing around the Jeep bouncing the bathroom key and attached brass dolphin all over the hood and doors. He was screaming so loud, and had continued to beat the car when she came out, she wasn't sure he heard her yelling at him.

She took a deep breath and pulled the trigger. She had intended to shoot above the Jeep and scare the man off, but it was so heavy, she missed a few feet lower than she'd been aiming. The bullet slammed into the top portion of pump number two, shattering the new plexiglass Marlboro ads she had just put up there yesterday. A shower of plastic and the louder-than-expected boom stopped the man dead in his tracks. She ignored the trickle of pee running down her leg and shouted at him.

The maniac—who had somehow gotten a hand inside the car and was holding onto a small handbag—scrunched his eyes in confusion and she realized that she might have been speaking Russian, or maybe a mixture of Russian, Yiddish, and English. Whatever it was, the man's temporary bewilderment evaporated as she raised the gun again.

The man did not wait for her to speak or fire the gun. He turned with a shriek and sprinted away from Dion's Quik Mart, still holding the brass dolphin and purse in his hands.

Katerina would have gone after him to retrieve it,

but the woman in the Jeep needed her. She was sitting on the center console, her head buried in her hands, sobbing. Katerina sat the gun on the hood of the Jeep and tapped on the side window.

"You're safe now, devushka," she said, just loudly enough for the woman to hear. "The bad man is gone. You can come inside and we will find out why the police refuse to come."

The girl inside looked up, her mascara running in black streams down her cheeks. When she realized the man was gone, she opened the door and stepped out. Her knees buckled under her, but Katerina caught her in her arms and walked her inside.

The girl sniffed and said, "I think I peed myself."

Katerina laughed, a hoarse, deep bark, "As did I. We will find something to change into."

"Thank you," the girl said with a smile.

Katerina outfitted the girl with a pair of hot pink panties from the back of the shop with a bright red image on the front and the words, "Tasty Cherries," a pink and tan tank top sporting a pair of antlers and the message, "With any Luck, a Buck in the Truck." The only shorts she could find for the girl—whom she learned was called Cinnamon—were a pair of

330 • DAVID BERENS

black shorty-shorts with a white handprint on each buttock.

The old Russian woman apologized that these were the only clothes she had for Cinnamon, but the girl—who looked quite ravishing in the makeshift outfit—seemed not to be worried about it. In fact, she pulled out a carefully folded wad of cash from her wet pants and handed it to Katerina.

The grandmotherly owner of the convenience store tried to refuse the money from the girl, but she had insisted and sealed the deal with a hug and a kiss on each of the woman's cheeks.

"How about we try the police again?" Cinnamon asked, scrubbing the dark trails of makeup from her face with a wet wipe from behind the counter.

"Not before you tell me why is this man trying to break into your Jeep?" Katerina wagged her finger as she said it.

The girl relayed an incredible tale involving her fiancé, or boyfriend, or something of that nature being killed by the flamboyantly dressed man. At first, Katerina had thought it might be a love triangle gone wrong, but quickly determined that the Jeep beater was gay and only friends with Cinnamon. She tried desperately not to raise an eyebrow when the girl had told her that he had also killed his own fiancé, or boyfriend, or something of that nature. Try as she might, Katerina could not make much sense of Cinnamon's story, but what she did know was that the girl was in danger and needed to be in the care of the police—even if she doubted the quality of that care.

Katerina had dialed 1-1-2 a few more times before telling Cinnamon that she was going to lock the store and take her down to the police station herself. Stubbornly, her champagne gold 1987 Buick Skylark —Morty's pride and joy—refused to start. She cranked it several times and banged her fist on the dashboard for good measure, but it quickly became apparent that it wasn't going to budge.

"We will have to take your car, devushka," she said, tossing the keys into her purse.

"My car?" Cinnamon tilted her head sideways, obviously confused. "What do you mean, my car?"

Katerina pointed her thumb back toward the gas pumps. "Yes, your car. Your, how do you say it, Daisy Duke Jeep."

"But I don't know where the keys are."

The old woman held up a single finger. Dangling from it, with a pink fluffy rabbit's foot, was Gary's key ring.

And that was how a 74-year-old Russian widow

wrapped in a creamy white cotton shawl and a 20-something-year-old stripper dressed in ... well, you remember it from earlier ... ended up cruising north on the Overseas Highway in a 1980 Daisy Duke model Jeep CJ-7.

34

With One Headlight

TROY BODEAN COULD NEVER BE CALLED an impatient man. If there was something worth taking your time doing, he was all for taking it. However, Dante Caparelli was apparently the type of person who chose a radio station, listened for approximately ten seconds, then flipped to the next station just as everyone else in the car—namely Troy —was getting into the song playing. The old mafia boss had scanned flippantly past The Eagles, The Rolling Stones, The Doors, Van Morrison, and a smattering of Spanish channels to finally curse and turn the radio off. The silence hung between them like a cloud of Lysol—aromatic, but obviously covering something up.

As the first drops of rain splattered on the

windshield of the car, Troy turned on the wipers to find that they were dry-rotted and did very little to clear the glass. Dante shrugged and told him he'd never driven this, or any other, car. In fact, he'd mostly forgotten how to drive, having used a driver since the early seventies. That was the first mistake Troy had made on the drive. Once the old man started talking, he didn't stop. He seemed to feel it was necessary to fill the silence with incoherent ramblings about the club, the family, the sad state of American politics and their war on crime, and finally, about his son, Matty.

"I love that boy," he said, his voice thick with tears. "He was all I had. You ever had kids, Mr. Bodean?"

Troy's mind wandered back to the boy Ellie Mae and Daisy Mae Gallop had claimed was his. He wondered where T.J. was now and how he was doing. The last he'd seen of him had been seventeen hundred miles north of Islamorada. He opened his mouth to say something, but Dante continued without waiting for his answer.

"He was a good kid, you know? Okay, so maybe he wasn't gonna take over the world, but running the family business, yeah, he coulda done that."

Troy tried the wipers again and only succeeded

in smearing the windshield into a greasy mess. In the growing darkness, he reached down and turned the headlights on. They were dim and did little to light the road ahead of them. Troy wondered if they were old and faulty like the wipers. Dante, however was on full tilt now, his lips flecked with spit as he railed about his son's killer.

"If I ever find the slimy son of a bitch who did this to my boy, I'm gonna take a pipe to him like Mickey Mantle to a hanging slider. There won't be a bone in his body I ain't gonna break. This guy is gonna wish he'd never been born."

Troy was afraid to interrupt Dante, but thought more than once about reaching down and casually turning the radio back on. He rubbed his right palm on his thigh and slid it closer to the power button. Before he could reach out and turn it on, Dante suddenly grabbed his arm. *Dangit.* He'd made his second mistake. He was sure he was headed back into the old man's office to be bound, gagged, shot, or taken out for a swim in the middle of the ocean wearing concrete shoes.

"Hey, cowboy," Dante said, a strange glint in his eyes, "you ever managed a strip club?"

Troy let out a breath he hadn't realized he was holding. "No, sir. Worked as a disc jockey at The

Peppermint Hippo back in Vegas, but that didn't work out like I planned."

"Cause, ya know, I ain't got no manager now, what with Matty being ... gone and all."

Troy wasn't sure how to answer that. "But, what about Sully? He's your man, right?"

Dante flipped his hand as if throwing off a bug. "Eh, Sully's a good guy. Real good people. But in the brains department, he's a couple bricks shy of a load, if you take my meaning."

Troy explained that he was already gainfully employed at the Islamorada Tennis Club. Dante said he knew about that on account as he had put a tail on him. Troy almost clicked together the puzzle pieces between that fact and the appearance of the strange assassin that had shown up there when he saw the red and blue lights blazing in the rearview mirror.

Dante whirled around to look out the window at the police car coming up behind them. "Jiminy Christ, what the hell do these overgrown Boy Scouts want now? You weren't speedin' were you?"

Troy shook his head as he eased over to the shoulder of the road. "No, sir. Kept her right on the limit the whole time. Not sure what this is about."

In the back of his mind, he wondered if perhaps

the car was stolen and the cop had run the plate. He played the arrest scenario over and over in his mind and in each and every one, he ended up behind bars.

"What should I tell him?" Troy asked Dante.

"Son, you just let me do the talkin'. Ain't no rent-a-cop gonna take me in."

Troy swallowed back the anxiety that was threatening to close his throat. He reached into his back pocket and pulled his wallet out. He fished out the driver's license that had expired four months ago and rolled down the window an inch. The rain was heavier now and sprinkled his left arm as the officer approached.

An impossibly bright LED flashlight blazed into the car, blinding Troy and infuriating Dante. The old man grumbled something about not going down like this, sending Troy's pulse into three-digit territory. Trying desperately to keep calm, he asked the cop the ubiquitous question.

"Is there a problem, officer?"

For an eternity, the silhouette behind the flashlight just ran the beam back and forth over the license. Troy wondered if the man was going to make a big issue over the fact that it was expired. An oddly familiar voice spoke through the spattering rain.

"You've got a headlight out," he said. "Step out of the car, please."

Troy suddenly realized why the lights had been so dim when he turned them on. "But I—"

"Step out of the car, now."

"Yep. Yes, sir," Troy said, raising his hands in surrender.

He reached down and opened the door, swinging it past the officer. He stood up and allowed the officer to turn him around, place his palms on the roof of the car, and frisk him. Then, seemingly sure that Troy wasn't a threat, the officer pointed his flashlight back into the car.

"Well, well, well," he said. "If it isn't Dante Caparelli."

And that's when Troy realized where he recognized the voice. It was Ian Bass, the FDLE Officer who had suspected he was The Cowboy Killer. Something tickled the back of Troy's mind, something about the case Ian was actually assigned to while he was undercover at the Islamorada Sheriff's Department—a mafia case.

"I've been looking into you for quite some time, Dante. Been up to no good, eh?"

Dread filled Troy just long enough to fill the split second between Ian's question and the impossibly loud bang. Ian Bass flew backwards, sparks and fire slamming into his chest. A vision of his buddy, Ned, being killed in Afghanistan crashed through walls of denial, sending Troy spinning back from the car in a daze.

"Get in, cowboy!" Dante was yelling. "Let's get the hell out of here."

Troy stared at Ian's motionless body lying in the middle of the Overseas Highway near mile marker eighty and decided that he was indeed going to get the hell out of here, but not with the murderer in the black Lincoln Town Car in front of him. He turned and sprinted away as fast as his aching knee would let him. He dove off the road into a swampy tangle of trees. The murky black water came up to his waist and he wondered if he'd made his third mistake.

He could hear the old man yelling and watched from under the twisted mangrove roots as Dante scooted into the driver's seat. The door slammed shut and the tires erupted into screeching motion. The car fishtailed and swerved back and forth on the road as the mafia boss struggled to remember how to drive. In a few seconds, the car was roaring away, crossing into and out of the proper lane.

When the sounds of the night took over around him, Troy began to trudge his way out of the mire and back onto the road. As his feet hit the pavement, he heard Ian Bass groan. He hobbled over to the man, hooked his hands under his arms, and dragged him off the highway. He knew he probably shouldn't, in case there was some kind of spinal injury, but he figured a moved spine was better than a crushed spine if a car happened along.

With a huge gasp and more grunting, Ian sat up. Troy was shocked, certain the man had taken a fatal bullet to the chest. As if he'd heard him, Ian opened his shirt a couple of buttons to reveal the mushroomed slug resting in the outer folds of his bulletproof vest. He picked it out between two fingers and held it up in the beam of the police car's headlights.

"Thirty-eight," he said. "Thank goodness your buddy doesn't use a bigger gun."

"Now, hold on just a second here," Troy started, attempting to defend himself.

But Ian held up a hand. "Not now. Which way did he go?"

Troy pointed and said, "That way."

"Help me up and let's get on him. Time is of the essence now that he knows I'm onto him. If I don't get him in the next twenty-four hours, he's gone."

Troy helped him up and walked him over to the driver's side. "You sure you're okay?"

"I'll be fine," Ian said, wincing as he pulled himself up into the Islamorada Sheriff's Department Ford Explorer. "Hop in."

Troy started around the front of the SUV, but Ian stopped him. "No, no. In the back. Can't have a civilian riding up front."

Troy glanced over his shoulder at his hiding spot in the mangroves and wondered if he could make a break for it. He decided that he couldn't and slid into the back seat of a police car … again.

He tried to remember how many times he'd seen this exact view, but gave up when the number rose past ten.

35

Losing It In The Keys

GARY JOHN SUSKIND stumbled down the road with a gait resembling someone lost in the desert or a tourist three sheets to the wind. His pullover was torn in several places and his jeans were soaked through on the right side with rain and sweat. At first, he'd chalked up the odd one-side-only pattern of the wetness with the sideways nature of island rain. But as he slowed to a wobbly walking pace, he'd realized the pain in his side wasn't just a stitch from sprinting.

He dabbed his fingers in a particularly wide gash in the light sweater and found they came away red. He gasped and stopped in the road. He pulled open the tear and saw a matching gash in his side halfway up his ribcage. He tore the shirt away under his arm and let the rain wash the congealing blood away.

He gingerly touched the fresh wound and winced at the stinging pain shooting up under his arm. The old woman at the gas station must have grazed him. In the darkness, he could easily see that he would require plastic surgery—the horrendously expensive kind of plastic surgery employing thousands of micro-stitches—to keep it from being visible to his ever-burgeoning Instagram following. If there was one thing he knew for sure, it was that none of the top male influencers—even those who had obviously had some work done—on the platform had any visible scars. He leaned his head back, shaking the brass dolphin and its dangling bathroom key at the dark sky in the falling rain.

"Why?" he yelled. "Why would you bring this deformity upon me?"

But he knew why. He had been a party to the deaths of two people he loved. First, Matty, then Dani. If only he'd listened to his instincts. Matty wasn't interested, he liked girls. Actually, Matty didn't seem to show interest in either sex according to Cinnamon. Gary shook the thought away and started ambling down the street again. And why had she gone psycho on him back at the gas station. He still couldn't figure that out.

Now all he had left in this world was Dani's purse. He wondered if she might have some gauze or a bandaid or something. The sooner he could get something on the gunshot in his side, the better the scarring would be.

Tears and rain streamed down his face as he sat down on the side of the road and began to rummage through the bag. It seemed strangely empty, as he tossed aside pointless objects: paperclips, hair clips, lipstick, cotton swabs, and a ticket stub from Les Miserables at the Waterfront Playhouse. He wadded up the cotton swabs and dabbed them at the wound, but hadn't found anything to hold them on—no tape or bandages or anything like that. He stuck his hand back into the bag and came out with a strange prize. Matty's finger and the ring. He pulled his arm back in classic quarterback fashion—or at least what he imagined that might feel like—preparing to fling the ring and the finger as far into the mangroves as he could. He wanted no connection between Matty and his gruesome death to be anywhere near him. But before he could throw it, he heard a strange squeaking sound coming up the road, closer and closer. This section of the highway was dark, but he thought he could make out the shape of a person riding a bike, headed straight towards him.

He squinted, trying desperately to make out more detail thinking what a terrible night it was to be riding a bicycle. And then he began to laugh, a strange, foreign sound. To his ears, it sounded like a mixture of Cesar Romero's rendition of the Joker and a stray Key West rooster announcing dawn. The figure riding in the deluge got closer and seemed to intentionally surge through a puddle on the side of the road in front of Gary, splashing him with what smelled like a vile mixture of mud, water, vomit, and urine.

Gary could only laugh harder as the man on the old green bike looked over his shoulder and shouted at him. He had a myriad of strange little cuts on his face as if old acne scars had decided to erupt and burst open and his arms were covered with mud and bits of rock.

"Get a job, ya bum," the man yelled.

Gary laughed again and shook his head. *Who's the real bum here, fella?* It struck him that there was something familiar about the man, even in the dim light and sheets of rain. He thought he might have heard the man muttering about tourists and bums and corrupt politicians as he disappeared into the night.

As the highway went dark and empty, the rain continued to drizzle down on him. It was salty and warm, like a medicinal bath. Gary looked down and realized he was still clutching Matty's finger. The heavy ring on it glinted and a thought occurred to him. Much like Dani had said, before being eaten, this ring could bring in a couple grand. It wasn't likely to pay for all his plastic surgery, but it would put a dent in it.

Headlights broke through the night and grew from pin pricks to saucers in no time. Air Brakes hissed as the old Winnebago slowed to a stop in front of Gary. He shoved the finger into his pocket and tried to wipe his face. The passenger's side window rolled down about an inch and the man inside craned his head to put his lips up to the opening. Gary jumped up out of the muck.

"Hey, there," a kindly voice said. "You doin' okay, son?"

The accent reminded Gary of his favorite television show, *Jersey Shore* on MTV, but the man's face was all Ian McKellen. The man had a slight lisp and spoke softly, so Gary stood on his tiptoes and leaned a little closer.

"I'm okay, thank you."

The driver leaned over and said, "Are you sure? You lost or something?"

Gary could now see that both men wore bright, Hawaiian shirts, one with a pink background, and one with a purple background. The passenger wore a rainbow lei around his neck and the driver wore a pair of rhinestone-encrusted glasses.

"I might have been," Gary said, smiling, "but it looks like I've been found."

MARTIN RUSSO, who was sitting on a pink satin donut-shaped pillow in the driver's seat, looked as if he'd walked off the set of *The Soprano's*—only the gay edition. Thick, dark, wavy hair combed back on his head showing off an incredible hairline, considering his obvious age, and slightly grey temples under the faux gemstones on his glasses made him look distinguished if not downright yummy. If not for the purple Hawaiian shirt and cutoff denim shorts—slightly shorter than appropriate—Gary might not have known they were "playing for the same team."

His partner, Frankie Russo, was a bit more ... obvious. He wore the pink Hawaiian shirt and a grass skirt, and the ubiquitous rainbow lei. He had been the one to bring Gary into the RV, get a towel to dry him off, and found some suitable clothes for him to change into. He also passed Gary a couple of large bandages, some medical tape, and a brown bottle of hydrogen peroxide to clean his side. In the light of the cramped bathroom, the wound didn't look as bad as Gary had originally thought. Maybe with a little Neosporin, he could reduce the scarring.

Once he'd changed and transferred Matty's finger to his new pants pocket, Martin had pulled over and let Gary toss the filthy old clothes into a dumpster. Frankie was the more outgoing of the couple. He turned his captain's chair all the way around to engage Gary, who was sipping a cup of wonderful green tea with honey and some other secret ingredient that Frankie would not divulge, in what could only be called delightful conversation. Every so often, Frankie would try to include Martin.

"Isn't that so, Marty?" he'd ask his partner, who had obviously tuned them out.

Martin would smile and wink at Frankie. "It is, my dear."

"So, is there a shelter or somewhere we can take you, Gary?" Frankie asked after a time.

"Oh, no," Gary said, finishing off his tea. "I'm not homeless. I just lost my ride."

Martin turned to look over his shoulder at Gary. "Yeah, and I'm Saul Morganstern."

Gary did not know who Saul Morganstern was, but chose not to make an issue of it. "No, really. I have an apartment, back on Upper Matecumbe."

"That's north, right?" Frankie asked, laying a soft hand on his knee. "Marty, we've got to turn around. The least we can do is give this young man a ride back to his place, right?"

"It is, my dear," Martin said, slowing and guiding the Winnebago into a wide arcing u-turn.

"Thank you so much," Gary said. "When we get to my place, I can get you some money."

"Absolutely not!" the two men said in unison. "A friend in need is a friend indeed. You just remember us and when you pass this on to the next poor soul, you tell them Uncle Marty and Aunt Frankie send their regards."

"Oh, so I'm the woman now, eh?" Frankie asked over a mischievous smile.

Martin only winked in reply.

"So," Gary said, hoping to interrupt the obvious flirting, "what brings the two of you to Islamorada?"

"We're just passing through," Martin said.

"It's an annual thing for us," Frankie added. "We have a German friend on Key West with a charming little place on Eaton. He goes back to the homeland to visit family and we take up residence to house sit for him."

"Very nice," Gary said.

"Mmhmm," Frankie agreed, licking his lips. "And we live the Conch life all the way through Fantasy Fest one street over from Duval."

"Sounds delightful."

Frankie's mouth dropped open and he turned to look at his partner. "Marty, we absolutely must host our new friend for the parade, don't you think? We have that futon in the living room that makes a surprisingly comfortable bed. Isn't that right?"

"It is, my dear."

And so the plans were made rumbling down the highway in the pouring rain. Plans that would never come to fruition.

36

Gator Crossing

DANTE CAPARELLI CURSED his inability to keep the car in between the lines demarking the proper lanes on the Overseas Highway. His palms were as sweaty as a pimple-faced kid asking his crush to the Junior Prom. It also didn't help that he could barely see past the end of the long, black hood. Nor did it help that his windshield wipers were older than his son would've been today. And the fact that one of his headlights was out made the whole thing an experiment in thrill-seeking. He glanced in the rearview mirror, still no sign of the overzealous cop or the cowboy. That eased his mind, but not his crotch.

All of this evening's stress behind the wheel, plus his oversized prostate and a combination of stronger-than-necessary alpha blockers had his bladder on full. He imagined it looked like a distended water balloon in the hands of a teenager hell bent on filling it with as much liquid as possible without popping it. Through the smear of his windshield, he saw yellow and white LED lights hazing into view ahead. As he got closer, he could see it was Dion's Quik Mart. He'd been here on one or two occasions when a rich—and gullible— customer ordered some kind of fancy-schmancy beer they didn't have on tap.

With his eyes directed at the glowing sign above the station, Dante turned a little too soon and hit the curb leading into the parking lot hard. A squirt of urine shot out of him like a water pistol and he squeezed his thighs together tightly to staunch the flow. He wasn't fully sure he'd be able to stand up out of the car without another trickle escaping. His doctor had warned him if he held it in on too many occasions, he would risk losing more and more control over his urethra.

He glanced down at the gas gauge and decided he'd empty one tank and fill another while he was here. Unfortunately, he wasn't sure of two things: Did Dion's have a public restroom? And did he remember how to pump gas?

Either way, he was gonna take a piss whether it be in a toilet or behind the building against the cinder block exterior of the Quik Mart. The gas, he figured, was like makin' love—and he'd always been a champion in the sack, at least up until he married his fourth wife, Jackie, Matty's mother.

He pulled his car close to pump number one, the other one was busted up like a repo man had gotten a hold of it. He jumped out of the car, clenching everything below his waist as tight as he could. He tiptoe-sprinted around the building and found a door with a gender-neutral bathroom icon. Under that, in black marker, the next Will Shakespeare had scrawled, "Don't hate me because I'm beautiful, hate me because I did your dad." And then, in another, darker, handwriting, "Go home, mom. You're drunk."

Dante had seen more than his share of stall jokes, and he wouldn't have read it, except for the fact that the door was locked with a large Stanley padlock. He tugged on it a couple of times, swearing at it in Italian. He considered just emptying his bladder all over the door, but then caught sight of a camera—probably fake—above the door, just out of reach.

He swore again and hopped back around the

building to the front door. It was locked as well, but with a couple of hard shakes, the bolt let go and the door swung open. Without waiting to locate the clerk, he called into the air, "Yo, I need the bathroom key."

Nothing. The only sound was a low, steady hum emanating from the fanciest beer cave he'd ever seen in the Keys and a buzz coming out of the fluorescent lights above him. "Hey, anybody here? I gotta take a leak."

He walked behind the counter and rifled through the envelopes, receipts, assorted pens, toothpicks, and personal adult items that couldn't be kept in plain view. There was no sign of the key, but there was a medium sized crowbar with the words, "Theft Deterrent," written on the side. With the bar in his left hand, Dante took two steps from behind the counter, then looked at the register. He glanced around the store, now absolutely certain that no one was here, and then back at the silent checkout counter. With the crowbar, he could be in the cash drawer in seconds, but what was he, a petty thief? He decided he wasn't going to do that. He did help himself to a handful of the cheap cigarillos with the plastic tips on them. Above his head, a similar camera dome eyeballed him until he swung the bar up and smashed it open. As he suspected, the smoky glass only concealed the fact that there was no camera hidden behind it. He could've just pissed on the door and been done with the whole affair— which reminded him that he still needed to go and bad.

An electronic chime startled Dante and he looked up to see a soaking wet man leaning a green bicycle up against the outside of the building. He thought he recognized the man dressed in a pink Ralph Lauren polo, pale stone shorts, and Sperry Docksider shoes, but even when the man walked through the door, he couldn't place where he knew him. Later, it would come to him that this was the reporter who had written an exposé on Woody's and how it was in danger of becoming a mafia hornet's nest. But without realizing this fact, he simply held up his prize of Swisher Sweets and said, "Have at it, young man. Looks like it's a free day. No staff."

The man, who looked as if he'd spent a few nights outside, sleeping on a park bench, eating from a dumpster, launched into a tirade about the "whole degenerate attitude becoming more and more pervasive in the Keys. They oughta burn the whole thing down to the ground and start over."

Dante stuffed the miniature cigars in his shirt pocket and said, "suit yourself ass-wipe."

He brushed past the ornery bicyclist and headed around back to take care of business.

TROY WATCHED in slow-motion horror as Ian Bass barreled at high speed—almost sixty miles an hour, which qualifies as insanely fast in the Keys—toward the log-shaped creature trudging across the Overseas Highway. Water and muck dripped from the ancient beast's limbs and body as its eyes glinted deep and black in the after storm mist rising from the asphalt. Apparently, his faculty for speech was momentarily frozen, so he reached up and banged on the cage separating him from FDLE Officer Ian Bass in the front seat. This turned out to be a mistake as Ian had yet to see the massive alligator crossing the road and looked over his shoulder to see what all the fuss Troy was making was about.

If they had been in a normal police cruiser, the front bumper might have pushed the gator for a bit giving it a fighting chance. As it was, the Islamorada Sheriff Department's prized Ford Explorer, confiscated from a Tavernier drug bust last summer, sat approximately twelve inches off the ground. Troy guessed it must have about a six inch lift kit on it and some of the biggest off-road wheels he'd ever seen on an Explorer. It was high enough that the rambling creature served as a perfect ramp. They launched the SUV up and over it like the black and gold Pontiac Trans Am Burt Reynolds had sailed over the collapsed bridge to escape Buford T. Justice in *Smokey and the Bandit*.

If Troy had been able to roll down his window, he might, under any other circumstances, be led to belt out a good old fashioned, "yeehaw." But his love for animals, even the sharp toothed ones, filled him with instant concern and dread for the alligator. Ian's driving was expert, though. They hit the ground and bounced with a skid. The Explorer jerked to the right and swerved to a stop so sudden, Troy thought they might flip. In fact, the passenger's side wheels lifted off the ground for a second, then slammed back down.

Ian looked through the cage into the back seat. "You okay back there?"

Troy pulled himself up out of the floorboard. "I'm alright, partner. Just a little shook up is all."

He picked up his tumbled cowboy hat and placed it back on his head, scooting toward the window to see what had become of the gator. It lay in the middle of the road, upside down. It's body appeared to be intact, but from this distance, Troy couldn't see if it was still breathing.

"Let's go," he said.

"Go?" Ian asked. "Go where?"

"We gotta go back and check on him."

"Looks like a female," Ian said, peering into the steam. "And we've got more important things to do right now."

Troy didn't ask how the man could tell it was a female, but figured he was probably right. It was probably out hunting for food. Might have babies nearby.

"But she could be—"

"Could be dead," the police officer interrupted him, "or could be alive. There's nothing you or I can do for it in any case. And the longer we mess around here, the farther away Dante gets."

Ian put the SUV in gear. Troy pulled his phone from his pocket and scrolled through to a browser. He began to peck out a search for animal control.

"Yo, cowboy," Ian said, his tone suddenly gruff. "Just what the hell do you think you're doing?"

"Callin' it in," Troy said with a shrug. "I'll give 'em a mile marker and they can come check her out and see if she's—"

Troy was stopped short by the black hole of a gun pointed at his face.

"Sorry, man," Ian said. "I can't let you do that."

The FDLE gave some nearly incomprehensible reason concerning the department horning in on his case, but Troy wasn't listening. He was trying to connect the call without looking down at his phone. He punched the button and it started ringing.

The window next to him buzzed and rolled down a few inches. "Toss it," Ian said, jerking his head toward the opening.

"But, I just got this one. It's a—"

"Now," Ian Bass said, jabbing his pistol into the cage, causing it to rattle.

Troy glanced down to see that his call hadn't gone through. He took a deep breath and hurled the phone out, watching it bounce and splinter across the pavement. Ian holstered his gun and eased the Explorer back toward the road.

"It's probably dead anyway, Troy," he said as they headed into the night after Dante.

Neither of them saw the alligator begin to stretch its legs.

37

Guns And Ammo

THE ISLAMORADA SHERIFF'S DEPARTMENT, formally, the Monroe County Sheriff's Office - Islamorada Substation, occupied a modern-yet-quaint stucco building with two stories of square windows looking into the lobby. As Cinnamon and Katerina pulled in, the parking lot was empty except for a single white Ford Taurus cruiser and a pink moped propped against the side of the building. The side of the police car was emblazoned with a wide forest green band outlined with yellow stripes and a star shining at the front end. A giant American flag flapped in the heavy, moist air, a single amber bulb beaming up at it.

Just beyond the glass doors, Cinnamon could see a receptionist—probably the moped driver—sitting at a desk running a file over her nails, smacking an unfortunate piece of gum, and blabbing away into a wire headset. Behind her, she could see a couple more desks, all vacant. To the left, down a short marble-floored hall, she could see a door proclaiming: Sheriff Paul S. Puckett, Jr.

She shoved through the front doors with Katerina shuffling along behind her. The girl at the desk didn't look up. She kept talking to whomever was on the other end of the call. Cinnamon crossed her arms and waited. No effect. Ximena Suarez—as declared on her nameplate—continued to chat with her friend, pulled out a bottle of nail polish, and proceeded to paint her nails.

Katerina pushed forward and said, "What is the meaning of this? We have been waiting here for over five minutes. We have emergency and need to speak to—"

Cinnamon didn't wait to hear the rest, she just walked around Ximena's desk and headed down the hall towards the sheriff's office. The girl jumped up, walked three steps in an odd looking duck waddle, her legs wrapped in a tight pencil skirt. The headset snapped her head back, she reached out her hand toward Cinnamon like a swimmer caught in a riptide.

"No, no, no," she wailed. "You cannot just barge in back there."

Cinnamon turned around and said, "We need to see the sheriff."

"But you need an appointment," the receptionist whined.

At that moment, she caught a glimpse of her nails. Apparently, she must have marred the finish on one of her fingers. She pulled it back in to examine it.

"Oh, geez," she whined. "Look what you made me do. This particular shade of Killer Coral is perfect for my Fantasy Fest outfit and you ruined it."

Cinnamon felt her mouth drop open in awe at the girl. "Um, correct me if I'm wrong, but Fantasy Fest isn't for a few weeks, right?"

The left side of Ximena's mouth jumped up into a knowing smirk. "Girl, you gotta test the color first. You never know how it's gonna look on your nails until you put it on."

Cinnamon shook her head, trying desperately to think of a sensible reply to this, but came up with nothing.

Luckily, Ximena, now full on grinning at her nails, had something to add. "But I don't know. I am in love with this color. If it doesn't match perfectly, I think I'll just buy a new dress."

"Okay, thank you, lady," Katerina said, jumping in. "Can you tell the sheriff we are here now and we need to see him?"

Ximena made a show of squeezing back into her chair and shuffling the pages of her calendar—which Cinnamon could see were ninety percent blank.

"Yeah, sure," she said, smiling up at them. "He doesn't have anything on his schedule until nine o'clock. That's when *Matlock* comes on."

Ximena picked up her phone to buzz the sheriff, but Cinnamon didn't wait for the formality. She grabbed Katerina by the elbow and pulled her down the hall.

THE FROSTED glass door swung open a little too fast and banged noisily against the wall. Behind a steel desk that might have come from a thrift shop, sat a pudgy man with pink jowls and thin white hair. He wasn't old, but he wasn't that young either. Cinnamon couldn't decide whether his tan was sprayed on or earned on a fishing boat. Either way, he was ruddy, but not altogether unhandsome.

There were a dozen photographs, varying in age, of the man sitting at the desk, shaking hands with people Cinnamon guessed were politicians. She had never taken any interest in politics, but she could almost smell the heavy cologne and illicit money wafting from the pictures.

A scarecrow of a coat rack stood in the corner with a wide-brimmed, olive-colored hat with a black band holding a gold badge on the front. Below that, a black umbrella poked up looking very much like it hadn't been outside in the rain in months. Cinnamon wondered how the man had patrolled the island without it the last few wet days.

In the few seconds before he noticed them, she saw the man was studying a *Shots and Shells* magazine. A woman with impossibly large boobs, wearing an impossibly small bikini, holding an impossibly big rifle, posed on the front in what could only be described as a tantric position with her gun. *Must be the swimsuit issue*, Cinnamon thought. Guns and sex and probably a lot of stories defending the Second Amendment—a testosterone pumping mixture for sure.

The man finally noticed them and jumped like he'd been shocked with a defibrillator. His chair nearly toppled as he slapped the pages of the magazine shut and shoved it into his desk drawer.

"How did you ladies get in here?" he demanded, looking over their shoulders toward his office door. "You can't just barge in here like that."

Katerina, nonplussed by the man's demeanor and certainly not interested in being bullied away, plopped down into one of his guest chairs.

"Ximena!" he called past them. "Ximena didn't you—"

His office door swung open and the receptionist, still blowing on her nails, shuffled in. "I'm so sorry, sir. They rushed right past me, I couldn't stop them, because my nails were still wet and—"

"Cheezit crackers," he blurted out, interrupting her. "I don't pay you to sit out there and do nothing."

"I am so sorry, Mister Puckett," she pleaded. "Please don't fire me. My kids will go hungry if I don't bring home the raviolis and tapatias."

Cinnamon almost laughed but thought that this woman probably meant what she said. The sheriff sighed heavily.

"I'm not going to fire you, Ximena," he said, his tone softening. "But when I'm busy, I really need you to screen the crazies—not the two ladies here, of course—but all the other crazies who come to see me."

The woman with the outlandish coral nails looked utterly confused, leading Cinnamon to believe that there hadn't been any *crazies* visiting him for quite some time. She decided it was time to get down to business.

"Sheriff," she started, picturing the finger wearing the mafia ring that she had found in Dani's purse earlier, "I have information on a murderer rampaging his way through Islamorada."

Paul Puckett bolted upright in his chair faster than she would have imagined he could. "You know about the killer?"

"I do," Cinnamon said, looking over at Katerina, who nodded in support.

She relayed the story of Matty—her boyfriend or fiancé or whatever they had been—going missing, and then the part about finding his finger in Dani's purse.

"Okay, wait, I'm lost," the sheriff said, looking up from his yellow pad and his scrawling notes. "Who's Dani?"

She explained that Dani was Gary's boyfriend and that Gary had come to her telling her that Dani had been killed by an alligator. But she had found

Matty's finger in Dani's purse and connected the dots.

"So," Paul said, drawing a line between some of his notes, "you think Gary killed this um, Matty, fella, and then killed his boyfriend ... um ... Dani?"

"Exactly."

The sheriff leaned back in his chair. "Does this Gary person wear a cowboy hat?"

Cinnamon was confused. "I uh, I don't know. I don't think so."

"And how did you know this was your boyfriend's finger? Does he have a mole or scar or something?"

"No, it wasn't just the finger," Cinnamon explained. "I recognized Matty's ring."

"There was a ring? On the finger? Lots of people wear rings, you know," he said, holding up his left hand, displaying his wedding band.

"Yes, but this one is a very particular kind of ring. It's like a class ring for—" She hesitated to reveal the pedigree of the ring and the family behind the crest engraved into it.

Thankfully, the man wasn't paying very close attention. He was back to studying the nearly illegible notes on his yellow pad. "Could you describe the ring for me?"

Cinnamon proceeded to describe the ring with its carefully engraved Celtic style vines climbing one side and the Caparelli family symbol on the other. The fine work was so detailed, even the lion's head representing the family's ancestors had a twinkle in its eye. The cap was a square with a maze of rose gold dotted with small diamonds at each corner. The center was a large ruby Matty had once told her represented the blood bond of all those who wore the ring. All in all, pretty impressive craftsmanship. She told the sheriff everything except for the fact that it was a mob family ring. She watched as he finished scrawling on his pad. He leaned back, folded his hands behind his head, and chewed an invisible toothpick as he stared at his notes. For a few seconds, she wondered if he had gone to sleep with his eyes open.

SHERIFF PAUL PUCKETT tried to keep his face impassive, but he'd never been well known for his poker face. Even the guys down at the lodge could tell when he was bluffing, so he'd stopped playing years ago. As soon as the girl—young, pretty, not green, but not jaded yet—had mentioned the lion with the sparkling eyes, he thought of Veronica

Sanches Puckett, the woman he had once called his wife.

Veronica—he called her Vero for short—insisted on opening a handmade jewelry store during their first year of marriage. She poured her life's savings of nearly four thousand dollars into setting up shop in the Tavernier Towne Center strip mall between Bill's Liquor and Dillon's Pub & Grill. She claimed that the heavy tourist traffic would be willing to shell out big bucks for hand-crafted fine jewelry depicting the flora, fauna, and flavor of the Keys. While her four grand had been a nice start, the rest of the fifty needed to get her shop off the ground had come from Paul's retirement fund.

Not that her work wasn't good. He slid his desk drawer open slightly and saw his wedding band sitting between the staples and the paperclips. The detailed relief of a great white whale with a mermaid riding atop was the perfect image to capture their union. Pushing the drawer closed around his great white whale of a belly he made a mental note to put going to the gym back on his calendar.

In three months, she had burned through all of his cash and the shop was in danger of closing. He'd skimmed everything he reasonably could from various drug busts and small-town robberies, but it wasn't enough to pay the bills. That was until Veronica's aging uncle, Javier Romero Sanchez had come through town caravanning a shipment through to be loaded on a couple of cabin cruisers parked on the lesser-known Missouri Key. Vero had made her famous ghost chili pepper tamales complete with pork, onions, green peppers, ghost peppers, garlic, and the secret ingredient spicy arrabbiata sauce in place of tomato sauce. Javier excused himself to the bathroom, complaining of heartburn and had never come out. His heart couldn't take the red hot meal and gave up while he sat sweating on the toilet.

Thankfully, Paul had a few friends on the wrong side of the virtual tracks in Marathon that were willing to take care of Uncle Javier's body in exchange for half of the contents of the trailer he'd been delivering. The two large cases of untraceable cash were enough to float Oceanic Treasures By Vero for another six months. As the unpaid bills began to pile up, so did the tension between him and Veronica. Without another serendipitous haul of drug money, the sea inspired jewelry store would be sunk—along with their marriage.

And that's when the order for a very special ring

dinged into her inbox. At first, Paul had thought it was for a one-of-a-kind graduation ring for one of Miami's patrician class, but upon closer study of the specs, he recognized it for what it really was—a mafia family ring.

He considered turning the information over to the FDLE, but when he saw the number of zeroes attached to the order, he decided to let it go. That and the fact that Uncle Javier's trailer was still parked out back with a few assorted items still in the back. He'd have to get rid of that stuff before the next election scrutiny started for sure.

Two weeks later, Vero had delivered the ring— the ring Cinnamon was describing—for a large envelope of cash. She hadn't taken anything with her when she left. It must have been enough money for a whole new start. He hadn't heard anything from her until he got the divorce papers. With the whole marriage being an exercise in dirty dealings, he figured it would be best to sign without confrontation.

"Sheriff?" the girl—who admitted she worked as a dancer on Islamorada—said, bringing him back to the present.

"Right. Right," he said, turning the subject away from the ring. "So, one thing I'm still unsure about …

why would Gary want to kill Dani? Or Matty for that matter?"

The girl shook her head and shrugged her shoulders. "I have no idea."

He scratched a meaningless doodle on his pad. "Mmkay. Well, where is Gary now?"

The old woman sitting next to her—who had at some point brought out a couple of knitting needles and begun work on a multi-colored shawl or scarf or something—looked up and said, "running down the Overseas Highway."

Later, Paul would find out that she left off the second concluding half of that statement, "after I shot him."

38

I Shot The Sheriff

TROY'S WRISTS ached something fierce. They were behind him, but he could feel Ian Bass's shiny, never-before-used handcuffs biting into the tender skin left by Dante Caparelli's plastic zip ties. At least these binders had smooth edges and weren't cutting into his skin. After Troy had decided to make a phone call—a call that ended with his phone being flung out of the Explorer at highway speed—Ian had decided it was in both their best interests if Troy were bound. He wondered how many times he'd been told by a police officer that being handcuffed was for his own good. Too many.

He wasn't goin' anywhere and to the best of his knowledge, he wasn't under arrest, but since they had barreled over the poor gator in the road, Ian

Bass hadn't been himself. The officer was leaned forward, peering over the dash, white knuckles clenching and unclenching on the steering wheel. Occasionally, the man would mumble to himself and Troy thought he heard something about the big one getting away and following in his father's footsteps, but he couldn't be sure. When they came up behind a slow tractor trailer, Troy decided to argue his case to be released.

"Officer Bass," he said, keeping his tone passive and calm, "I know there are certain regulations and such about transporting crimin—er, I mean people in the rear seat of a police vehicle, but—"

Before he could finish his plea, the radio crackled to life. Ian shushed him and turned it up.

"Ian, where are you?" a voice called over the static.

Troy glanced up at Ian Bass, but he didn't seem to react. "You gonna answer that?" Troy asked.

"Not until he uses proper protocol."

As if the voice on the radio heard him, it sighed heavily and said, "Officer Bass, what is your 10-20?"

And after a few seconds, the man on the line added, "Over."

Ian picked up the receiver, "This is Officer Bass, I am headed north on US1 just past eighty-one."

"Whip it around would you? I've got information about a man who may be connected to two homicides. Latest has him hoofing it south."

Ian twisted the wheel without any apparent release of the accelerator. With his hands cuffed behind him, Troy was thrown across the SUV so hard, he slammed into the door behind Ian, his hat tumbling to the floor. (Neither of them realized that the door had been damaged and was now unlocked.)

He managed to right himself as the siren and lights blared into the night over his head. As they flew into the night, headed back the direction they came, Troy listened as the man on the radio continued with a detailed description of the murderer, his clothes, and warning to be careful, he is armed.

"Did he have on a hat?" Ian blurted out.

"Huh? What's that?"

"Was he wearing a hat?" Ian demanded.

Troy could hear the man on the radio asking someone else the same question. "Nope. No hat that we know of. Why do you ask?"

Ian reached down and turned the volume dial on his CB radio until it clicked off. Troy expected the man to explain what was happening to him, but he didn't. Instead he just mumbled to himself more.

"Must have ditched the hat," Ian said, speaking to his hands on the wheel. "S'gotta be him though. I've got him now."

Troy wasn't sure who the officer was talking about, but a tingling in his spine told him this wasn't going to end well.

"MARTY," Frankie said with a huff, "leave the poor boy alone. He doesn't want to hear about your exploits at Woodstock. Hell, nobody his age even knows what Woodstock is for crying out loud."

"I'll bet you a lap dance he does know," Martin Russo called over his shoulder.

He and Frankie had switched driving duties a mile or so back and now Martin was trying desperately to engage Gary in conversation. Gary tried his best to look nonchalant as he peered through all the massive, rectangular windows watching for the cops. He figured he was about as safe as he could be with these two birds. No one would ever suspect him to be cruising south toward Key West in a couple of gay tourists' Winnebago. He glanced past Martin and saw that the gas gauge was creeping ever lower and guessed they'd have to stop for gas soon. He'd say he had to pee and disappear.

Just as he had the thought, the RV—which was large enough to sleep seven—screeched to a halt. Martin, who had not fastened his seat belt, was thrown out of his captain's chair into the floor. Gary, who had buckled up, was thrown against his belt so hard, it dug into his collarbone and chest. He felt the wound on his side tear open and begin to ooze with warmth. He was bleeding again and wondered if he'd torn the gash and made it bigger. He idly stroked the pocket hiding the finger and the ring—his ticket to some nice plastic surgeon's office in Miami.

"Jesus Christ, Frankie," Martin said, pulling himself up from the floor. "What the hell was that all about?"

"First, you don't believe in Jesus, so please refrain from using his name in vain, it is offensive to me."

"Yes, dear," Martin said, sulkily.

"Second, would you look at that?"

"What am I looking at?" Martin said peering out through the windshield, his hand at attention over his eyebrows.

"Do you ever wear your glasses?" Frankie huffed. "It's an alligator. Across the road. Biggest one I've ever seen."

"Jesu—I mean, Jiminy Cricket," Martin said, his eyes widening. "Is it ... ?"

"Dead? I don't think so. It hasn't moved since we stopped and it looks like it's laying upside down."

"Can you go around?"

"I could go on the shoulder over there, but it looks pretty soft. I'm afraid we might get stuck or take a tumble into the mangroves."

"Gary." Martin looked over his shoulder as he spoke. "How's about you and me check this thing out. I bet we can slide it over enough to get around."

"Oh, I uh, I'd rather not."

Gary's mind was filled with visions of the gator that had taken Matty and then Dani. He was definitely not interested in getting close to another one, even if it was dead. He felt tears welling in his eyes and couldn't be sure if they were tears for the loss of his two friends, or tears of fear at the beast who had taken them.

"I ... I ... I can't," he stuttered. The terror must've been obvious on his face.

"I gotcha, son. It's okay to be scared. Let me and Uncle Frankie take care of this." Martin said, patting Gary's shoulder.

"Oh, so now I'm the gay uncle in the relationship?" Frankie said with a smirk.

"Frankie, come on. Let's see if we can roll it off the road."

Gary watched as the two old men took the metal steps slowly down from the RV. He wondered if this was his moment. He could just start running and get away from them. But there was something new in his mind, curiosity. He was glued to the windshield watching Martin and Frankie approach the alligator like Steve Irwin, the Crocodile Hunter. He could almost hear the dead adventurer's voice saying, "Aww, ain't she a beauty. Look at the size o' those teeth."

When they finally reached the massive roadkill, Martin reached out and tapped it with a sandaled foot and skipped backward away from the animal. Gary held his breath and waited. Nothing happened. Frankie moved closer to the gator's head and bent down, hands on his hips. He cocked his head back and forth in an odd movement and then reached down to pull something out of the alligator's mouth. In the amber glow of the street lights, Gary saw him hold up a jagged triangle of orange plastic. He leaned forward, his forehead pressing against the back window. His breath fogged the glass and he rubbed his forearm against it to clear a round spot he could see through.

Martin—apparently emboldened by Frankie's find—reached down between the jagged teeth silhouetted in the night and jerked on another piece of something wedged in between the daggers of death. He held it up and Gary's blood went ice cold. It was a shred of cloth—pink camouflage cloth. Everything clicked into place.

Gary jumped backward off the bench seat in the rear of the RV. It was the same gator that killed Matty and Dani. He could still see the two men creeping around the beast's girth and decided that it was definitely time to make his exit. He was certain that the evidence they were holding would connect him somehow to the deaths of his friends. The Islamorada police would bungle the job, but they would send it on up to Miami and the Feds would get involved. They would most likely find a microbe or fiber or speck of DNA linking him to the crime and he would go to jail forever. And being the attractive man that he was, Gary knew exactly what would happen to him if they put him in an orange jumpsuit. For a split second, he pictured himself in prison regalia and thought he would look mischievously sexy—orange had always been a good color for him.

He was deep in his penitentiary dream when he

heard the high-pitched scream. He leapt back to the window and the veins he thought had gone cold went colder still. He felt as if someone had injected him with ice water and froze as it raced through every capillary and artery in his body. Frankie and Martin were standing on opposite sides of the alligator and between them, the thing was snapping insanely large jaws, turning its head back and forth, deciding which target was the tastiest.

In a move so fast, Gary could barely see, the gnarly creature flipped itself over and began to lunge in circles at the two men like a puppy chasing its tail —only this puppy was armed with a jagged set of razor sharp teeth. Frankie was running just in front of the alligator's tail, his arms flailing like a used car lot's inflatable waving guy. Martin was stumbling backward, precariously close to the gator's mouth. He had one hand out, Heisman trophy style, attempting to hold off the maw that was closing in on him at blinding speed.

"It's not dead!" Gary shouted at the glass, realizing as soon as he said it how obvious that was to the two men outside.

It's not dead, he thought, I have to kill it. I have to save them. He reached for the gun in his waistband only to find that it wasn't there. It hadn't been there since he had thrown it into the swamp after Dani was killed.

A sudden bump outside sent the RV rocking back and forth. Gary saw that the men were now running circles around the Winnebago. He saw them, through side windows, then the back, then the other side, then the windshield. It was Frankie in the lead, Martin next, and the gator last. Gary was shocked it hadn't gotten one of them yet. It must still be in a daze from whatever had caused it to be lying in the middle of the road.

Frankie shrieked as they all made another 360 around the back of the RV.

"Gun!" he shouted as they rounded toward the driver's side. "Get the gun in the glove compartment."

Gary was momentarily confused. Who was Frankie shouting at? He watched as the man stared right at him through the front windshield again, jabbing his finger toward the passenger's side in the shape of a gun.

"Gun!" Gary yelled, again realizing it was a stupid thing to say. "I've got it. I mean, I'll get it."

He dove toward the front and slid into the passenger's seat. Jerking the glove compartment open, he tossed aside a raft of random papers:

registration, gas receipts, and extra napkins from McDonald's. Finally, he uncovered a holster and pulled it out. It was smaller than he expected. He jerked the gun free and saw that it looked kind of like it was plastic and he wondered if it was a real gun or a flare gun or something. On the end, near the open barrel, he could see the engraved logo: GLOCK. He'd heard of them, but this one was much smaller than he had expected. The police would later find the empty GLOCK G42 .380 caliber registered to one Martin Russo apparently tossed into the mangroves at the scene.

Without realizing that this gun was much too small to do any real damage to the alligator, Gary shoved the thin, aluminum door open, banging it against the side of the Winnebago. As Frankie, then Martin, then the roaring gator raced past, he jumped down, skipping the two metal steps and landed heavy on the road. Frankie apparently decided their circle pattern was getting them nowhere and decided to turn left and sprint toward the dark, swampy area on the side of the highway. *Genius*, Gary thought.

He raised his arms and started running after them, screaming and firing the tiny gun as fast as he could. He saw sparks fly off the pavement and distantly heard the pop of the GLOCK in his ears. He realized as he watched Martin's shoulders pinwheel around that he'd missed the alligator, but shot the man running just in front of it. Martin uttered a strange grunting cough and went down to a knee, clutching his right arm. Before Gary could be shocked, the gator snapped his jaws down on Martin's leg, made a sudden course change around Frankie, and began to drag the old man between his teeth into the murky black swamp. Frankie's shrill cries echoed up and down the road as the alligator raced past him. He reached out and kicked at it to no avail. He chased after it, swinging his arms and slapping at the beast, but it ignored him now that it had caught one of them.

Gary raised his arms, realizing that he still had the gun, and fired three more times until the gun was empty. He hit the alligator with two out of three of the bullets, but it never even blinked. He threw the gun at it and it bounced off the gnarly tail and flew into the mangroves. Frankie was still chasing after the creature when Gary grabbed him by the arms and hauled him backward, both of them falling into the road.

Frankie tried to get back up, but Gary held him until he stopped screaming.

"It's too late," he said as Frankie wailed. "He's gone."

The night grew quiet as the older man's sobs began to slow. Somewhere in the brush, they heard a final scream and Frankie passed out. Gary wondered if this was the time to bug out or if he wanted to see what he'd really look like in prison gear. Neither of them saw the car stopped just a hundred yards away from the RV, idling, one headlight out, the other dim.

39

That Rings A Bell

FIFTEEN MINUTES before the alligator took Martin Russo off into the night, Dante Caparelli dabbed at the urine soaking the crotch of his pants with a handkerchief. He cursed his aging prostate for allowing him to get all the way to the back of Dion's Quik Mart before finding his zipper stuck. Any normal adult male would have been able to hold it long enough to loosen his belt, pull his pants down, and complete the job. He'd gotten it almost to the last notch before the sensation of squeezing a water balloon erupted between his hips.

"No, no, no!" he yelled as the acrid smell of piss blossomed out in a dark stain on his slacks. "Jeezus frickin' Christ."

He considered taking them off to wring them

out, but thought better of it. He would just have to wear it until he got back to Woody's. He had a few extra things in his office and it wasn't likely anyone would notice his accident in the dim black-lit club.

He was nearly there when he happened upon an odd scene—even for the Keys. In the glow of headlights (not his, but a large RV parked askew in the center of the highway,) he could see two men sprinting in circles around the vehicle with—he squinted into the darkness, cursing his poor night vision—an alligator chasing them. He inched his car closer, and considered blowing his horn, but he didn't. He wasn't sure if it would scare the gator, the men running from it, or if it would enrage the creature.

He reached down between his legs, stretching to feel around under the seat. The smell of his own urine stank and he cursed when his head tapped the horn on the steering wheel. But like many other features of the old Town Car, it didn't work. He felt around, his fingers brushing the cold steel of his personal pistol. With a heave and a deep breath, he was able to grab it.

When he looked back up, another man had joined the fray, but this one was chasing the alligator and waving something at it. When he got close, he watched as the third man began to fire recklessly. He ducked when he heard a ricochet ping off something nearby.

With something near popcorn munching entertainment value, Dante watched as the man in the back proceeded to wing the man just in front of the gator giving the beast time to chomp down on him and drag him into the mangroves. The man in the front began to chase after them in hysterics, but the guy with the gun hurled it after the fleeing alligator and grabbed him. He turned him around, yelling something at the man, but Dante couldn't tell what he was saying. And then the man who had been in the front of the whole macabre parade fainted.

Dante eased closer still and thought there was something oddly familiar about the guy who'd been blasting the gun, but he couldn't place it. The man who had fainted finally came to and began wailing and thrashing about again. The gunman slapped him hard on the cheek and it seemed to do the trick. He helped the frantic man up and they walked toward the RV—still idling and purring away like a two-ton box of a kitten.

Before they could get in, Dante stepped out and met them, his gun drawn. The younger of the two men yelped. His eyes met Dante's and the flash of recognition darted across them to be painted with fear shortly after.

"Don't I know you?" Dante asked, wagging the gun at him.

"Do you know this man, Gary?" the previously frantic man asked.

The man named Gary said nothing. He turned and sprinted away. With Dante's hobbling speed, he probably would've gotten away except for a sudden thrashing and a low growl in the direction the gator had made its exit. Gary stopped suddenly and began to edge his way back toward them.

"How's about you and me and this guy," Dante jabbed a finger in Frankie's chest as he said it, "get a drink at my bar and figure this whole thing out? Eh?"

Gary swallowed and raised his hands into the air. "Guess we don't have much choice, do we?"

"Nah," Dante said.

DANTE HAD PUT them in the back of his car, activating the child locks so they couldn't get out. He almost laughed at the fact that this was the one thing still working on this old heap. He made a promise he was going to get something new when this was all over, maybe a Cadillac DeVille—do they still even make those things? Eh, didn't matter, he was gonna get something with leather and cool A/C and plenty of bells and whistles and all that.

The man named Gary was sitting diagonally behind him, studying his feet. Tears were streaming down the guy's face and he was rocking back and forth. He kept muttering something about losing his true love or something like that.

"Oh, Dani, Dani, Dani," Gary moaned, "I can't believe you're gone. It's all over now. I'm sure to be taken out for a long boat ride and—"

"Hey, kid," Dante growled, interrupting him, "can it. You ain't got nothin' to worry about. I just want to get a feel for what the hell is going on around here."

Gary sniffed and swiped his hand across his nose, but he didn't calm down. In fact, he grew more and more hysterical. So much so, that Frankie was jerking on his door handle, trying to get out—at forty miles per hour.

"Jeezus, kid," Dante said, channeling his inner father, "shut your mouth or I swear to you I'll come back there."

"And what? Shoot me in the face?" Gary yelled, snot bubbles popping in his nostrils.

"I just might, ya frickin' idiot."

The car swerved all over the road as Dante alternated between turning around to try and reach the man and looking in the rearview mirror.

"Fine by me," Gary shrieked, "I'll just be with my beloved Dani then."

"That's it," Dante slammed on the brakes.

The car lurched sending Gary and Frankie both hurtling into the seats in front of them. In one swift motion, Dante reached over the passenger's seat and grabbed Gary by the collar. He intended to slap some sense in the man, but then hesitated. He was holding something in his right hand—a gun, or maybe a knife.

Dante peered down to get a closer look, his hand reaching for his own pistol. As his eyes focused, he could see it wasn't a weapon at all.

"Is that what I think it is, kid?"

Gary said nothing. He just shook his head from side to side and pulled against Dante's grip on his shirt. The old man's grip gave and Gary slammed back into his seat, his hands in his lap, turning a small object over and over.

Dante reached up and tapped the dome light. Nothing happened. He rammed it with his palm and an amber beam of dim light shone into the back seat.

"Christ almighty," Dante breathed, "is that a finger?"

Gary didn't answer, but just moaned and sobbed uncontrollably.

Dante leaned over the seat and saw that, yes, indeed, it *was* a finger. Something glinted in the low light as Gary ... well ... fingered the finger. And then Dante saw it, glistening in all its golden glory and wet with Gary's tears.

Matty's family ring.

40

Strangers In The Night

AROUND THE SAME time that Dante saw the Caparelli family ring on the disembodied finger in the back of his Lincoln Town Car, Troy Bodean and Ian Bass happened upon Martin and Frankie's Winnebago. It was literally sitting in the middle of the Overseas Highway, lights on, engine on, nobody home.

Ian Bass approached with his gun drawn, fully expecting a cartel of drug dealers to come pouring out of the RV like a clown car. Troy watched from the back seat of the Explorer, wondering how he was going to get out of the car if Ian got shot. After an eternity of suspense watching Ian poke around inside the Winnebago, the officer waved at Troy through the large rectangular back window. He gave Troy the universal all clear sign and then disappeared back into the forward regions of the large family-style trailer. The sound of air brakes squelched into the night and the RV began to creep ahead and drift to the side of the road—Ian was clearing the traffic lane.

Troy wondered if Ian was concerned with tampering in a possibly evidence filled vehicle, but then again, there was no crime as of yet. For all they knew, this could be a simple case of—actually, Troy couldn't think of a single, simple scenario for this, but he left well enough alone. As Ian pulled the large vehicle onto the shoulder, Troy could see a black puddle of liquid out in front of where it had been sitting. Even though it was dark, he could tell what it was—blood. Had to be blood. It pools and congeals like nothing else on earth. Ian jogged back toward the car as Troy waged an internal battle over whether or not to tell him about the puddle.

As it happened, he would never get the chance to bring it up.

FIVE MINUTES before Troy and Ian discovered the Winnebago and the puddle of blood, Cinnamon Starr and Katerina Kuznetsov were flying past mile marker eighty-one at a speed normally reserved for the Concorde or a Space Shuttle. Cinnamon had composed herself and was applying makeup in the non-lighted visor mirror in Gary's 1980 "Golden Eagle" model Jeep CJ-7—aka the Daisy Duke version of the popular SUV.

Having gained no confidence whatsoever in the Islamorada Sheriff's Department to actually do anything about the deaths of Matty Caparelli or Daniel Kane Kotlerson—Dani for short—Katerina had told Cinnamon that she'd be happy to drive her home. In truth, the old Russian woman was having the time of her life, speeding around town, shooting at strangers, and harassing the local police. She couldn't remember ever being this excited since her husband had gotten his prescription for his little blue pills.

"It's fine," Cinnamon said. "Just take me to Woody's. You can take the Jeep up to Dion's and I'll catch an Uber after my shift is over."

"Are you sure, malyshka?"

"Yeah. I'm probably safer there than anywhere else." Cinnamon said, her eyes scanning back and forth on the road. "I mean, Gary's probably on his way to his apartment and he's my next door neighbor. I sure as heck don't want to be there when he gets home."

Katerina opened her mouth, then closed it, apparently unsure of what to say.

"And besides, Matty's dad is my boss at Woody's. I'm probably safer there than anywhere else."

She felt tears sting the back of her eyes, but promised herself not to cry, she had spent way too much time on her mascara to let it run down her cheeks. Then again, maybe she could pull off some kind of Rob Zombie goth dance with the right amount of black around her eyes.

"He's probably sitting in the dark, waiting on me to come home so he can kill me like the others."

She lost her battle with the tears and they streamed down her face.

"Oh, come on, now," Katerina said, handing Cinnamon a Wendy's napkin she found in the center console. "I have no doubt you would kick his ass before he could do such a thing. God, look at those legs!"

Cinnamon couldn't help but laugh, until she noticed they were about to slam into the back of a police SUV. Without thinking, she reached up and grabbed the wheel and yanked it hard to the right. The Jeep careened off the road onto the soft shoulder and suddenly, they were about to ram into the back of an RV. She jerked the wheel left and they nearly jumped back onto the pavement. The wheels barked as they fishtailed into oncoming traffic and back into their lane, barely missing a silver Toyota Sienna full of chaotic kids.

When Katerina regained control of the Jeep, she started laughing. It began as a nervous titter and bubbled into an infectious giggle. When Cinnamon joined in, it erupted into a full-on, eyes-watering belly laugh for both of them. The anxiety of the situation broke the dam and they both laughed so hard that Cinnamon wondered if they might need another change of pants.

Struggling to catch her breath, Katerina asked, "You are sure about this? You want me to take you to work?"

Cinnamon nodded as she spoke. "Yes, if Gary comes after me there, I'll have a whole bar full of chivalrous knights ready to come to my damsel-in-distress aid. Katerina looked doubtful, but couldn't think of any reason not to take her to Woody's.

Neither of them gave another thought to the roadblock of an RV and a police SUV they had just blown past.

. . .

TROY FELT the Ford Explorer rock back and forth as the white blur zoomed past the passenger's side onto the shoulder of the road. His door protested with a loud metallic screeching noise and a high-pitched squeal like fingernails being dragged across a chalkboard. It looked for all the world like the racing vehicle was going to slam into the back of the abandoned Winnebago, but at the last second, it veered back onto the road without hitting it. Ian Bass wasn't so lucky. He'd been sauntering back to the police SUV, just inside the solid yellow line marking the outside of the traffic lane, when the white car —*maybe a pickup or Jeep, yeah,* Troy thought, *it looked like it might've been a Jeep*—nearly tilted up on two wheels to avoid colliding with the RV.

The front passenger's side wheel bumped over the front half of Ian's right foot. Though the officer had on boots, Troy felt sure they weren't steel-toed or protective in any major capacity. He felt sure of this because Ian was hopping around on one foot, holding the other between fingers laced under his shoe.

He thought he had heard just about every swear word known to man during his time in Afghanistan, but Ian proved him wrong. There were words that made Troy turn away, spewing out of the officer's mouth as he limped back to the car. He slid in, gingerly and Troy could see the shoe was smashed pancake flat. He thought whatever was inside that shoe was broken in a way that could only be compared to shattered glass. Ian was still swearing and panting so hard that Troy thought he might hyperventilate.

When he finally managed to slow his tirade, he looked over his shoulder. "Did you see it?"

"See what?" Troy asked.

"The Jeep?"

"If you're meanin' the one that just ran over your foot, yeah," Troy shrugged as he said it, not sure what the officer was getting at, "I saw it all right. What about it?"

"It's Gary's," Ian said, twisting his hips to his right so that he could push the gas pedal with his left foot. "The serial killer prick just tried to take me out. He must know I'm onto him."

Troy thought about this and concluded that there was absolutely no way that this Gary person could know that Ian was on his trail. The SUV lurched forward and Ian yelped in pain.

"You know," Troy said, leaning his forehead on the metal grate separating them, "I could help out if you'd just—"

"Not a chance, cowboy," Ian Bass said, his knuckles as white as his cheeks on the steering wheel.

Troy slumped back into his seat, his wrists aching from the cuffs. As they picked up speed, he felt a cool draft of air coming from somewhere to his right. He shook it off without realizing that his door was ajar.

41

Le Voyeur

CHAD HARRISON FELT the strings of sanity losing their tenuous hold on his composure as he pedaled furiously in the darkness of mile marker eighty-one. His beach-classy date night outfit was a soggy, muddy mess. The rusted fenders on the "borrowed" bicycle did next to nothing to staunch the rooster tails of road spray splashing him in the face and back. If Jackson Pollock had chosen highway sludge and linen as his medium, it would've had cleaner, simpler lines than Chad's clothes.

He pedaled in a fury, driven by all that had happened to him in the last couple of days. He clenched his teeth and spat epithets around like watermelon seeds.

No one heard the story he was telling about how

his kayak—the one prized possession he had kept from his first marriage—had been stolen, pirated out from under his nose. He imagined a vagrant selling it to a local pawn shop that would not care if it were not properly purchased and would demand no proof of ownership. And then, a thought occurred to him. It wasn't a sane thought by any means, but it came to him in a flash and he began to chuckle at the possibility.

"Jenise, you sly witch, you," he called through fits of coughing laughter.

Jenise, his ex-wife of fifteen years, had bought him the kayak as an anniversary present and, in his eyes, was the only thing of any excitement that had happened in their marriage. If he had known how down-to-earth and sensible Jenise was going to be, he would never have married her. Maybe that was what he'd wanted in the beginning, but a strip club and pornography habit—not the filthy internet porn, but the classy, magazine kind shot with soft focus filters and closed legs—had turned him into a bit of a pervert. He tried on more than one occasion to get her to expand her horizons and she had brushed him off with little more than a giggle.

"Oh, Chad. You know good girls don't do that sort of thing," she'd told him.

And she was right, but he discovered he could get the girls up in Miami's red light district to do those things—for a price. So, he'd claim the paper was sending him on story after story and he'd have to travel nearly every weekend. Jenise had been oblivious. She was proud of her husband and his amazing work ethic, which was similar to her own. So industrious she was, that one weekend while he was away, she had taken it upon herself to clean out the attic of their Islamorada bungalow. She found a black suitcase with strange instruments made of chrome, plastic, leather, and rubber. She had to run an internet search to discover the medieval uses for most of them.

When he arrived home that Sunday night, she met him at the door with a suitcase of her own. She handed him her attorney's business card and said they would work out the details in court. The only things Chad had been allowed to keep were fifty percent of his earnings, the house in Islamorada, and the kayak.

He raised his fist in the air, shaking it wildly at the menacing clouds overhead. "If you took my kayak, I'll cut your—"

His thought was interrupted by a bizarre scene solidifying in front of him in the steamy aftermath of the evening's rainstorm. He stopped the bike with a screeching protest from its rusty brakes. Something big and boxy—maybe a tractor trailer—was standing still, the motor running in the middle of the highway. He pedaled forward slowly and the whole wild thing played out in front of him.

He watched as men, maybe three of them, ran circles around the idling RV he'd thought was a trailer. Then there was gunfire, one of the men went down, and then a gator—holy crap, that's a big alligator—dove on him, dragged him away off the side of the road. Even with the slo-mo he was experiencing while watching it all happen, it only took a few minutes from the chase, to the shots, to the gator chomping one of the dudes. He put his left foot down, preparing to race his bike onto the scene to help. Unfortunately, he never noticed the fact that his special order Orlebar Brown boat shoes had come untied, a shoelace dangling precariously near the single gear between his ankles. Before he could launch the bicycle forward, he saw a car stop at the far end of the scene, silhouetting the two remaining men in the dim beam of a single headlight.

There was some talking, some smacking of cheeks, the drawing of a pistol, and eventually, the two men who'd been left in the wake of the alligator attack, getting into the car with the new man on the scene. Chad, who wasn't feeling particularly like himself heard a voice inside his head tell him to stay back. He had a short argument with the voice.

"Do you know who I am?" He asked the voice.

"I do, I'm you."

"You're who?"

"You."

"Me?"

"The one and only."

"Exactly, which is why I'm confused as to why there seems to be two voices in my head right now."

The third voice kept quiet, but somehow, Chad knew it was there, lurking, waiting for the right time to be heard.

He shook his head to clear the zany, and for the time being, it worked. As the car with the three men —the two alligator hunters and the older guy with the pistol—pulled away, Chad pushed off and cranked twice on the bike's pedals wondering at the sheer incompetence of the Islamorada Sheriff's Department. That this could happen in the middle of the Overseas Highway with nary a blue light or siren anywhere nearby was at the same time shocking yet not surprising at all.

Before he could get very far, a sudden tsunami

of road grime, sewer filth, and something that smelled like wet cat, splashed up on him from a vehicle screaming past him. He raised a hand, dripping with the grossness of the rooster tail spewing up from the SUV's tires, and gave the driver the middle-finger salute. As he did, he saw the green and yellow reflective logo on the tailgate of the Ford Explorer.

"Why is it okay for a cop to blast his way across the island at that speed?" He yelled to the disappearing vehicle.

"You of all people should know that's how the local-yokels operate around here." Voice number one said.

"Did you really expect anything different?" The second voice couldn't help but chime in.

"Kill," voice number three hissed, feeling it was finally his time.

"Wait, what?" Chad said, startled by the new voice. "What did you just say?"

Voice number three remained quiet, but pleased that he had planted the seed.

"I think he said there's a hill up ahead," voice number two said, covering for his counterpart.

"Oh, shut up," Chad blasted, pushing forward again. "All of you keep quiet so I can just get back home. Then I will deal with the police in my own way."

He could have sworn one of the voices called him something vaguely homophobic and offensive, but he couldn't be sure. The bike lurched forward and the shoestring that had been white before the evening started, wrapped around the gear and got hopelessly tangled in the chain. It jerked Chad forward so hard that he launched over the handlebars, leaving the bike and his left shoe tumbling along behind him. Reflexively, he threw his hands out in front of him to catch himself.

As he flew toward the rutted pavement, he remembered the piece his counterpart at the Seattle Times had penned just yesterday. Chad had laughed that the prestigious paper would print such a stupid article, but as he fell, he realized he was too late to heed its advice.

"Pivot to your side, tuck your head into your chest, and avoid the FOOSH at all costs," Kate Moriarity, senior wellness editor had penned. "FOOSH, or falling on outstretched hands, is a sure way to concentrate all the force on your wrists. The risk of breaking one, or both, is quite high."

Chad had nearly spit out his coffee reading the ridiculous acronym, but now, as he saw the ground rushing up at him around the outline of his hands, he knew exactly what was going to happen.

The jolt and following excruciating pain in his arms had so many textures, it was hard to follow them all. The first sensation he had was the skin on his delicate palms grinding along what felt like bits of broken glass and sandpaper. The second, located squarely in his right wrist, was a snap. If a fracture can feel clean, this one did. The third pain, like the third voice in his head, felt evil. It wasn't in his wrist, but farther up. It was closer to the elbow than his hand. And unlike the other break which had a sudden, twig-snapping feel, this one was more ... splintery. He was certain the x-ray of that one would have the doctor shaking his or her head and calling in others to take a look at the complexity of the thing.

He pulled his hands in close to his stomach after the first gut-wrenching impact and tumbled for at least ten feet. He rolled to a stop, flat on his back, head lying in an inch deep puddle of cat urine. It had to be pregnant cat urine as it stank with the sharp acrid odor of a litter box that had never been scooped.

Looking up at the clearing night sky, he tried to slow his breathing. Both arms throbbed from the shoulder down to his fingertips and he was sure his palms were oozing blood and puss, but he dare not look. Not yet. He didn't want to see what was going on down there until he'd had a second to come down from the initial shock.

An intense white point of light with a long tail streaked across the sky. Then another. They were followed by dozens more and Chad recognized them as the Perseid Meteor Shower.

"It's beautiful," he whispered, tears forming in his eyes, then running down his cheeks and into his ears.

Thankfully, the other voices were quiet. He realized as he lay and watched the startling fireworks display in the night sky that—in his forty-something years as an inhabitant of the Keys—he had never seen the famous meteor shower. It was a constant visitor this time of year, but Chad had never taken the time to come outside and watch the show. He was about to make a resolution to change his life, to stop and smell the roses, to be a more positive influence on the world, when he heard the rumble.

It was distant, but coming on fast. Part of what he heard was engine noise from some kind of truck. There were also undertones of low and deep vibrato, maybe oversized tires with big knobby tread.

Realizing that he couldn't use his hands to lift himself up, he cursed his recent lackadaisical attitude toward his abs. He had to roll over on his side, get a foot up under his body and raise up to one knee.

As he did, he was blinded by the high beams of something. Piercing white headlights, small, round, close together, shone into his eyes like paparazzi flashbulbs. He had never actually been the subject of the paps, but he'd been near a few celebrity frenzies that had left ghosts of white circles on his eyes for days.

"I'm dead," he whispered and screwed his eyelids shut as tight as they would go.

Big tires make a strange sound when they grind to a halt. They don't sound anything like the wheels of ordinary cars, screeching and screaming. They make more of a groan or maybe a moan. Chad waited on the impact, his bladder emptying its comforting warmth down his thighs, but it never came. He could feel the heat and hear the pinging of an engine just inches from his face.

He opened his eyes and saw the distinctive grill of a white Jeep CJ-7. It tickled the back of his mind and he was sure it should be familiar. But like the lyrics to an old song you knew back in high school, but could only remember the first line, it was there, but then gone.

The doors of the Jeep opened at the same time, spreading like an angel's wings and Chad tried to say something. His voice caught in his throat at the sight of the two women walking toward him. He didn't know the old broad in the passenger's seat, but the other girl—young, pretty, nice legs, firm butt— snapped the hazy memory into focus.

He knew the girl, oh yes, he knew her. She was the wench who'd been talking about his kayak at Robbie's. He started to lunge at her, reaching out his ruined arms, but the pain lanced up his arms, into his shoulders, and finally up into his neck.

He tried to scream at her, but all that came out was a moan. A strange, Quasimodo sound echoed out of his throat and for a second, he thought it was the third voice making itself heard. He slumped back to his knees and tucked his arms back into his chest.

"Ugh, look at this Svo-lach'," the old woman said, jutting her chin at him. "The vagrants have gotten so bad since we moved here. Look, he's even pee-peed on himself. What a wretch."

"Olga," the younger woman said, her tone softer and kinder, "Don't be so cruel. I mean, look at the poor man. He's obviously homeless and starving."

She pulled out a wad of cash and held it out toward him. *Condescending witch, don't you know who I am?* He considered for a second about taking the money out of spite, but realized he couldn't, his broken arms wouldn't allow it. He gritted his teeth and shook his head.

"See?" The younger woman said, tucking the money away. "He has too much pride to take any money."

"Whatever," the woman called Olga said, crossing her arms in a huff. "He might be homeless, but he doesn't have to be homeless in the middle of the road."

The younger woman leaned down, her face close to his. She smelled good, like Linda. Was that Chanel she was wearing? He was about to snap at her with his teeth, but before he could, she hooked her hands under his arms and pulled him up. The pain was so intense that he nearly fainted. He couldn't support his own weight and allowed the woman to drag him to the side of the road. As they reached the shoulder, he saw that his single remaining shoe had come off and was lying on its side near the white center line of the highway.

The young woman pulled out the money again and dropped it into his lap. "I know you don't want to take it, but you look like you really need it. Consider it a gift and pay it forward one day."

"Come on, Cinnamon," Olga said. "Let's go wash your hands of this filth."

As the headlights of the white Jeep disappeared down the road, and he limped over to retrieve his shoe, Chad Harrison's voices came back.

"Pay it forward?" Voice number one asked. "What a load of crap."

"Oh, we will pay it forward," voice number two said. "She'll get exactly what she deserves."

And voice number three finally got to come forward to be heard in earnest. His message was a simple one and for once, Chad agreed wholeheartedly.

"Kill."

42

Back To The Beginning

DANTE CAPARELLI almost spit in the water he was carrying back to his office for Gary, but he had two glasses—one for the gay Winnebago guy who had just lost his husband-type-thing and one for the idiot who had killed his son—and he was afraid he would mix them up. While he had cause to be pissed at Gary, he had no beef with the other guy.

"Why you even givin' 'em any water, boss?" Sully asked as he locked the door behind them. "In my estimation they don't deserve nothin'."

"Because, Sully," Dante said, as if instructing a third grader, "I want them to be able to tell me what the hell I just witnessed on the road down there."

Sully shrugged his shoulders in a classic

fuhgeddaboudit move and sat down in a chair beside the door.

Outside the office, the now ubiquitous banging of the band was in full swing and hearing what was being said was difficult at best. Woody's was packed tonight, rain always had that effect, so Dante had told the band to be on their best behavior.

The lead singer—Big Dick, aka Jack Snipes— had said they'd been rehearsing with the new drummer and the sound was close to normal. Dante was promised the reckless Keith Moon wannabe would be on his best behavior tonight or he'd be gone. They would all soon find out that this was a prophetic statement in every way. As they roared into "Break on through to the Other Side" by Jim Morrison and the Doors, Dante handed the two men sitting at the far ends of a well-worn leather couch the glasses of lukewarm water. Gary drank his down in one gulp. Frankie just stared into the glass in his hands, his lips pursed in distaste. The poor man looked as if he was trying not to make direct contact with anything in the office, including the couch.

Dante ignored him and pulled out a massive bottle of antacid tablets. He shook out the last three chalky TUMS and popped them into his mouth. His belly hadn't been feeling well since he'd come to work this morning. The whole damn world was going insane and his ulcer didn't appreciate the extra stress.

Long, silent, anxious moments hung in the air just under the cloud of hazy smoke. Frankie stifled a cough and Dante shot him a glare that he felt sure made the man squeak, but the pitch was too high to hear over the band.

"Can I get another glass of water?" Gary said, looking up under swollen eyelids.

The sassy kid had sobbed all the way to Woody's and wiped away enough snot to fill a milk jug. Dante had given him his handkerchief and Gary had soaked it through and through before they'd gone a mile from the Winnebago.

"I think you've had enough," Dante growled. "What I really need from you now is the details."

"The details?" Gary's eyelashes fluttered.

"Can you believe dis guy?" Dante asked Sully over his shoulder.

Like a good mob wise guy, Sully echoed, "can't believe it, boss."

When he turned back around, he smacked Gary across the cheek. It immediately flamed into a red handprint and Frankie yelped in surprise—this time loud enough to hear over the band.

"I'm askin' the questions, here, yeah?"

"Yes, sir," Gary nodded, cradling his cheek in his hand.

"Now, let's try this again, shall we?" Dante leaned forward and put his hands on his knees. He was six inches from Gary's face. "The details I would like to hear are the ones that pertain to my son and his untimely demise. Capiche?"

Whatever had been holding back the water inside Gary suddenly burst. Dante was sure the floor beneath his feet was going to be a puddle soon as much as the kid was sobbing. He was soon a bubbling, gurgling, hyperventilating, gasping, convulsing mess. Dante pulled back his hand to slap Gary's other cheek, but Frankie suddenly spoke up.

"Hey, mister," he shouted, wagging his index finger at Dante, "I don't know you, but you do not realize what we have both just been through. I just lost my husband to a vicious, man-eating monster. Gary, from what I've been piecing together in the last few hours, has lost two people, one of whom I understand was your son. Well, you just stop and consider that we've lost people, too."

Dante rose out of his chair faster than he himself thought possible and was close to punching Frankie in the mouth. Somehow, Sully managed to grab his arm and hold him back. When he was finally composed, the bar manager let him go. Dante straightened his tie and sat back down.

"The difference, Mary Kay," Dante inhaled long and slow as he spoke, trying desperately to ignore the pain in his chest, "is that your bosom buddy here killed my son."

"It's true," Gary sobbed. "It's all true. I should never have gone out there. All I wanted was to take Matty on a kayak ride out into the mangroves. A little wine, a little cheese ... I thought it might make him more ... amenable to my advances."

Dante's mouth twisted up as if he'd eaten a rotten lemon.

"It was the same alligator," Gary continued. "It has to be. He ate Matty, and then Dani when we tried to go find the kayak."

"And then my Marty," Frankie added, sniffing.

Dante shot a questioning glance over his shoulder at Sully. "You buyin' this?"

"I dunno, boss." Sully sucked air over his teeth. "I mean, the only way to really know is to go back out there. See if Matty's really gone."

Dante stood, walked to his desk, and picked up a hot-dog shaped napkin. He unrolled it slowly to reveal the finger with the Caparelli family ring still on it.

"This is," his voice caught behind the lump in his throat, "all that was left of my boy?"

Gary nodded vigorously. "Dani found it when we reached what was left of the kayak."

"But you didn't see nothin' else of his body?"

"No, that was it, but the alligator was huge and—"

"Sully, my friend," Dante interrupted Gary, "looks like you've finally had a smart thought."

"I did?" the white-haired bartender asked.

He turned back to Gary and leaned close again, holding the finger up under his nose. "Since you seem to know exactly where this kayak is, and since you're the one who took Matty out there in the first place, I think it's only fair that we take you out there."

Gary's mouth dropped open and he began to tremble and shake like a patient with a high fever. "No, no, no," he moaned.

"It's perfect," he pulled the ring off the finger and tucked it into his jacket pocket, "we'll let this gator finish what he started. Nice and tidy-like."

"You can't do this," Gary sputtered. "You just can't take someone out into the—"

He looked over at Frankie and scooted toward the man. Frankie pulled away from him as if his hands and arms were covered with leprosy.

"Frankie," Gary motioned at Dante and Sully as he spoke, "you've got to tell them. They cannot do this!"

Frankie turned to Dante and raised a hand like a school child asking to go to the bathroom. "Could I get a ride back to my Winnebago since it's on the way?"

THE FOUR OF them ducked out the back door and walked around the building to Dante's car. He shoved Gary into the back seat and slammed the door. Sully slid into the driver's seat and the old Lincoln fired up with a protesting sputter. Frankie raised his arms as Dante walked around and opened the passenger door.

"What about me?" he asked, his tone threatening to be indignant. "You said you'd give me a ride."

"I said nothin' of the sort," Dante said. "Besides, this ain't the kind of ride you want to be takin'."

Frankie opened his mouth to say something, but Sully rolled down his window before he could.

"Yo, Elton John," he snorted, letting his left arm

dangle out the window, pistol pointing at the ground. "Tell your story walking before we decide to take you with us."

Frankie turned and ran, not one-hundred percent sure he was heading in the direction of his RV.

43

Brawlin' After Midnight

WHEN CINNAMON STARR waved goodbye to Olga as she pulled away in the white Jeep with the big gold eagle on the hood—she told the old woman to park it at the Quik Mart and she would Uber to it after her shift—the sound inside Woody's changed from music to what she could only describe as a train wreck. Either someone was juggling steel trash cans or the band had taken on a whole new, demolition derby metal direction. She was so afraid to open the front door that she never saw Dante, Sully, and Gary sitting in the black Lincoln Towncar in the parking lot.

When she finally worked up the courage to go in, the sonic wave pushed at her like the fly stopping air machines that destroyed her hair every time she shopped at Walmart. The music was unrecognizable, with no discernible tune or tempo. It was as if each member of the band was playing a different song and playing louder and louder to be heard over the others. She lowered her head and shoved into the bar.

Inside, the noise was substantially louder and she wondered if she would have permanent damage to her ears after tonight. The girls were all sitting at tables, holding their hands to the sides of their heads, as were most of the patrons. No one was dancing.

The band looked as bad as they sounded. Cinnamon thought they all looked like they'd just come back from Bonnaroo and should've stayed home to sleep off the drugs.

John was shouting rather than singing and the few words she caught of the lyrics made her cock her head to the side in confusion. Is that "Midnight Rider?"

She had never heard a death metal version of the classic Allman Brothers song, but here it was. What should have been a rolling, Southern rock style guitar lead, was a screeching, squealing, eardrum piercing wail that made her head hurt. The bass player was sitting in a chair, surprisingly, not playing a single note. His face was impassive as if all of this was completely normal.

And then there was the drummer. The dude had rolled in a week ago when the band was without a rhythm section and claimed he would be better than any percussionist they had ever had. He had managed to dent more cymbals and break more drum heads in that time than Cinnamon had thought possible. The guy was dripping with sweat, hammering away at the tiny drum kit as if he was forging a battle ax—maybe in his mind, he was. *Mjolnir, eat your heart out*, Cinnamon thought, ducking through the tables toward the bar.

She jumped onto an empty stool next to an angry looking man holding out a twenty dollar bill. He held a piece of paper in one hand and the money in the other and was scanning back and forth behind the bar. Cinnamon noticed quickly that there was no one there. No bartender? Strange. Wonder where Sully is?

"Here, sweetheart." The man shoved the twenty and his receipt at her. "I'm outta here. This is ridiculous. Man can't even enjoy a good booby bar anymore. Do you kids call this crap music?"

He didn't wait for an answer and speed-walked out the door. Cinnamon was vaguely jealous as she

watched him disappear. She walked behind the bar
and popped open the cash register. She stuffed the
bill and receipt in and slammed it shut. As she did,
she heard the booming voice of Big Dick over the
cacophony.

"You are fired, you jackass," he shouted. "If you're
a drummer, then I'm Heidi Klum."

That got a tentative laugh from the crowd, maybe
they thought this was part of the show.

It wasn't long before they realized it wasn't as the
drummer continued to bash the drums with one
hand and flip Big Dick off with the other. Dick, aka
Jack, had taken to performing the long sets that his
band was famous for whilst sitting in a chair. He'd
done so ever since the gout had gotten so bad in his
ankles that his leg from his knee to his feet was a
swollen, tree trunk of painful knots. His love—or
perhaps addiction—to high gravity beer made him
look like he was standing atop two tubular sacks of
golf balls. He could no more stand for more than
twenty minutes straight on stage than he could stand
on the surface of the sun.

When the drummer tipped his cowboy hat back
and flung a drumstick at Jack, the behemoth of a
singer had finally had enough that he stood up. The
entire bar full of drunks, strippers, strippers'

boyfriends, and mobster types gasped collectively. It reminded Cinnamon of watching the Jerry Springer show when they had an envelope-opening *you're-not-the-father* moment. The room seemed to suddenly be devoid of oxygen as the guitar player stopped playing and Jack took two wobbly steps toward the drummer.

"Whatchu gonna do, fatass?" the drummer cackled, flinging his remaining drumstick at Jack.

The wooden missile whizzed past the corpulent singer and smacked Harley Doug on the right side of his face. It whacked like a Rocky Balboa punch to a hanging side of beef. (If you don't know who Harley Doug is, picture a defensive end-size biker dude with a slick, bald head, fists like cantaloupes, a long, graying goatee tied in two wiry braids, and an indiscernible number of tattoos covering his arms in a tapestry of naked women and various symbols of death.) The air that had gone out of the room seconds earlier, wooshed back in as people exhaled in disbelief as Harley Doug stood up.

His face twisted in rage, all sunglasses and grinding teeth. He clenched and unclenched his fists in time with his grunts and snorts like a bull readying to charge the matador. Jack had lurched to a stop, the Titanic had hit its iceberg. Before

Cinnamon could comprehend what was about to happen, Harley Doug took four, heavy steps toward the stage, bent and picked up a fallen crash cymbal, and smashed it on top of the drummer's head.

Cinnamon was sure it was going to flatten the drummer's skull, but as fate would have it, his stool —a cheap piece of yard sale crap that had always a faulty hydraulic lift lever—collapsed under him as the brass Zildjian cymbal hit him with a splashing bang worthy of John Bonham's epic drum solos.

Jack Snipes watched his band erupt into an instrument throwing brawl, clutching his chest. Later, he would find out he had survived what doctor's sometimes call a widow maker heart attack and would need a stent in his left anterior descending artery. After that, he would live another six months. But for now, he turned his head to the left and vomited a foul mixture of half digested buffalo wings and beer on the table of frat guys that had stopped in on the way to Key West. He wasn't altogether disappointed as the obnoxious boys had been hurling insults at the dancers all night.

The boy who had gotten the worst of the river of barf all over his custom coral Ralph Lauren polo with the lime green embroidered logo and the leader of his gang of college idiots, stood and flipped their small table. Seventeen empty bottles of beer and a half full bottle of Jaegermeister went flying. Each bottle seemed to have radar and hit a patron who had not yet been involved in the brawl.

Cinnamon watched as the fight spread like a virus through the room and before she could move, every single person in the bar was throwing a punch or a kick except for her. She picked up the phone at the end of the bar and dialed Dante's number.

"What?" he snapped when he answered. "This better be frickin' good. I'm doin' business right now."

"Dante," she yelled into the receiver, "it's me, Cinnamon. Where the hell is Sully? The floor looks like WrestleMania came to town and they're all getting in a practice bout."

"What the ... where are you? Are you inside?" Dante demanded.

"Yeah," she said, looking over her shoulder as Harley Doug threw someone—maybe the weird drummer guy past her.

He slammed into the back wall behind the bar, smashing into the bottles of liquor there. Glass and alcohol rained down around her as he fell between the sink and the dusty margarita machine.

"Jesus, Dante," she shouted. "This is about to get out of control."

As she said it, she realized it was the understatement of the year, maybe the decade. She could barely hear Dante yelling something to someone in the background.

"Me and Sully are on the way in," he said. "Just keep that shit from getting too rowdy and we'll cool it down."

The old man hung up and Cinnamon dropped the receiver, not bothering to hang it up. As hot and loud as it was, she looked down and a sudden icy chill shot into her spine.

The drummer was staring up at her, his eyes glinting. Blood trickled from a myriad of cuts to his face and his teeth were pink from a busted lip. Amazingly, his cowboy hat was still stuck on top of his head. But that wasn't what frightened her. No, what really terrified her was that the dude was ... laughing.

He hacked and coughed and spat blood as he howled with laughter.

"Now, this is what I call a party," he said. "You ready to dance, chica?"

Cinnamon turned to run, but his hand grabbed her ankle and she fell. Glass bit into her palms as she tried to crawl away, but he had her in a grip so strong it might as well have been a vise. Strangely, he had her leg in his right hand, and in his left he held a Zippo, flickering gently sending a spray of bright sparkles out all around them, reflecting off the broken bottles.

"Where you going, sweetie?" he pulled her back toward him. "Pleased to meet you. Hope you guessed my name."

44

Light My Fire

TROY AND IAN were nearing mile marker eighty on the Overseas Highway when a Jeep raced past them going the opposite direction. Though it was mostly a blur, it was obvious to Troy that it was a very unique Jeep made popular by a very unique actress, Catherine Bach, on a very unique TV show from the early eighties called The Dukes of Hazzard. The eagle on the hood flew past them, wings outstretched, as if it were diving to skewer a rodent for dinner.

"Well, I'll be," Troy said, just before Ian Bass jerked the wheel, preparing to pull a U-turn to intercept the vehicle.

Ian picked up the radio and was about to call in the sighting of the 1980 model Jeep CJ-7 that belonged to the murderer who had last been seen walking down south of Dion's Quik Mart. Troy was slammed into the passenger's side door of the Explorer and the door popped open. It swung open and he was thrown halfway out of the car and found his right elbow, right hip, and right leg dangling over the road as it screamed underneath the SUV.

Fortunately, he had somehow managed to grab the buckle of the seat belt under his butt before he was flung completely out of the open door. He squeezed it with his fingers, but felt it slipping as sweat dripped down his wrist. His Outback Tea-Stained straw cowboy hat flipped off his head and flew out into the night, tumbling down the road.

"What the hell are you doing back there?" Ian yelled.

"Tryin' not to end up a grease spot on the highway," Troy grunted.

Thankfully, Ian swerved a bit and Troy's weight shifted back into the car. The door slammed shut and locked tight. *That was close*, Troy thought as he fought to get his breathing under control. And then he realized with a start, that his hat was gone—*the* hat. For a long time it had been part of what defined him, part of his character, part of his ethos.

"Say, officer," he said, turning to look over his

shoulder through the back windshield, "you wouldn't want to turn around and go back for my—"

His thought stopped abruptly as he turned back around and saw the smoke and flames dancing out in front of them like a lava lamp after it really got going. The sky was dark, but an orange glow lit up the trees surrounding the strip club known as Woody's. Smoke billowed out of the top of the building, roiling toward the sky like a nuclear bomb had gone off inside.

"Dangit," Troy gasped.

He felt the Explorer slow as Ian comprehended what was happening, then abruptly he sped up again. Troy wondered why he wasn't calling this in. Had to be a four alarm or five alarm fire, though he doubted there were that many fire departments on the island.

"Must've had some kind of kitchen fire," Ian said.

Troy tried hard to remember if they served any food at Woody's. All he could remember ordering there was beer and the occasional shot of something or other. He squinted to jog his memory and then it came to him. Fries. They served something called sour cream and onion potato wedges. He did have a plate of those one night and guessed maybe they were deep-fried in a vat of grease—a vat that probably didn't meet the current safety codes. And then he realized he was worried about the wrong things. Cinnamon. What if she was in there? What if the fire was so big no one could get out. She would be burned alive with all the other ugly dancers. Big Dick and the Extenders would be a great loss if they were trapped inside as well.

"Hurry," Troy muttered, his eyes suddenly wet with tears.

"Goin' as fast as I can, cowboy," Ian snapped.

Troy felt the familiar surge of anxiety wrap its fingers around his spine. His lungs tightened and his breath became ragged. The awful image of Ned, gunned down in Afghanistan, raged in his mind. He tried to shove it away, but it insisted on taking over. He watched as his friend pulled himself, legs gone, bloody mess from the waist down, toward him. He reached out to grab Ned's hand, but the gunfire started again, pelting the sand between them. He looked up to see the flames bursting out of the end of a rifle above and raised his arms to shield his eyes from the sun. He must have fainted at that point, because the next thing he knew, they were screeching into the parking lot at Woody's.

The scene was almost as bad as that wretched day when he lost Ned. The inferno raged out of the building like Beelzebub himself was trying to escape —*maybe he is*, Troy thought. People were streaming out of the building like ants as Ian rammed the police SUV into park. He was about to jump out when Troy snapped out of his stupor.

"Backup, dude," Troy yelled. "You gotta call for backup. Get the fire department out here. Heck, get all the fire departments out here."

The FDLE officer wavered for a second.

"I know you wanna be the hero," Troy said, "but this is bigger than you. You gotta call for help on this one."

Ian Bass stared at the burning building, the flames flickering in his eyes. For a long time, Troy didn't see him move a muscle, not even to blink.

"You're right," he finally said, leaning back into the vehicle.

He picked up the CB radio mic, snapped the power on and hailed the Sheriff's station.

"Puckett," he shouted over the chaos, "I've got a ... a, um, 10-70 or wait, it's a 10-73, hell, I don't know. It's a damn big fire down at Woody's. Whole back side is going up."

"Are they barbecuing or somethin' down there?" The Sheriff sounded as if he might have been asleep.

"What? Barbecuing?" Ian snapped. "No, sir. It's

burning. Fire everywhere. Roof's going to fall in soon. Better hurry. I'm going in to see if anyone's stuck inside."

He flipped the mic aside and slammed the door shut.

"No!" yelled the Sheriff. "Do not go in. The fire department is on the way. Ian? Are you there? Repeat. Do not go inside!"

But Ian Bass was ducking into the building through a wall of flame. Troy Bodean wondered if the fire would reach the Explorer and cook him alive while he sat in the parking lot. He could feel the heat through the tiny crack Ian had given him for air. It was as if someone was trying to dry his hair through the slit with a blow torch. Then he remembered the door had been flung open when they turned around. He twisted his body around and put his feet up against it. He kicked hard, but only succeeded in sending a jolt of pain into his knee. For a few long seconds, he just lay flat, waiting for the ache in his compromised ACL to subside. Through all the hysteria outside, he swore he could hear someone howling the lyrics of "Sympathy for the Devil."

45

Molotov Cocktails

DANTE CAPARELLI WAS surprised how quickly the scene inside had gone from rowdy to explosive—literally. Something smashed to the right and fire burst up onto the wall. A bottle? *Jeezus*, Dante thought, *somebody's throwin' frickin' Molotov cocktails in here*. Before he could take another step, two more flaming bottles smashed around the stage. But for all the fire, the stupid idiots beside the stage were still fighting.

"Sully, see if you can get to the phone and call the—"

He was interrupted by a bottle flying past his head and slamming into the cigarette machine. He and Sully hit the deck and for the first time in his life, Dante regretted not having the carpet redone.

Even in the smoke-filled foyer, he could smell the mold and rot in the black sticky berber. Orange and yellow fire swarmed over the machine and the smell of old Winstons wafted through the room.

Dante raised himself up on his elbows and screamed into the air. "Who the frick is throwin' those?"

But, his voice was not loud enough to be heard over the cacophony of the bar fight, the band—who were not playing, but rather throwing things at each other—and the screaming of dancers trying not to get hit by a flying missile of flame.

"Sully, you idiot," Dante growled, grabbing the man's shirt sleeve and twisting it tight. "Do something!"

THE NEW YORKER grinned under his thick mustache. He would later recount in his statement that he was used to this kind of thing in the Big Apple and that he thought his time to prove himself to his boss had finally come. He reached around behind his back and produced the pistol that he'd found under the old man's seat in the car. It wasn't much of a gun, but, a few well-placed shots could go a long way in a situation like this. He scanned the room, but the smoke and the haze coming from the now furious walls of fire made it difficult to see. Close to the stage, he could just make out the figure of a lanky man with a hat on. It clicked in his mind. The drummer. *He's gotta be the asshole responsible for this mess.*

He raised the gun and fired. The pop was barely audible under the crashing of bodies into tables and chairs. The man he'd shot froze. *Got him*, Sully thought. But then his target stumbled, fell to the ground, crawled a few feet, and then collapsed. Below the smoke cloud at the ceiling, he could see he'd shot Jeffy "Fast Fingers" Farmer, the lead guitar player. *Dammit*, wrong guy. He felt a slight twinge of sadness for Jeffy's soon-to-be widow and their three snot-nosed rugrats, but he didn't have time to dwell on it.

He looked past where Jeffy lay and saw another rangy man swinging something around his head. Without hesitation, Sully aimed and fired again. He was rewarded with another direct hit. His second target fell to his knees, dropped the mic stand he had been holding and slumped face forward to flop on top of Jeffy. Unfortunately, he could now see that he hadn't taken out the drummer, but rather the keyboard player, Rick "Ivory Tickler" Kevinson. As far as he knew, Rick didn't have a wife or kids, but he did have three cats that might not get any kibbles tonight.

With some of the noise dying down, Sully could hear a voice yelling—no, singing—to his right. In disbelief, he rolled over to see a man standing on top of the bar, holding a bottle with a towel stuffed in the neck, and a zippo lighter about to touch it off.

"Ha!" Sully yelled. "Gotchu now you son of a b—"

He was about to pull the trigger when a black Army boot the size of a Volkswagen Beetle slammed up into his hand. He was certain that all of his fingers were broken as well as most of the bones in his wrist. The pistol flew up and away from him and disappeared into the smoke.

He clutched his hand and looked up to see who had kicked him. At that moment, Harley Doug's bowling ball of a fist smashed into Sully's face, crushing his nose and sending brilliant sparkles dancing in his eyes.

"You bastard," Harley Doug growled. "You killed Jeffy and Rick."

Sully tried to tell him that he hadn't intended to kill those guys, but rather the maniacal drummer. Unfortunately, all that came out through his swollen lips was a bloody, mucus ball that Doug mistook for him spitting at the man.

The second punch turned out the lights in Sully's vision.

WHILE SULLY HAD BEEN ASSASSINATING members of Big Dick and the Extenders, Dante had been inching through the bar, hiding under tables and behind overturned chairs. He couldn't see far, but the occasional flash of light guided him toward the source of the liquor bombs being thrown around the building. Of course, they were coming from the bar—a veritable ammo dump of high octane alcohol. The balls of crashing fire flying all around the bar continued to soar over Dante as if J.R.R. Tolkien's Balrog had dropped into Woody's for a drink. But as he army-crawled up under the lip of the bar between two wobbly stools, he got a good look at the source of the fiery barrage.

It's that frickin' drummer, he thought, gritting his teeth under pinched lips. Above his head, he could hear the man's boots clomping around on the yellow-varnished bar top. Over the storm of noise, he could also make out the guy's ranting. Something about taking them all down with him. He'd see them all in hell. Blah, blah, blah.

Dante had heard this kind of thing a million times. When faced with death, a person has a distinct reaction. To Dante's thinking, there were about four of them. Most people that come to the realization that they are about to die, will usually cry hysterically and beg for mercy through dripping snot. Some do the opposite and go far away into their minds, quiet and soulless. And then there are those who will bargain for their lives. The family had turned quite a nice profit with those types.

But the fourth kind, the kind that this drummer was clearly a part of, was the rebel. This was the type of person that decided if he was going out, he was going to go out in a blaze of glory. And not only that, he was going to try to take someone out with him. This kind of idiot was the most dangerous kind, resigned, frenetic, emboldened, and reckless. If he got lucky, he'd take down someone before he got his final reward.

The good news—Dante coughed in the thickening smoke, wondering if there actually could be any good news—was that this kind of victim was usually flying blind, no plan, no exit strategy, and no brain. It was likely that this guy had his sights set on distant targets, spots in the bar where he could fling more fire to the distant dingy edges of the building. Dante decided to wait until he saw two bottles shoot out from over his head and then he'd make his move. He grabbed one of the legs of the nearest stool and jerked it back and forth until it broke free. He knew it would because Sully had repaired—or at least claimed to repair—this particular stool several times.

He crawled up to his knees, pain lancing into both of his hips. He cursed his age and decided maybe it was finally time to look into what his doctor had called "total hip arthroplasty" for both of his degenerative joints. A clear bottle with a royal blue label—*probably the Sambuca*, Dante thought—arced over his head, directed toward the stage. It smashed into the bass drum and burst into a ring of flame like a New York City bum's barrel had been overturned. The next projectile he saw made Dante cringe. The glass bottle with a mustachioed face molded into the side contained the expensive, and quite tasty, Rey Sol Anejo Tequila. He'd paid over five hundred dollars for that bottle and now it was sailing through the air with a bright flaming tail chasing after it. It smashed into the dusty, unused jukebox by the front door and sent the shattered remains of old 45 records flying.

Dante jumped up faster than he would have thought possible, and true to his roots as a young New York Yankees fan, he swung the broken stool leg like a 19-year-old Mickey Mantle hitting his longest home run. The makeshift bat caught the unsuspecting drummer on the back of his calves and hit the man with such force that he did a complete backflip and landed face down, sprawled down the full length of the bar.

Dante raised the stick to hit him again, but then caught sight of someone else crouching down behind the bar, just a few feet away, under the dangling receiver of the telephone. Recognition finally clicked in as he squinted through the ashy air. Cinnamon. *Holy Christ*, Cinnamon was trapped behind the bar, sobbing and trembling uncontrollably while this madman was conducting his arsonous assault.

Dante put a hand to the side of his mouth to shout at her and ask if she was okay, but the words never came out. He hadn't noticed the cowboy hat-wearing drummer grab a bottle from the well. He lit it and smashed it on the top of Dante's head. The old man never heard Cinnamon scream as he dropped to the floor.

CINNAMON STARR WATCHED in horror as the raving lunatic drummer smashed Dante with a bottle of cheap rum. Thankfully, the white strip of cloth the man had tried to light wouldn't catch fire. But, he hit the owner of Woody's so hard, Cinnamon was sure that he'd killed the man. When she suddenly realized she was screaming, she clapped a hand to her mouth and blinked away the tears. Something inside her snapped. It was the little girl inside her who'd been bullied back in high school for having developed awkwardly during her Freshman year. Little did those adolescent pricks know that she would eventually fill out into the Senior class's "Most Attractive" girl—back before it was deemed politically incorrect to award such things.

She decided she'd had enough from this dude and began to form a plan to take him out.

46

Dazed And Confused

TROY CLINT BODEAN could only watch in horror as his most recent bar of choice on the sleepy little island of Islamorada blazed up into a towering inferno of fire. The old painting of the wood-sided car on the front of the building was curling and flaking off in pieces that floated around and settled like Autumn's first leaves. The steady stream of tourists, strippers, and random locals had stopped flowing from the building's warping front door. The glass had shattered into a million pieces and smoke billowed out, the demons escaping hell.

Troy had tried the door a few more times only to find it locked. It had popped open at fifty miles per hour on the highway, but not here parked safely in the only handicapped space on the lot. He took a deep breath and tried to concentrate, but that only left him coughing and sputtering from the heavy smoke. He wondered if Cinnamon was still in there. He couldn't say where she was and he hadn't seen her come out with the others. At this point, he wasn't sure there was much else to do but watch it all burn to the ground and wait for the dogs to come.

Somewhere in the distance, he heard a siren start yelping into the night. He leaned closer to the open window to see if he could tell where it was coming from and how long it might be before they arrived. As he did, he caught sight of a man sitting in the car next to the police SUV. It was dark enough that he couldn't make out much more than the fact that the guy was rocking back and forth and making odd, gasping sounds. He glanced up at the nudie bar and then back at the guy. Surely, he wasn't doing what it looked like he was doing. Troy brushed the sophomoric thought aside and began to yell out the one inch crack at the guy.

"Hey, buddy! Yo. What's goin' on over there?"

The man either didn't hear Troy, or was ignoring him ... or too lost in his pornographic fantasies to care. Troy inched his chin up toward the top of the open window and tried again.

"Hey there, friend," he yelled as loud as he could. "How 'bout a little help here?"

The man stopped rocking and Troy saw the silhouette of his head turn toward him.

"Yeah," he said, nodding his head furiously, hoping the man could see him. "Over here. Can I impress upon you to kindly open this door for me? I've got friends in there and I need to see what the heck is going on, if you don't mind."

The man leaned forward and Troy could see his eyes now. They were ringed in dark grey patches and sunken so deep in their sockets that he wondered if the man was a junkie on a fix. Maybe that was why he was acting so strange. Tear tracks striped the man's face. Beyond hope, he reached up and opened his car door.

Troy laughed and spoke up toward the opening with his lips protruding like a fish gasping for air ... or rather, water.

"I got friends in that building over there, fella. I don't know what you're doin' here, but I thought I might've seen a buddy get out of your car and run in there." Troy pleaded his case to a man with dead eyes. "Yeah, so, if it ain't too much to ask, would you just help me outta here?"

The dude stood and stretched as if he'd been on

a ten hour drive for a family vacation. He showed absolutely no sign of urgency and Troy decided the guy was definitely hopped up on something.

He nodded his head down toward the door handle on the outside of the SUV.

"There it is," he said. "Right down there. That chrome handle there. Just give it a quick tug. It's only locked from the inside."

The man shrugged and started to mumble and point toward the building. A section of the roof detached and slammed down next to him not five feet away. Smoldering bits of wood and metal steamed as they hit a puddle in front of the black Lincoln Towncar the man had exited. For his part though, he didn't even flinch.

Troy strained to hear what he was saying, but all he could make out was that he had brought all of this on everyone and he deserved what he was going to get.

Even though he wasn't talking directly to Troy, he thought it might be best to engage him in conversation to expedite his escape from this late model Ford Explorer.

"Now, now," he said, trying his best to sound like an old buddy from high school. "This ain't a time to be worried about blame and such. Why don't you let me out and we'll get this whole thing under control lickety-split."

The man shrugged and laid his hand on the door handle. He didn't pull on it though, but simply stood there, fingers looped through the faux chrome and stared into the flames licking through the empty door frame.

An impossibly loud shriek echoed out of the building and startled Troy. So desperate it was that he couldn't tell if it was a man or a woman who had uttered it. It was the perfect soundtrack to the moment and it spurred Troy to get this thing going.

"Dang it, dude," he said and leaned back and cracked his forehead against the window. "Open the dang door."

He immediately regretted the head-butt as his vision began to swim and he felt like vomiting. He wondered if he'd given himself a concussion and figured it wasn't his first and very likely wouldn't be the last one he'd ever get. But the bump against the window did the trick. The man jumped and voluntarily—or maybe involuntarily—jerked on the door handle. It popped open and Troy fell out, directly on his chin. His hands were still locked behind his back and he realized that this was going to be a major problem if he was still planning on running inside.

"Much obliged," he said, pulling himself up to his knees. "Say, pardner, would you mind to check up front and see if there's a key to these cuffs up there somewhere? Usually, the cupholder, or maybe tucked up in the visor."

He knew it was a long shot, but the man shrugged and ducked into the front of the Explorer. He emerged with a tiny keyring sporting two silver keys. "You mind to do the honors?"

Troy turned around and extended his aching hands. He felt the cuffs fall away and then reached out to shake the man's hand. He flinched and backed away like a stray dog who'd been beat one too many times to trust anyone.

The entire right side of the building collapsed and cinders exploded into the air above them. Troy felt himself duck and raised his hands to block anything from falling on him. The other dude just stared into the embers of the ruined remains of Woody's.

"Okay, then," Troy said, mustering his courage.

A siren rang out down the road and he considered waiting for the firetrucks to arrive. As he looked back, he saw something fluttering above the back end of the SUV.

"Well, I'll be danged," he said, stepping back to the rear of the vehicle.

Spinning atop the CB radio antenna in the evening breeze, circling lazily, like it didn't have a care in the world ... was his hat. He put a foot up on the bumper and grabbed it. He slid it on his head and turned back toward the nearly extinct strip club. From this vantage point, he could see all the way into the bar. A dude was standing on the bar, walking back and forth, two bottles of liquor—one in each hand—spouting flame from dangling bits of cloth. And behind him, huddled under the nearly empty shelves of booze, Troy could see Cinnamon, crouching as far away from the guy as she could get.

There was no time to wait for the cavalry. Once again, Troy knew he was going to run into danger, maybe even certain death, to save the girl.

He left the dude who had let him out of the cop's car standing in a daze and ran through the open door without slowing down. If he had one thing on the mad bomber, it was the element of surprise. It was unfortunate that he hadn't checked the back of the Explorer and found what Sheriff Paul Puckett referred to as his Islamorada Crowd Control.

47

Who'll Stop The Rain

TROY BURST THROUGH THE DOOR, absolutely certain that he could hear the "Flight of the Valkyries" reverberating through the flaming timbers in the remains of the roof. He hoped in vain that the choppers were coming and then, in a sudden moment of clarity, he realized he wasn't in Afghanistan. *Dude, this is Islamorada*, he told himself. *Get a grip, Troy. This is no time for an episode*. The one psychologist he had agreed to see before they discharged him had insisted on calling them episodes. After twenty minutes, Troy said he was all good, a bit more fishing and layin' in a hammock would do the trick and he didn't need to set up another appointment. The doc had chased him down the hall until Troy wheeled on him and thumped him in the chest with a single finger. He'd flopped down onto his back, his white coat rumpling around him. After that, Troy had walked out past two orderlies, a heavyset nurse with a lazy eye, and a handful of applauding veterans without incident.

As he cleared the blazing threshold, a flaming bottle of something flew over his head and smashed in liquid fire behind him. He ducked just in time, the Molotov cocktail singeing the peacock feather in his hat. The searing heat of the projectile must have been the last straw for whatever was still supporting the header above the door, because it collapsed like a house of cards in a hurricane. The exit was now as impassable as a velvet rope to a tourist on South Beach.

That's one way to keep customers from walkin' out, Troy thought.

He pulled himself up to a crouching position, his knee protesting all the way, and squinted through the smoke and fire. Of all the things he expected to see, he estimated that what he saw was literally the last thing he would have guessed would be playing out in front of him.

On top of the bar, a flaming bottle of something in either hand, naked as a jaybird, stood the drummer for Big Dick and the Extenders—whom

Troy realized were not playing at the moment. The lanky man didn't have a stitch of clothing covering what his mama had brought him into the world wearing, except for one thing. A singed, straw cowboy hat. In a sudden moment of clarity, the thing Troy had been trying to remember, the fact on the tip of his tongue, the déjà vu feeling of recognition snapped into place.

It was him. The man who Troy was watching dangle his body across the bar hurling fiery death around at every square inch of Woody's nightclub was the same man who had murdered Earl Heskett and held him and a few new friends hostage in the back of Benny's World of Liquor. Because the dude had stolen a straw cowboy hat from the store and disappeared—originally, he'd taken Troy's hat off his head, but eventually it came back like it always did —the authorities had started calling him The Cowboy Killer.

That incident had made the bus ride down to the Keys quite memorable and the kid who had perpetrated it all was now raining brimstone on the one and only bar Troy had enjoyed in Islamorada. Troy took an awkward duck-walk step forward, trying to stay below the thick smoke, but a hand clamped down hard on his ankle. He kicked at it, but the grip remained firm. He turned to see who had a hold of him and was shocked to see Ian Bass lying on the floor, outstretched like a soldier on the battlefield.

Ian pulled at Troy with surprising strength, hauling him backward behind the overturned, charred jukebox. It was just enough cover to keep the Cowboy Killer from seeing them.

"What in the hell are you doing in here, Troy?" Ian gasped.

The FDLE officer was holding his right arm tight against his abdomen. Troy could see that his sleeve was burned away and the man's skin was charred. He probably had third degree burns.

Seeing Troy's eyes, Ian said, "He tagged me with a bottle as soon as I walked in the door. A pretty damn good shot. Knocked my gun out of my hand."

Ian jutted his chin toward the gun lying on the floor, ten feet across a smoldering bed of coals that used to be the carpet.

"I can't get to it," Ian explained. "My right arm is burned and feels like it's broken. Can't crawl at all and if I stand up, he'll see me and hurl a vodka bomb my way."

Troy nodded. "So, what's the plan, then? Get out, call the cops?"

"I am the cops, Troy. But to your point, I called the *cops*, remember? Puckett is probably trying to finish his solitaire game before he comes to check it out. And as for getting out, that ship has sailed."

In reply to his statement, the roof above the front door lurched and fell a few feet in a splash of brilliant embers. Troy was reminded of a log in a fire pit reaching its breaking point where the fire had eaten through the center of it and it split in two, tumbling in half throwing sparks into the sky.

"There's only one thing that will get us out of this alive, Troy," Ian winced in pain as he said it, his face looking more pale than it had a second ago. "You've got to get that gun. I think I have two shots left. That's enough to take this guy out. I know you had time in the service. This is your time to take out the bad guy and win the war."

"Whoa now," Troy said, raising his hands in a double high-five. "I was just an officer chopper taxi pilot. Only combat I ever saw got my buddy's legs blown clean off."

Ian studied him with resignation. Troy wasn't sure exactly what the man was seeing, but he nodded. His face became that of a poker player laying down his last card.

"The girl, your friend, Cinnamon," Ian said, his

eyes flitting toward the bar. "She's behind the bar. The naked bomber there has her pinned, she can't get out."

Troy felt a blast of icy cold reality hit him. "Dangit."

He glanced over at the gun. Seven feet away, maybe eight. If he could get to his feet, it was two big steps, then he'd have to aim and fire. The guy would surely get a chance to throw at least one bottle at him. He figured his best bet was to wait the guy out a few seconds. Let him discharge a couple more cocktails, then go while he was reloading. Fireballs shattered the VIP room—in which nothing but regular lap dances happened—and Troy jumped for the gun. He took a step and was greeted with an explosion of flame and glass at his feet. He leapt backward and fell flat on his back next to Ian. The FDLE officer patted Troy's leg putting out a small flame threatening the hair on his shin.

"Dude is good," Troy said. "Like *Nolan Ryan* good. How the heck is he flinging those things so fast?"

"He's been doing it for a while now," Ian said. "And he's pretty accurate, too."

Great, Troy thought. *Kid coulda been an MLB*

contender, but he's here in my bar, in his birthday suit, killing people with burning alcohol bottles.

"I kept hoping he'd run out of ammo," Ian said, "but they just keep coming. Can't move or he hums one right at us."

"We gotta get him to look away for a sec." Troy peeked over the edge of the jukebox. The Cowboy Killer, still prancing around the bar, did indeed have his head on a swivel. Anything or anyone that moved, paid for it with a fastball of fire. "What we need is a good old fashioned distraction."

WHICH IS EXACTLY what Cinnamon Starr was thinking as she inched away from the naked man stalking the top of the bar. She had a plan. She wasn't one hundred percent sure it would work because nothing in the building was up to current fire codes, but she thought it was worth a shot.

48

The Cavalry

TROY WAS ABOUT to suggest that Ian jump up and shout waving his one good arm to distract the Molotov flinger, when he saw a hot pink blur run out from behind the bar. Everything slowed down like a John Woo film. The one pretty dancer at Woody's nightclub darted out in long, gazelle-like strides—an impressive feat in the nine-inch heels she was wearing. He saw the little red box on the wall she was running for and realized what she was doing. She yanked down on the handle, sending the fire alarm into action. The bell trilled through the air with ear-splitting volume. Troy could hardly believe it was so loud amidst all the chaos. His first instinct was to watch the action sequence, enjoying the first-rate direction, brilliant special effects, and Oscar-worthy acting, but Ian smacked him on the arm. He yelled the word "go" but it came out in the low rumbling growl of slo-mo.

"Goooooo," the FDLE officer shouted.

Troy snapped back to reality. He dove for the gun as the sprinklers came on. He rolled onto his side, raising his arms to aim at The Cowboy Killer. He pulled the trigger and the click was deafening. He pulled it again and again. The Glock clicked like a metronome keeping time for "Flight of the Bumblebee." Troy shot a glare over at Ian. Somehow, even with a bad arm, the man shrugged and held up his palms.

Troy glanced back up at the man on the bar, certain he was about to get a flaming drink to the face. All he saw was the man's lily-white bottom staring back at him. Cinnamon had distracted him alright and he was not happy at all.

He screamed, "No, no, no! That's not the plan. The plan was to send all of you to hell. This place is a bastion of indecency and filth and the devil's workshop."

Troy thought that was an odd thing to say standing on the bar completely naked, but the man was obviously one brick shy of a full load anyway.

He screamed again, but it was unintelligible

gibberish spat through his spittle covered lips. Troy watched as the kid reached down, picked up a bottle, and lit it with a Zippo. Instead of throwing the bottle, he launched himself down from the bar and ran straight at Cinnamon. Her eyes were wide and she became a deer in the headlights, frozen to the spot to the right of the fire alarm. Troy willed her to move, but she didn't. He wondered if she thought the guy was like a T-Rex whose limited vision could only see movement. That obviously wasn't the case, because he was tromping right at her.

Troy jumped up. His knee buckled and pain shot through his thigh. Not now, he thought. He massaged his aching tendons until he could stand. He lurched like a fast Zombie toward The Cowboy Killer who had raised his arm into the air. He looked like the Statue of Liberty, a Smirnoff torch held high in one hand—if the statue had been a man, without a dress, wearing a cowboy hat.

Not going to make it in time, Troy thought. He leapt toward them, hands outstretched, watching in horror as the flaming bottle began its slow arc toward Cinnamon.

Troy opened his mouth to scream, but the voice that came out was not his. He fell to the ground, his knee refusing to take him any farther. The bottle the man had thrown at Cinnamon smashed just above her head and didn't explode. It must have been thick glass, Troy thought as it bounced away harmlessly. The screaming—that hadn't been his—continued and he turned to see what was happening. Through a wall of flame, fire dripping all around on non-flammable curtains, posters crisping and flying away like Autumn leaves, and sequins melting into silvery pools of mercurial goo, the man who had freed Troy from the Explorer burst in, arms raised Evel Knieval style. If only the dude had a motorcycle, it would've looked like a Vegas stunt, as it was, it looked like the stupidest thing Troy had ever seen anyone do—running into a building that was seconds away from collapsing into a fiery, flattened pile of burning rubble.

The guy, who Troy would later find out was named Gary, sprinted through the smoke and flame like a man on a mission, or a Kamikaze flight. He was two steps from the bar when the most serendipitous thing occurred. Troy watched as a body—a body Troy had thought was a dead man—stirred. Though the man's silver hair was drenched with blood and his face was a mask of dark congealed fluid, Troy recognized him. Dante. It was Dante rising from the dead. As he made it up on all fours, he looked in the direction of the door and obviously saw Gary running toward him. His eyes became huge white orbs, glowing against the mask of blood on his face. The terror there reminded Troy of similar looks he'd seen on faces during his short, but dreadful time in Afghanistan.

Dante opened his mouth and screamed, but Troy couldn't hear anything over the sudden cracking of a timber above him. He rolled to his left, guessing at the safest direction to move. A massive piece of the rafters above him slammed down, angled just over his head. Cinders rained down on him burning tiny pinpricks on his arms and legs. Ian, whom he had bumped into when he rolled, slapped his good hand on Troy's back to put out several small spots that had ignited.

Troy looked back toward the bar to see Gary take a step up on Dante and launch himself like an Olympic vaulter up and over the bar. His right foot took off from the old man's back and his left hit the edge of the bar at full speed. He jumped hard and flew into the air. The Cowboy Killer had just put his hands up to grab Cinnamon when the missile named Gary slammed into him.

Cinnamon must have seen what was coming, because she ducked just in time for the two men to crash into the wall behind her. The Cowboy Killer's head smashed into the drywall, leaving a bowling ball sized hole in it, but Gary wasn't through. He began raining blows down on the man's head, shoulders, and back. The dude squirmed enough to roll over under Gary, but Troy thought that was a bad idea. The punches were now landing on his face and chest. One punch glanced off the guy's forehead and his cowboy hat went sailing away to catch fire and burn up in a flash.

"He's gonna kill him," Ian croaked. "You've got to stop him."

Troy didn't hesitate. He jumped up, Ian's empty Glock in his hand. In ten obstacle-course-like steps, he was on him. The Cowboy Killer was bleeding through a sickening grin, his teeth stained red from blood running from his nose. A strange thought entered Troy's mind. He wondered if this is what the kid had wanted to happen. Maybe he couldn't stop the killing and needed someone to stop him. Why else would he take a job as a drummer in Islamorada rather than continue south and hop on a boat to Cuba? As Troy stared down at him, a flash of recognition painted the man's face.

"Hey," he said pointing up at Troy. "I know you.

You're the guy from Benny's liquor store ... with the hat."

Gary's arm pulled back and Troy knew if he let the fist fly, the man on the ground—the now-completely-naked Cowboy Killer—might not make it out of here alive. Troy raised the Glock and smacked Gary in the back of the head. He crumpled forward in an awkward bloody hug over the man.

At that moment, the sky opened up and water began to rain down on them from all sides. The firemen had finally arrived in what Troy imagined were nanoseconds before the total collapse of Woody's nightclub in Islamorada:

13 UGLY GIRLS AND 1 PRETTY ONE.

49

The Sheriff Is Near

SHERIFF PAUL PUCKETT jumped out of his car, ran two steps toward the smoldering, wet mess of a building that used to be Woody's. Even though the Islamorada Fire Rescue Station #20—or the Bernard Russell Station, named for its founder—was only three blocks away, the trucks had been delayed arriving for a staggering thirty minutes. Linda "Big Boobs" Morganstern's prized Bengal cat had managed to claw its way to the top of a thirty-foot palm on Marathon. The fifty-thousand dollar cat found itself stranded with no limbs to make its way back down on. The seventy-five foot ladder truck had been dispatched to deal with that. Cheeca Lodge had commandeered the use of the two pumpers to fill a newly repaired pool. Normally, they wouldn't have been used at this time of night, but the owner of the famous resort had put a big, fat campaign check into Paul's hands requesting both trucks to get the pool filled before the pending arrival of a semi-famous starlet the next day. Though he was not directly responsible for the operations of the station, he could certainly influence what they did and didn't do in relation to non-emergency activities. Amidst the screams and flames, he could see his reelection efforts floating up and away with the sparkling embers.

Apparently, there were a few people with serious injuries on their way to the hospital and a couple of people had been shot during the blaze, but for the most part, the building had taken the most damage. Oddly, the back corner of the building Paul recognized as Dante Caparelli's office—another wacky story altogether—was still standing. He took two steps toward the sizzling, smoking, dripping mess and stumbled on a piece of the front door. He reached out to stabilize himself against a black Ford Explorer parked in the first space. His hand smudged through the ash on the vehicle uncovering the familiar logo of the Islamorada Sheriff's Department.

"Holy Christ," he gasped, realizing it was his station's SUV.

He rubbed at the window with the back of his hand and peered inside. Ian Bass sat in the driver's seat, cradling one arm to his stomach and talking on a cell phone with the other. He jutted his chin up to indicate that he saw the sheriff and mouthed the words, "hang on." He glanced into the back seat and saw an ash-covered man, skin and bones, completely naked, sitting alone, his head lolling back and forth. His face was a mess of bruises and blood and both eyes were swelling. To Paul, he looked like he might've just stepped out of Auschwitz or climbed down off a cross—a strange juxtaposition of images indeed. Next to the man, on the sooty rear bench seat, sat a cowboy hat, tattered and burned. Ian rolled his window down, apparently finished with his call.

"Got him, Sheriff," he said, his face looking almost as bad as the poor man's in the back seat.

"Huh?" Paul said, shooting a glance back at the guy, who looked up and grinned through bloody teeth. "Got who?"

"The Cowboy Killer," Ian said with pride.

"You mean to tell me that's the ... I mean, he doesn't look like he could ..."

"I'll kill you, too, pig," the man in the back seat hissed.

"Well," Paul had stepped back at the man's outburst, "I suppose you did. How in the world did all this happen?"

Ian relayed the story of how Gary John Suskind —the man whom they had thought might be the infamous serial killer—was not The Cowboy Killer. He had, however, been involved in the deaths of two other people.

Paul Puckett scratched his head, not sure how all the pieces fit together.

"Okay, wait," he said, "So, this guy (he pointed to the man in the back seat) is The Cowboy Killer."

"Yes."

"But the guy who took him down is also a killer?"

"It's a long story," Ian said, "Anyway, he and Troy—"

Paul held up a hand to interrupt him. "Troy? Who's Troy?"

"Troy Bodean," Ian explained. "He's the first guy I thought was The Cowboy Killer, but he's not either. In fact, he helped Gary take down the real killer."

"I am thoroughly confused." Paul stared at the remnants of the building as the fire hoses continued to rain on the dying red coals. "So, who's going to jail?"

"The FDLE is sending a caravan to pick up Jasper."

"Jasper?" Paul asked.

Ian looked over his shoulder and hooked his good thumb toward the now dozing criminal in his back seat. "He is. Jasper Obadiah Hurlbutt. The real Cowboy Killer."

"But how did the FDLE know he was here?"

Ian reached into his back pocket and pulled out his badge. He licked his lips and inhaled slowly as he showed it to the sheriff.

Paul Puckett whistled through his teeth and rubbed the sweat from his forehead. "So, you're FDLE, eh?"

Ian nodded.

"Guess this means you won't be coming back to work tomorrow?"

Ian shook his head. "Nope."

A long pause settled between them. Paul shuffled back and forth trying desperately to process all that was unfolding around them.

"What about Gary?"

Ian pointed toward the portion of the building that was still standing. In an untouched booth toward the back, a man sat wrapped in a blanket across from an older man with a paramedic bandaging his head.

Paul walked into the building—or rather, the mucky grime of wood and ash that might've been a giant's campfire after it had been extinguished. He stepped carefully through fallen ceiling joists, pieces of broken and melted vinyl records, and broken glass … lots of broken glass. He would later learn that forensics would estimate that ninety-seven Molotov cocktails had been used in the assault that would be called Florida's Largest Wood(y) Fire in the newspapers.

As he approached he could hear Gary speaking to Dante in a series of sobs and sniffs. Apparently, this whole thing had started with Gary trying to woo Matty by stealing a kayak and taking him on a secluded boat ride. That had ended with Matty being eaten by an alligator. And then, when he'd taken his sometime boyfriend, Dani, out to find the remains, the gator—possibly the same one—had eaten Dani.

"I was just trying to hide the kayak because the whole world was looking for it and I figured if they found my prints on it and maybe Matty's blood that they would," Gary looked up at Dante, "that you would … kill me. Or I'd go to jail or something."

Dante said nothing. The old man's eyes were glazed over and blood oozed from a bandage on his head. The paramedic looked up at Paul.

"Concussion," she said. "Might not remember much about this. He's going to need a few days in the hospital to assess the real damage."

She helped Dante up and walked him slowly through the wreckage toward the ambulance.

She was surprised when the injured man stopped to speak to the couple sitting on the curb outside the building. A pretty young woman wearing, well, almost nothing, was dabbing a bit of gauze under the brim of a cowboy hat.

"You're the damn drummer that did all this, right?" Dante demanded.

"No, sir," Troy pulled himself to his feet and faced the man, helping Cinnamon up to stand beside him.

"That guy is headed to jail for a very long time," Woody's only good-looking dancer said.

Dante nodded his head. "His playing was definitely a crime."

Troy smiled, "Ain't that the truth."

"You play, kid?" Dante poked a light finger into Troy's chest. "Got an immediate opening."

"Nope," Troy raised his hands. "Can't play a lick on anything but a fishin' pole."

Dante grimaced.

Troy thought about it for a second. "But if you're looking for a real pro, you should try Ronnie Hobgood. Best I've ever heard and I think he's looking for work."

Troy reached into his back pocket and pulled out his wallet. Though it was sopping wet from the fire hoses, he found an old card Ronnie had given him and handed it to Dante.

"Thanks, cowboy." Dante said.

"It's Troy, sir. Troy Bodean."

Dante shrugged his shoulders. "Thanks, Troy Bodean. Now get the fuck out of my bar."

With that, the paramedic pulled the old man away toward the ambulance.

"Ain't much of a bar anymore," Troy said, surveying the damage in the pale purple haze of dawn.

"Sure as hell isn't," said Cinnamon. "Looks like I'm out of a job."

"What'll you do? Head back home?"

"No," she said with a slight downward turn of her

eyes. "I might try that revue in Key West at Bourbon Street. Dani won't be working there anymore and they'll need someone to fill in."

"Isn't that a drag bar?"

She shrugged.

"But ... you're a girl," Troy said, waving his hand along her body like she was a prize on the Price Is Right.

"Ha," she laughed. "Thanks for noticing. Anyway, sometimes they hire women. Maybe I'll just be the most convincing drag queen on Duval Street."

Troy grinned. "That you will. Thirteen drag queens and one pretty lady."

"What about you?" she asked, hooking her hand into his elbow.

"Guess I'll be headin' back to the tennis club. Season's about to start and I want to get that place ready so I can hightail it outta there when the head pro gets back from Miami."

She stopped and looked into his eyes. "You're ... you're leaving? But ... why?"

He brushed a stray hair off her forehead. "It's just kind of what I do, darlin'. Besides, this place ain't quiet enough for me."

She laughed, but tears threatened to well up in

her eyes. "A rambling cowboy. Well, I hope you find what you're looking for out there."

Me too, he thought as they walked away from the crater left where Woody's used to stand. *Me too.*

"WELL, KID," Paul said as he loaded Gary into his patrol car, "you might be off the hook with Dante if he can't remember any of this."

Gary looked up. His face was streaked with tears through a thick layer of ash.

"As for the theft of the kayak," he paused to scratch his chin, "you'll need to come with me."

He was not looking forward to calling Mr. Self-Righteous Reporter, Chad Harrison. He would have to relay the bad news that the kayak was destroyed, but at least this time, he had the thief in custody.

50

Just Desserts

FRANKIE RUSSO WALKED WITH PURPOSE, like an Olympic speed walker on ... well, on speed. The shock of the burning strip club had worn off and the pain of losing Marty had come storming back. His heart ached and his throat was sore from uncontrollable sobs. What had it been ... thirty years ago? Or maybe thirty-five? He could remember it like it was yesterday, walking into that place near Walker Square—God he did not miss Milwaukee. He'd been searching for a new haunt and was drawn to the bright, shining neon rainbow sign out front. He could almost remember what the name of it was ... it was on the tip of his tongue and he—

He froze. It couldn't be, could it? He squinted into the rising sun and could almost see the image of

Marty standing out front smoking a cigarette trying desperately to look macho and sexy at the same time. His dark hair was slicked back and he wore a Freddie Mercury mustache and a Queen t-shirt. Behind him in all its tubular glory glowed the bar's name: Woody's.

"Of all the crazy coincidences," Frankie muttered as new tears welled in his eyes.

He looked up at the sky. It was going to be a beautiful day. As he looked down, he could see the big, boxy shape of the Winnebago ahead. Thankfully, it had been pulled to the side of the road.

"What do I do now?" he asked no one.

Something caught his eye ahead on the side of the road opposite the RV. A squat little building of stucco and red roof tiles with a distinctly Spanish appearance sat tucked in a scruff of mangroves. He walked a bit closer and saw a statue standing out front. A man stood in a boat riding on the waves, one arm outstretched toward the west. Frankie found the sign revealing that the man in the boat was San Pedro—or Saint Peter.

"Of course," Frankie smiled and looked at the sky. "Thank you, Marty."

Though he was no Bible scholar, he knew that

Peter was a fisherman, or a fisher of men. Marty had sent him a sign to carry on to Key West, the biggest fishbowl of men east of San Francisco.

"I will continue on to Fantasy Fest in your honor, Marty. I love you so m—"

He took two steps and was bowled over by a man he hadn't seen racing toward him on a rusty bicycle. He'd been so distracted by the statue of San Pedro that the oncoming bike had taken him by surprise.

The man who'd knocked him down yelled, "Suck it, ya bum!"

He looked down at his clothes, soaked and sooty. He did look like a bum. But that was no way to treat someone down on his luck.

"Screw you, jerk!" He yelled at the wobbling bike disappearing away from him.

CHAD HARRISON THREW up the finger as he flew past the vagrant he'd just plowed into. He chuckled to himself. It had most definitely not been an accident. He scored himself ten points for putting the bum in a mud puddle. *Bonus.*

He pedaled on, unaware that the collision had loosened the chain on the bike—a karmic occurrence that would come back to haunt him all too soon. The morning mist was burning off and the day was already proving to be the warmest he'd felt this month. He swiped at a trickle of sweat running down his temple in irritation. Off the side of the road, in front of a shack of a building that used to be a quirky little art gallery, he saw a sign announcing:

`NEW MANAGEMENT! ADULT NOVELTIES, LIQUOR, AND TATTOOS`

Nice, he thought sarcastically. *Living here just isn't what it used to be.*

He could remember when he'd bought the bungalow back before the tourist boom—or at least before it got so commercial that it drove most native Floridians out. There was a time pre-dating all of that crap, that he could ride his bike up and down Islamorada in the middle of the Overseas Highway and never see another car, or shop, or person for that matter.

And with all the pollution caused by the damnable influx of human garbage, enjoying the water was a toxic affair at best. Not that he could enjoy that either.

"Damn thief!" he yelled, throwing a fist into the air, cursing the as-yet-un-caught kayak purloiner. *Can't even keep a boat under your house without chaining it up*, he thought. *And that stupid hillbilly of a sheriff can't even track down a single lead on the thing. I'll see him run out of office before I'm through. He'll wish he'd never heard of me by the time this is over.*

Though he wasn't yelling at anyone in particular, his face twisted into some strange contortions as he ran over the whole thing in his head. A group of cheerleaders in a passing convertible thought it was funny enough to post a snapshot of him on Instagram with the caption: *Crazy dude yelling at the sky. Only in the Keys.*

But Chad Harrison, known to a very few rabid fans as Cap Wayfarer, would never see the embarrassing post. At that exact moment, his untied shoelace flopped inside the loosened chain. He'd forgotten to tie it the last time this had happened. The whole thing turned into a knot that a salty sailor would be proud to call his work.

With a jerk, his tangled left shoe wound tight into the chain and jerked him hard to the side. His bike went sailing off the road and toward the marshy muck. He flew past the round, tennis ball shaped sign with peeling blue letters announcing the entrance to the Islamorada Tennis Club. He pulled hard and was able to get a little slack for his left leg, but in doing so, he'd pulled the lace tight, binding his foot even more inside the shoe. He was still moving fast and out of control when he hit a deep pool. He crashed in, splashing wildly in the slimy mire. Try as he might, he could not get his shoe loose from the bike. He was tangled inexorably in the rusty gear and couldn't stand. As it was, he could only flop around on his right foot to keep his head above the grungy water.

He struggled on, picturing the gruesome scene in the movie, *Saw*, where the lead character had to cut off his own foot to try and escape to save his family. His heart pounded in his chest as he plunged under the surface and clawed at the damnable shoelace. He jerked on his foot trying to free it, but nothing would work. Stars began dancing across his vision and he knew he was about to pass out. He wondered if this is what it was like to drown.

And then it came to him. He would have to go under, find the bottom, let the bike rest and give him some slack. Then he should be able to loosen the shoe. The more he fought it, the tighter it got. His lungs burned with effort, but he figured it could only be seven or eight feet deep here at the most.

He concentrated on slowing his breathing. He was tired, damn tired. But if he could get free, he could crawl back to his house, climb into the hammock and rest for a month or two.

Steeling himself, he took a deep breath and let himself sink. Visibility was less than zero. As he sank down into the swampy marsh, he wondered if he'd made a mistake. What if he couldn't get the shoelace to let go. If he couldn't get loose, he was exhausted and would never make it back to the surface.

After what must've only been seconds, but seemed like hours, the bike finally rested on the bottom. Amazingly, as soon as the weight came off his foot, the shoe opened up and he jerked his foot free. With his last bit of strength, he pushed off and rushed toward the surface. He broke through laughing and gasping for air.

He pulled himself up onto the tangle of roots of a nearby mangrove and flopped over on his back. He wasn't sure how long he lay there, but when he finally lifted himself up to get the lay of the land, he realized he could no longer see the road. He had no idea which way was out. He eased himself up to a sitting position, aching from the ordeal on the bike, and scanned the area around him. It all looked the same. All jungle and marsh, no solid land or road.

And then, he saw it. A flash of color. Something out of place in the green and black and brown. He squinted into the rays of sunlight dappling through the mangroves. There was definitely something there that didn't belong. He tried to stand and a sharp pain shot through his lower leg. He looked down to see his ankle swollen to the size of a grapefruit. *Odd*, he thought, *that the grapefruit gets such a bad rap. It's always a tumor the size of a grapefruit, never an orange, or apple.*

He pulled himself along as best he could, over the octopus-like roots of the trees, trying hard not to put pressure on his bad sprain. As he got closer, the object became clearer. It was smooth and round on one side, and jagged on the other, and as orange as a Monroe-Dade County construction sign. Chad Harrison had found his kayak—or what was left of it.

He lifted his hands into the air and bellowed in triumph. "Yes!" he yelled. "I knew it. I knew I would find it!"

He sat shaking his head piecing it all together. "Tennis pro. Or maybe the help. Somebody at that damned tennis club stole my kayak for a joyride. That's exactly what happened."

He laughed harder, his hands starting to shake. "I'm going to bury the prick who thought he could steal from me."

The odd echo of his voice rising across the water

got louder. "I'll own this tennis club before it's all through. You hear me, you bast—"

His tirade was interrupted by a low, guttural growl behind him. He jerked his head around so fast that he lost his balance and fell into the water beside the jagged piece of his kayak. At first, he was afraid he would sink again, but found the bottom to be about six feet deep. He was just barely shorter than that and had to hop slightly on his good foot to keep his head from going all the way under.

As he did, he saw the shape: long, black, and scaly. His heart thrummed again and his breathing bubbled the water in front of his face. The gator's eyes flashed yellow just above the surface, moving toward him. He hopped backward as fast as he could, but it wasn't fast enough. He swallowed a mouthful of swamp and coughed and sputtered as he flailed his arms, trying desperately to gain speed.

But he knew it was no use. An alligator in the water could swim nearly twenty miles per hour. It was only three feet away now and picking up speed, preparing to thrust at its prey. As the creature's toothy jaw opened wide, showing its mouth full of razor sharp daggers, Chad saw something sparkle. A glittering shimmer of something lodged in the beast's maw.

Just before it took him, the infamous author of semi-famous Florida Fiction novels *Frog Nuggets* and *Hammerhead Gal*, could see the source of the shining.

Are those ... sequins? As the mama gator slammed her jaws shut around him to protect her nearby nest of twenty-seven freshly laid eggs, Chad's last thought was, *who in the world wears pink, sequined camouflage.*

And then she took him under, along with the last, jagged piece of orange kayak he was holding tight in his hands.

Epilogue

TROY CLINT BODEAN felt sure that Lucas Walsh—the resident tennis pro of the Islamorada Tennis Club who'd raced off to Miami to win back his cheating girlfriend—wouldn't mind him borrowing the dusty Prince backpack for a bit. He stuffed a couple of dirty t-shirts, two pairs of khaki shorts, a Woody's t-shirt (that he'd found lying under the ash in the remains of the building) and a pair of green and purple flip-flops that sported a Wimbledon logo. The collector's edition flip-flops had been under the bag and were equally dusty. Lucas probably wouldn't care because he might never notice that the things were missing.

He swallowed the last gulp of a tepid Corona, no lime or orange—his preferred slice of fruit for the

Mexican beer, and tossed the bottle into a full recycle bin next to the refrigerator. It clunked against another one as it settled into the basket. Troy inhaled slowly.

"All used up," he said, tipping his charred cowboy hat at the mess. "But headed for better things, I reckon."

He looked around the apartment above the tennis pro shop. It was what some would call a crap-hole. The shredded green carpet and hole-ridden linoleum would appear to some to be a sign of disrepair, but to those who spent any time here, they would be signs of use—lots of loving use. Troy couldn't remember how many nights he had actually spent in the room, but the ones he could count ... they were good ones. Most of his time had been spent outside, on the island. He slung the backpack over his shoulder and walked out on the porch. He pulled the door shut, slamming it hard three times before it would latch. He turned the key, locking it, and slid it under the doormat that proclaimed:

IN TENNIS LOVE MEANS NOTHING.

He walked down the stairs dragging his fingertips along the bright pink bougainvillea that were blooming furiously as if to shout, "we want you, Troy."

He answered them in kind, "there ain't no livin' with, with a killin'. There ain't no goin' back from it. Right or wrong, it's a brand, a brand that sticks."

When he reached the bottom of the stairs, he saw Sheriff Paul Puckett leaning against the ash-covered Ford Explorer that he'd been in just two days earlier. The sheriff looked tired, bags under his eyes and pale. But he wore a smile on his face that almost seemed real. He stood as he saw Troy hit the last step.

"There's no going back," Troy muttered.

"If you're hoping I'll shout for you to come back as you ride off into the sunset, well, I might," Paul reached out a hand.

Troy took it and shook it like the man was an old friend. He hadn't been around the sheriff much, but in the short time he'd been down at the station giving his statement, he'd grown to like him, or at least not dislike him.

"I'm losing Ian, you know?" Paul said. "He's headed back to the FDLE with the glory of catching The Cowboy Killer."

Troy nodded. Ian had left the day of the big fire with the gangly man who'd reportedly killed a dozen people, maybe more since the day Troy had run into him at Benny's World of Liquor. *Lord, how long ago was that? A month? A year?* He had no clue.

The sheriff waved his hand toward the Explorer. "I can give you a lift, if you like?"

Troy shook his head. "Appreciate the offer, sir, but I've spent enough time ridin' around in the back seat of that thing."

"I'll let you ride up front," Paul laughed.

"That's mighty kind of you, sheriff," Troy touched the brim of his hat as he said it, "but I'll still pass."

"Afghanistan, eh?"

Troy tried not to let his face show any emotion. "For a short time, yes, sir. How'd you know?"

"A soldier knows a soldier, son," Paul said, picking imaginary dirt out from under his fingernails. "And also, I saw your file in Ian's things."

Troy wondered what that file would look like. He reckoned it might be seven or eight books worth of stuff. *The Troy Bodean Omnibus*, he thought, chuckling inside. *Probably not worth the paper it's printed on.*

"Pay ain't all that great," the sheriff continued. "The benefits ... well, they aren't all that great either, but you'd get to cruise around the island in this guy."

He slapped his hand against the hood of the

Explorer exposing the white paint under the soot from the inferno at Woody's.

"Much obliged, sheriff." Troy sniffed at the air. "But, that ain't really my thing. I figure I'll just head to the bus station from here and figure it out from there."

"Bus station, eh?" Paul Puckett reached out and took the backpack from Troy. He chucked it into the back and motioned to the passenger's seat. "Least I can do is give you a ride up to seventy-four. There's a Greyhound stop up there. You can ride in the front and I won't even cuff you."

Troy considered it for a second. It was only two miles, but he was tired, so very tired. "How can I turn down that?"

He got in and the sheriff clicked a button on the radio. Lindsey Buckingham was belting out the familiar chorus of "Go Your Own Way" by Fleetwood Mac. It was as if someone was scripting it all out. As Troy listened to the classic breakup song, he figured it was appropriate. He was, in a sense, breaking up with the sleepy little island town of Islamorada. As the sheriff droned on about the job at the police station, Troy watched the azure water swim by his window, wondering where he would go next.

"So, if I can't talk you into it," Paul said, pulling over at the bus stop, "where will you go from here?"

Troy extracted himself from the SUV with more aches and pains than he expected from such a short ride. He pulled his backpack out and pushed his hat down on his head.

"Ain't sure. Maybe south. Maybe north. Won't know until the wind kicks up and fills my sails."

Air brakes hissed as a bus pulled in behind them. He glanced up at the destination sign on the front of the Greyhound.

"Key West it is," he said, waving to the sheriff and stepping on.

THE END

TURN THE PAGE TO CONTINUE THE ADVENTURE

Afterword

Over these past few books, Troy Clint Bodean has become less mythical character and more old friend to me. When he isn't appearing on the screen as my cursor races across it, I wonder what he's up to, where he is, and what trouble has found him this time.

This book is the longest and most complex Troy book to date and I hope you appreciate the hard work I put into it. I want each of these to be better than the last, and I put a lot of time and effort into making them as good as they can be.

Though Troy is always fun to write about, it does me good to write about other people, places, and things. (See the Also by David Berens page for info.)

There is VERY likely to be another Troy book, but my attention is shifting to another project that will introduce a whole new character named Amber Cross. She will exist wholly outside the Troy Bodean Tropical Thriller universe and will likely be more "thrilling" as well. Her first book currently titled *Her Lost Alibi* is a thriller about a case involving a man imprisoned for a murder even though he has seven alibis stating he was a thousand miles away. Surely, he's innocent ... right? Find out in January in a massive anthology project I'll be involved in.

Don't worry, there is a way to keep up with all of this —sign up for my newsletter.

Please be sure to visit www.BerensBooks.com *and join the BeachBumBrigade Reader Group so you'll be among the first to know about my promotions, events and specials!*

Fair weather and following seas, my friends,

Also by David Berens

If you'd like to stay up-to-date with all of the latest from David Berens, be sure to join the BeachBum Brigade.

JOIN HERE: www.BerensBooks.com if you haven't already.

Troy Bodean Tropical Thrillers

- #0 Tidal Wave (available FREE exclusively to the BeachBum Brigade Reader Group)
- #1 Hat Check
- #2 Ocean Blue
- #3 Blight House
- #4 Stealing Savannah
- #5 Skull Island
- #6 Shark Bait
- #7 Dead End (Short Story)
- #8 Gator Bite

Made in the USA
Coppell, TX
27 April 2022

77136853R00305